What othe

Utterly ness.

Tim Hawtho

Its description of our service provision is **a brilliant work of fiction.**

Electricity company spokesperson

A **truly terrific** misrepresentation of the facts.

Unnamed person at the municipality

Not a bit like *The Da Vinci Code*, which was **a real page-turner!**

Somebody who knows a book reviewer at The Mercury

It is **simply stunning** that Ms O'Mara can get away with this.

Peter Labuschagne, Northern Natal Express

The author's comments about our customer service are **nothing short of hilarious.**

Helpdesk employee

The funniest book I've read in years was written by P. J. O'Rourke. *Home Affairs* is quite amusing, too.

Staff writer, Estcourt Echo

It takes place in Africa or somewhere, right? All that foreign humour; I just don't **get it!**

Parys Hilton

You have to read it to appreciate just how unwell the author is.

Clinical psychologist, Weskoppies

Published in 2007 by 30° South Publishers (Pty) Ltd.
28, 9th Street, Newlands,
Johannesburg, South Africa 2092
www.30degreessouth.co.za

Design and origination by 30° South Publishers (Pty) Ltd.
Printed and bound by Pinetown Printers (Pty) Ltd.

Cover design by Marot & Sanders (Pty) Ltd.

ISBN 978-1-920143-19-0

Bree O'Mara

Home Affairs

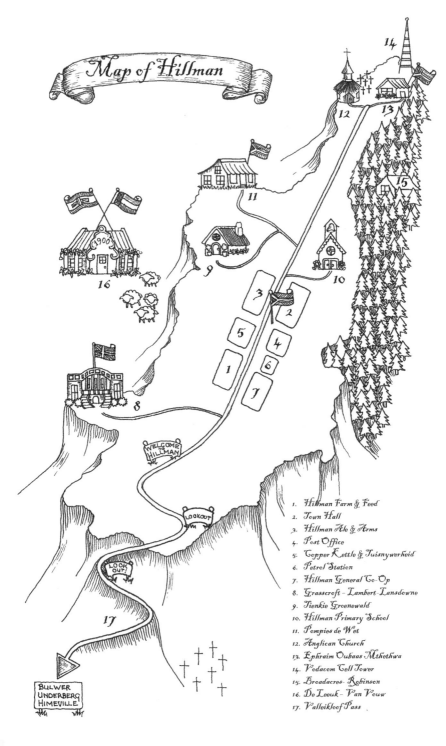

Map of Hillman

1. Hillman Farm & Feed
2. Town Hall
3. Hillman Ale & Arms
4. Post Office
5. Copper Kettle & Tuisnywerheid
6. Petrol Station
7. Hillman General Co-Op
8. Grasscroft - Lambert-Lansdowne
9. Tienkie Groenewald
10. Hillman Primary School
11. Pompies de Wet
12. Anglican Church
13. Ephraim Oubaas Mthethwa
14. Vodacom Cell Tower
15. Broadacres - Robinson
16. De Leeuk - Van Vouw
17. Valleikloof Pass

For Imelda and Ben,
How I miss you and your rapier wit

Foreword

There are very few facts in this book and those that do exist have been ruthlessly and shamelessly manipulated to suit my purposes.

While Underberg, Himeville and Bulwer all exist, and indeed many of my happiest childhood memories involve all three towns, the town of Hillman does not, so no amount of searching for it will locate it. Nor is there a Valleikloof Pass, although this pass is based on the Oliviershoek Pass near Harrismith, which I have driven up (and down) on many occasions, nearly to my peril. If you want to find a town like Hillman, however, you should know that its geography is based on the mountain town of Hogsback in the Eastern Cape, where the townsfolk are lovely and not at all like majority of the people in this book.

None of the characters in *Home Affairs* are real, so if a Dotty Gilmore or anyone else really does exist, I truly didn't mean *you*. Lady Lambert-Lansdowne is the only character based on a real person and the person on whom she is based featured heavily in my early life and possessed all the elements of her fictional counterpart (with the exception of her knowing any dodgy Germans, which I am only guessing she did not). She has since gone to the great polo event in the sky and will therefore no longer mind me plundering her many outlandish character traits in the service of humorous literature. I hope she finds everything perfumed and refined and to her liking up there, or woe betide whoever is in charge of housekeeping in the hereafter.

W. A. Hillman did, however, exist, and he did indeed hail from Chatham in Kent, serve in the Royal Engineers during the Boer

War, and perish on a battlefield in the same war. I found him just like Dotty does, on the Internet. I am sure that this is not at all how he intended to be immortalized, but I offer my thanks to the man nonetheless for his service to his country, his nutty, power-hungry queen, and my book.

Mike Sutcliffe is real and is in the process of changing many of the street and building names in Durban, which has incurred the wrath of many people in Durban, both black and white. Oh, and Ethekwini does indeed mean "bull's testicles".

The Mthethwa army was a noble fighting force and Dingiswayo was its chief. Dingaan, as I allude to in this book, was a bit of a nutter, but I in no way wish to demean the fighting brilliance of the man, even if he really did kill his half-brother Shaka (named, incidentally, after an intestinal beetle), who was also arguably a superior man in the ways I state in *Home Affairs*.

Winston Churchill really did say all the crazy things I attribute to him, and although he was a phenomenal leader, and my father—were he alive—wouldn't have a bad word said against the man (despite Churchill encouraging him to go and fight in a war when I'm sure he'd rather have stayed home and had a nice cup of tea), the fact that Winston said them shows just how far the Brits have come in their foreign policies, even if they still do go around meddling in other countries.

And before they all start vilifying me and issuing long, elaborately-worded-but-ultimately-nonsensical-press-releases denying my allegations of ineptitude, while I have had no personal dealings with any of the political parties mentioned in *Home Affairs*, I have had many frustrating dealings with municipalities, vehicle licensing departments, Telkom and other government offices and they are every bit as ghastly and officious as I have described them in chapter 16. And that *is* a fact!

If I offend you in the course of this book you either belong to any one of the political stereotypes pilloried herein or you haven't understood a word I have written. In either of these instances, I recommend that you use the book as a coaster (it will take two coffee cups side by side; I've tested it) or donate it to a school library, where hopefully it will become matric coursework so that the madness is not perpetuated by any side.

Bree O'Mara

(although I am thinking of renaming myself Tabitha Foxcroft-Bellington Avenue because I don't want to miss out on all the fun)

"The more things change, the more they remain the same."
(Plus ça change, plus c'est la même chose.)
Jean-Baptiste Alphonse Karr (1908–1990)

"The best argument against democracy is a five-minute
conversation with the average voter."
Sir Winston Churchill (1874–1965)

"It's all absolute poppycock; whole bally country's gorn to hell!"
Lady Eleanor Lambert-Lansdowne (d.o.b. never you mind)

Prologue

At precisely 5.30am on Friday the 12th of May 2006, two things happened in the Underberg town of Hillman, the first of which was that Mayor Dewaldt "Pompies" de Wet's trusty bullmastiff, Eskom, ran a slobbery tongue over his master's face, waking him from a rather pleasant dream in which Pompies was being smothered with kisses, having received a medal for bravery of some description.

On realizing—with some disappointment—that the attention given his face came not from either the postal mistress or indeed from one Mrs Esmé Gericke, Pompies sat up, put both feet in a worn pair of slippers, and ambled through to the kitchen to prepare a bowl of Woefies for Eskom and a cup of coffee for himself. From the window of his farmhouse on the western brow of the mountain, the mists were rising slowly to reveal the same pastoral idyll onto which he had gazed for fifty-eight years, three months and eleven days, give or take those times when he was too small to see out of the window; his week-long honeymoon in Mooi River; and the four days when he was away in Harrismith applying for Police College. (He didn't get in.) In the valley below, Van Vouw's sheep could be heard bleating as they did every morning, and in the distance he could hear the jangle of goat bells and the laughter of Oubaas' great-grandchildren as they herded their charges higher up into the hill. All was well with the world.

At exactly 5.30am further down the hill, a piercing alarm shrilled in Tienkie Groenewald's thatched bungalow, waking her from a rather less pleasant reverie in which she had been frantically sorting piles of mail that had been sent to the wrong address. Tienkie, postal mistress of Hillman and the former Miss Pasture Cattle Feed (Vereeniging, 1978), read her horoscope every week in the *Estcourt Echo* and knew a bad omen when she felt one. All was not well with the world.

However, in a large white colonial mansion set discreetly into the side of the hill and overlooking a tapestry of pine forests and pleasant fields as far as the eye could see, Lady Eleanor Lambert-Lansdowne slept on, blissfully unaware in her lavender peignoir of the earth-shattering events that the day held in store. She would wake only when Florence brought in her morning tea (at the far more leisurely and respectable hour of 7.15), together with the mail and her specially "imported" copy of yesterday's *Mercury*. To her the world simply did not yet exist.

Kobus "Dominee" van Vouw was already one full hour into his day, the business of sheep-farming having no place for the idle slumber that is the preserve of those with nothing better to do, and was rattling down the mountain in his Isuzu Raider with no thoughts of the world whatsoever bar that which was contained within the barbed-wire fence surrounding his personal 3,110-hectare kingdom: the farm of De Leeuk, home to four generations of sheep-farming Van Vouws since 1900.

At the very top of the hill, in a small, whitewashed house with running water, a telephone, a generator, and a well-tended yard with potted azaleas and hydrangeas, Ephraim "Oubaas" Mthethwa lay wide awake on his bed, having been unable to sleep since the previous night's discussion with his grandson, Alpheus. Like Pompies, he had lived in his house all his life, as had his father and his father's father before him. This rectangle of land was his world; the only world he knew. He heard Alpheus singing as he washed himself in readiness for a busy day at the Hillman General Co-op and watched his wife of forty-two years, Aggripina, hanging washing on the wire fence that surrounded the Vodacom cell tower, which stood just inside Farmer

Robinson's boundary. At 6.20am, a breeze stirred the mists that hovered around the mountain top, ruffling Aggripina's laundry, and Oubaas closed his eyes in acceptance of what Alpheus had foretold. To no one in particular he announced, "The world is changing."

The (abridged) history of Hillman

There is only one road into (and out of) the mountain village of Hillman, and in the one hundred and seven years of its existence it has never been tarred, widened, improved upon or modified in any way. It has no signs, chevrons, road-markings, arrestor beds or barriers, and has only ever once been the subject of a discussion involving either tarmac or "cat eyes". At the back of the mountain, on the sheer slopes of Reginald Robinson's pine forests, is one other dirt road, virtually impossible to reach and even more impossible to scale, save in a four-by-four with the most dogged determination. Nobody has used that road for years, not even Robinson himself, because it is as inhospitable to vehicles as the old man is to people traversing his land. A handpainted sign at the foot of his side of the hill says "Fokof!" leaving no one in any doubt as to the welcome they will receive should they attempt to approach Hillman via rear entry.

Nobody ever ends up in Hillman by accident. Largely forgotten by cartographers, it is reached only by going through Underberg and Himeville and taking a sharp right at the narrow dirt road signalling the onset of the notorious Valleikloof Pass, which climbs high into the hillside. One signpost at the very start of this dirt road announces "Hillman 8½", the "half" having been added in Tippex by Dorf "Doffie" de Wet at his father's insistence back in 1994, when *everything* seemed to be changing, and which he has retouched every year subsequently as part of the town's annual "maintenance programme".

When it rains—which is often—the road becomes a slalom, the nett result of which is that the village of Hillman can lay claim to boasting the highest percentage of widows per capita of any town in the greater Drakensberg area. The plundered shells of vehicles dating from 1946 to the present day comprise an unlikely museum at the foot of the Valleikloof Pass as well as forming a garden of remembrance of sorts to some of the town's former citizens. It also serves as a tacit warning to non-residents who feel they may just be intrepid enough to attempt the expedition.

And everyone in the village likes it this way.

Shrouded by mists and cloud for much of the day, the town of Hillman is accessed only by wending one's way cautiously up the slippery gravel road, up an incline that defies gravity and tests all but the stoutest of gearboxes. Just beyond the lookout point—at which most "foreign" vehicles decide there is nothing to be gained by proceeding any further—the road levels out and the mists clear to reveal a weather-worn signpost that says: "Welcome to Hillman. Est. (approx) 1899. Population 237".

Over the "7" (and again at his father's insistence) Doffie de Wet dutifully paints an "8" every year, and will continue to do so until the next population census, his father having been absent from his house the very evening the last census forms were completed in 2001.

Lacking both initiative and guile, Doffie had completed the census form accurately while his father attended to a pressing matter of concern to the town's postal mistress, Tienkie Groenewald, on the evening in question. Pompies had always impressed upon his slow-witted but diligent son to "always tell the truth" and Doffie has never failed in his obligation to do so.

Ms Groenewald herself, however, having lived in the land formerly known as the Transvaal, and therefore having acquired a good deal of worldly wisdom in her nineteen years in that province, saw no reason to state on her census form that the mayor of Hillman was in her house at that time of the census, enjoying both her ruminations on the state of the postal service as well as a second helping of some particularly fine skilpadjies with pap. Thus it was that Hillman came to have an official population 0.42% lower than its actual figure.

As to the date on which the town was founded, no one could state with any certainty. It was known that "Dominee" van Vouw's great-great-grandfather, Jacobus, certainly lived on the De Leeuk farm on the leeward side of the mountain in 1900 (these numbers being sculpted into the gable over the stoep of the farmhouse), but Oubaas Mthethwa has long claimed that folklore attests to the town having been there even before that. Verifying any claims concerning the founding of the town, however, are all but impossible since the Great Fire of 1919, which tragedy occurred during a spitbraai held in the main street to celebrate the end of the war (a war in which no citizen of Hillman had fought because it broke out during sheep-shearing season and everyone was busy).

Fearing that the coals of the fire were looking a little low, Pompies de Wet's great-grandfather, Hendrik, had thrown fuel on the embers, resulting in an almighty conflagration, which saw the end of a rather nice rack of lamb, Mrs Maude Struben's finest Sunday hat (and much of her hair), and the original Town Hall in which the archives were housed.

In the eighty-seven years since that fateful day no one has had the time or the inclination to try and salvage any remnants or artefacts of the town's history and the only certain dates that offer any proof of settlement are Van Vouw's front stoep and one legible gravestone in the Hillman Anglican Church's cemetery which states: "Here lies Günther Sibelius Berg, 56. Late of this parish following misadventure. 17 March, 1901".

In fact, not a great deal has changed in the town since 1919, the major additions being a new Town Hall (1920), indoor plumbing (1929), electricity (1937), a village post office (1947) a telephone exchange (1949), the establishment of the Hillman Agricultural and Domestic Science College (1954) and its closure (in 1970, due to lack of sufficient pupils). Analogue telephones came in 1979. The first CD player to make an appearance in Hillman did so in 1994, attached to the ears of Dominee's son, Neels, (who spent a year's pocket money on a Sony Walkman and his first CD: *Barbra Streisand's Greatest Hits*). Ten years thereafter the town witnessed the introduction of its first-ever computer, this being the prized possession of Mrs Dorothy "Dotty" Gilmore, president of the Ladies Auxiliary, who stunned and confused everybody when she announced that she wanted to "surf the net", prompting Mrs van Vouw (chairwoman of the Needlepoint Club) to take an impromptu sojourn to Pietermaritzburg where she enquired of every haberdasher in town if this was a new sewing technique of which she hadn't heard. They said it wasn't. Since 2000, however, every single resident of Hillman has been in possession of a cellphone, although this was not at all by design and was due in no small part to an oversight by old man Robinson, which he rues to this very day.

In 1946, Pompies de Wet's grandfather opened the first and only co-op and petrol station in existence in Hillman, the establishment of which coincided with the first motorized cars ever to make an appearance in Hillman (and, coincidentally, with the first motorized vehicles ever to disappear *off* the mountainside of Hillman), but aside from a coffee shop here and a feed store there, the landscape of Hillman today looks pretty much as it did the day Hendrik de Wet burnt down the Town Hall.

The Right Honourable
Pompies de Wet

As far back as anyone could remember the dorp of Hillman had always been a happy mix of English, Afrikaans and Zulu residents, with no one group outnumbering or dominating the other in any great way. How this peaceful co-existence came to be in a country as polarized as South Africa no-one could quite recall, and indeed nobody really questioned, but many assumed it was because the mountain was too inhospitable and inaccessible a place for people to pick fights with their neighbours over matters as trivial as tradition or language. Aside from occasional spats about whose sheep produced the best wool (Van Vouw would brook no argument there) or who was faring better in the Darts League tables (ditto the above), the only real point of debate concerned the history and establishment of the town of Hillman.

To settle the dispute once and for all, a meeting of the Hillman Town Council was convened following the mayoral election of 1998, attended by all the town councillors (i.e. every man over thirty still resident in the village who wasn't in Harrismith at the cattle auction that day), including Oubaas Mthethwa and his eldest son, Elias, and a veritable phalanx of women in pastel twin-sets from the Hillman Ladies Auxiliary and Needlepoint Club or HLANC (which, Mrs Gilmore and Van Vouw were at pains to point out, was not in any way affiliated with the other ANC but was a completely independent, non-governmental organization).

After quickly dismissing Doffie's suggestion that the town should be said to have been founded in 1981 because that was the year he turned ten and also the year Michael Jackson's *Thriller* was released (an album which Doffie would even now be crushed to know is no longer on the top ten of any current chart anywhere) a vote was taken by a show of hands confirming that the date on which the town was deemed to have been founded was 1899.

Everyone bar Doffie was generally satisfied with the vote: Van Vouw because that was the year the Boer War started and therefore the year that his ancestors took a break from sheep farming to teach the rooinekke a lesson; Lady Lambert-Lansdowne because that was the year her ancestors boarded a fleet of ships to come and teach the Boers a lesson; and Oubaas because today was the first time he got to vote democratically, having not yet received his ID book in time for the general election in 1994.

Pompies himself was happy with any reasonably plausible date because at least the town now had a history, a date on which it could hang the cap of its inception; a date which they could mark with fairs, festivals and spitbraais, the latter now being held in the middle of the Hillman Farm & Feed Store parking lot, away from the new Town Hall and with the strict moratorium (imposed in 1919) on the use of "fuels as incendiaries" firmly in place. And at these events, he imagined, he would preside over the festivities with some importance in his capacity as mayor, a position he had held somewhat by chance since May 1982 when during a darts competition in the Hillman Ale & Arms he had called foul over a play by Kobus van Vouw.

"Ag, rubbish, man," Dominee van Vouw had countered. "Who died and made you mayor?"

This gave the then-35-year-old Pompies pause for thought and in that very moment he had the germ of an idea. Mayor? Why not? The town had never had a mayor before!

Pompies had struggled to find guidance and companionship since the respective demises of both his father and his wife (the elder in one of the aforementioned accidents while going down the Valleikloof Pass in the rain; his wife, tragically, while giving birth to his only son,

Dorf, in 1971, at the end of what was said to have been a difficult pregnancy. What with all the drama surrounding the mortally ailing Maria de Wet, the newly born Dorf was passed in haste to Pompies who had gripped the infant's head rather too robustly between the pair of forceps by which he'd been delivered, resulting in the poor child's somewhat arrested development). A lawsuit never took place, however, because Pompies was too distraught over the loss of his beloved wife and because no member of staff at the Mimi Coertse Neo-Natal Clinic in Estcourt had been holding either the baby or the forceps at the time. In an instant, poor Pompies had lost the woman who had been the object of his affection since they were in Standard Seven at the Hillman Agricultural and Domestic Science College, and overnight he had to learn about parenting, something not a single male De Wet before him had ever done.

In just one year, Pompies had become sole heir to the Hillman General Co-op and Petrol Station fortune, and single parent to a gentle and loving, but clearly challenged, son. It made him both a viable proposition on the one hand and pariah on the other. With so many eligible ladies in the town, a man with capital—an entrepreneur even!—such as Pompies, was a rare commodity. He also had the singular distinction of being the only widower in Hillman, a status that won him a good deal of sympathy and extra helpings of melktert after church on Sundays.

But Pompies realized that if he was to make it as a parent he'd need help of the feminine variety. Few of the widows in Hillman, however, wanted the type of responsibility that they imagined young Doffie would present. It was tough enough in a town with no Checkers, no bank, a variable electricity supply, not a single Milady's outlet and just one school in which everyone was taught together, to say nothing of trying to raise a child who clearly required extra attention and care.

But here, eleven years on, *here* was a loophole, thought Pompies!

As mayor of Hillman he could command respect, exert authority ... and have legitimate access to the single, female citizenry of his town. Perhaps he could even get one of those gold chains with the dangly Krugerrand thingy on the front. And his own parking space! He was punchdrunk with the heady notion of all the advantages that such a title could bring.

Fuelled by copious amounts of Castle Lager and with only one boerie-roll each as buffering (the Boks were playing the Aussies that day and what with the extra crowds at the Hillman Ale & Arms, Mrs Gericke had only been able to make one roll per person), the assembled party began chanting a mantra that was music to Pompies' ears:

"Mayor! Pompies! Mayor! Pompies! Mayor! Pompies!" banging their beer mugs on the bar counter as they intoned.

"*Orrait*, then," he said, wiping his face on the back of his hand and looking Dominee squarely in the face. "If it's a mayor you want, it's a mayor you have!"

A huge cheer went up. The Boks had won two hours previously and everyone was full of the milk of human merriment. And beer. You could have announced you were going to fly to Saturn that evening and the response would have been no less enthusiastic or supportive.

"*Pompieeeeeees!*" yelled one cohort.

"*Mayyyyyorrrrrrrrrrrr,*" yelled another.

"*Vrystaaaaaaaaaaaaaaaaaat,*" yelled Klippies, son of Hillman Farm & Feed Supply store owner, Kerneels Klopper, but only because he couldn't think of anything else to shout. He was, in point of fact, fiercely proud of being a Nataller.

And so it came to pass. What had started in jest became fact, and putting his right hand on a used copy of *Personality* magazine, with a freshly drawn pint of Castle Lager in his left, Dewaldt "Pompies" de Wet solemnly swore allegiance to the town of Hillman, to its citizens and to the great Republic of South Africa, as mayor for the next four years. In the presence of the then proprietor of the Hillman Ale & Arms, Kobie Gericke (who has since joined the legion of Ale & Arms patrons who have gone to meet their maker at the foot of the Valleikloof), and witnessed by at least seventy-two residents, many of whom would need to be reminded of the incident the next day, Pompies was sworn in as mayor of Hillman for the next four years.

The title, while it offered no salary, parking space or—sadly—dangly gold chain, did have its advantages, however, and at least one of Pompies' ambitions—to whit, the adulation of the town's female folk of a certain age—did indeed come to fruition. From the day of his election, Mayor de Wet never wanted for a meal or a nice slice of homemade fridge tart, and he became the focus of the doting affections of many of the Hillman ladyfolk, including—but not limited to—Tienkie Groenewald and Mrs Esmé Gericke, both of whom became rivals for the attentions of the mayor and each of whom prevailed upon him for assistance with Matters of Importance Where Town Issues Where Concerned. He also had to endure a good deal of backbiting and gossip-mongering in the process, but the upside of his devotion to duty and to the denizens of Hillman was that this usually involved liberal amounts of good, strong coffee; Hertzoggies; hot meals, and the occasional brandewyn whenever the gravity of the situation demanded.

What he did *not* get, however, was assistance in the rearing of young Doffie, with the result that the boy grew up thinking that biltong and beer were two of the four main food groups and that the other two were boerewors and pampoenkoekies.

In 1999, one year after finally establishing when the town was established, and seventeen years after he was first elected mayor, the town held its first centennial celebrations and Pompies did indeed preside over the festivities as he had imagined, those being a sheep-shearing competition, an arts and crafts fair presented by the HLANC, a church picnic, and the crowning of the first Miss Hillman at a beauty pageant held in the Town Hall, staged by Miss Pasture Cattle Feed 1978, sponsored by Hillman doyenne of the arts, Lady Lambert-Lansdowne, and followed by the obligatory spitbraai. There were three entrants of suitable age (weight and features in proportion not necessarily being of vital importance given the paucity of candidates), all of whom were crowned variously Miss Hillman, Hillman First Princess and Hillman Second Princes (the embroidery machine having run out of gold thread before Mrs van Vouw could complete the second "s" on the sash). The first princess from that auspicious pageant, the lithe and nubile Koekie van Vouw, aged 15, would go on to become Miss Hillman 2003 upon her return from boarding school in Pietermaritzburg, fuelling her dreams of a more glamorous life away from the drudgery of sheep farming.

Doffie and his friend, Klippies, had both campaigned hard for a fireworks display after the spitbraai to mark the 100th anniversary of Hillman's accepted existence, but Mayor de Wet had put his foot down, fearing a repeat of the unplanned fireworks display in the town just eighty years previously. Instead, all the farmers shouldered their rifles and fired a twenty-two-gun salute into the night sky, Klippies not wanting to be left out of the festivities even though he had lost a foot in 1986 and was no longer a bona fide farmer.

All in all, Mayor Pompies de Wet—in addition to running the General Co-op and Petrol Station with a fair degree of efficiency and a good deal of bonhomie—acquitted himself admirably in his role of mayor. Under his aegis the town got refuse collection (in payment of a long outstanding debt he persuaded Dwayne Donovan to send his labourers in his bakkie once a week to collect refuse bags and take them to the dumpsite near Underberg; he also persuaded him to continue doing so long after the debt was repaid); he got new books for the Hillman Primary School (they were second-hand books from a flea-market in Martizburg, but he'd paid for and transported them and the children were at least reading), and he persuaded retired doctor, Theodore "Teddy" Miller, to set up a weekly clinic in the Town Hall, which dispensed medicines and medical advice to farmers, farmhands and anyone else who was poorly, free of charge, every Thursday.

He even saw to it that the new South African flag was raised proudly on the flagstaff which he had erected outside the post office in Main Street in the fervour of events in 1994. The occasion of its first raising drew most of the townsfolk except for Dominee van Vouw, who elected to stay at home and patch up his Vierkleur in case "all blerrie hell breaks loose now".

Upon rejection by the SAP in 1965, Dewaldt de Wet had taken over management of the petrol station from his father, earning, according to him at least, the moniker "Pompies". Twenty-three years later his son Doffie first failed agricultural college and then followed in his father's footsteps by also being turned down for the SAP. Subsequent to both of these disappointments, he worked for six years delivering mail for Tienkie Groenewald until 1994, at which time his father decided Doffie was ready to take over both the day-to-day management of the petrol station and assume the task of raising and lowering the national flag, which solemn duty was bestowed upon him in December of that year.

Doffie had inherited his father's love of all things military and, dressed in his petrol attendant's uniform and polished shoes, he saluted the flag with studied precision every day at 7am before setting off for the garage in the courtyard of his father's co-op, which he now managed with methodical diligence.

All in all, the town was operating smoothly and people were happy. Pompies' only regrets, and they were few, were that his precious Maria wasn't with him to share in his success, and that Dorf would never follow suit. Truth be told, Pompies also still regretted that the SAP had not seen fit to let him join their ranks when he had left school and he still failed to see why his announcement that he was "colour-blind" had been a problem for the police force of South Africa in 1965. But other than that life was good, if a little lonely at times. He had his bullmastiff for company, it was true, but the dog was called Eskom with good reason, because like the service provided by his namesake he kept going out. And with Doffie grown up and with his own circle of friends, the boy wasn't around as much as he had been. The mayor of Hillman was lonely at heart.

Once every four years, in around the middle of May, a group of residents would gather in the Hillman Ale & Arms of a Saturday afternoon after the rugby had finished, and with an air of solemnity, ably assisted by the difficulty they experienced when trying to stand after a punishing round of tequila shots, a spokesperson (that being the person who could best form whole sentences while remaining standing) would pose the question: "So, Pompies ou pel, you up for another four years, boet?"

Pompies would always seem to mull this over with the appropriate amount of gravitas due such a question, and then he would say: "Ag, ja wat. Why not, hey?"

And with that, he would be confirmed as mayor for another four years, the contract being closed with an oath uttered with one hand on a beer mat, pitchers of Castle all round, and a brandewyn or two to seal the deal.

In twenty-four years nobody had ever sought to contest his candidacy because everybody thought Pompies did a sterling job anyway, and in truth nobody else really wanted the hassle. The only person who even *thought* of putting his name forward was Dominee van Vouw, and that was only because Pompies had beaten him at darts in the League Final in March 2002. But Mrs van Vouw, being both observant and keenly protective over that which was hers, saw for herself a future in which the single and widowed ladies of Hillman would seek her husband's counsel, and summarily curtailed any notions of mayorship that her husband may be entertaining.

"Kobus," she had said that day (she only ever called him Kobus when she was cross with him; the rest of the time it was "Engel" or "Liefie"), and her eyes narrowed as they only did when somebody bought Dotty Gilmore's lemon meringue pie instead of hers. (The Tuisnywerheid had been started in 1994 when the world was officially coming to an end. In the gloom of the impending Armageddon the good ladies of the HLANC had recognized a gap in the market that could only be filled by cheesecake, baked goods and handmade toilet-roll holders. It was a co-operative, yes, but that didn't mean there wasn't healthy competition amongst the co-operators.)

"Kobus. You run for mayor, my boy, and I will completely forget how to make my Three-Chocolate Chocolate Cake!"

Kobus "Dominee" van Vouw was not a man to be easily threatened, but he recognized in his wife's warning the portent of a world of pain which not even the Hertzoggies of Ms Tienkie Groenewald could remedy, should he go ahead with his plan to challenge the incumbent mayor. Without anyone ever knowing that he had even considered the position he withdrew his candidacy and avenged himself by winning the League Final the following year with aerodynamic darts that he had sent to him by mail order from England specially for the event.

Balance having been restored, at least at the dartboard, Hillman went about its business, oblivious to life below the mountain and to the fact that upheaval had lurked on the mayoral doorstep for even a minute.

That is, until Friday the 12th of May, 2006.

The return of the prodigal Alpheus

At 6.07pm on Thursday, the 11th of May, Alpheus Mhlangana Senzangakona Mthethwa had arrived home at his grandfather's house, two minutes earlier than usual and in a highly agitated state.

"There's going to be an election, baba," he announced, breathless with excitement, sweat dripping off his brow.

"An election?" the old man said. "When?"

"On Saturday. At the imperialist shebeen."

Oubaas placed both hands on his walking stick and regarded his grandson with amusement. Twenty-three years old, idealistic and academically astute, Alpheus had been just eleven years old when the flag of the new country had been raised in the town square in Hillman. At that time, Oubaas recalled, his grandson's chief focus in life had been following in the gilded boot-steps of his hero, Lucas Radebe. As it did for many eleven-year-old boys in 1994, the dawn of a new day held little interest for young Alpheus unless it involved a football and goalposts.

Seven years later, having matriculated from high school in Harrismith but with no football contract in the offing, Alpheus had followed his father to Durban where he set about ingratiating himself in the cut-throat world of coastal commerce. The eighteen-year-old Alpheus had a dream, and his dream involved a BMW, a flash suit from Markhams, a gold watch and a pair of Ray-Ban sunglasses.

Despite good matric results, however, Alpheus' CV was a little scant on bankable experience, and Durban—democratic, progressive and BEE-focused though it was in 2001—offered few opportunities for a young man whose prior work experience comprised sheep-shearing for Kobus van Vouw, piece-jobs for Klippies Klopper at the Feed Store, and packing shelves for Pompies de Wet in the Hillman General Co-op during school holidays.

Having a vision, ambition and drive, Alpheus quickly discovered, was simply not enough, even in the New South Africa. What you needed were an education, capital and connections.

Education he already had in spades (one A for Maths; two Bs and three Cs, at that), so he set about addressing the acquisition of "capital and connections", assuming that once you had the former, the latter would come of its own volition. Or was it the other way round?

As months turned into years, however, Alpheus became disillusioned. His dreams of becoming a successful businessman with equity, a nice house and all the aforementioned accoutrements that are the hallmark of a prosperous man, seemed to be disintegrating daily. By 2004, he had only managed to acquire two things on his wishlist, both of which were items he sold by the dozen on a large cardboard display rack outside the Indian Market in Grey Street: a gold watch (well, gold-coloured, to be precise; he sold them in various shades of faux 9ct, 18ct, 22ct and platinum) and a pair of Ray-Bans (again, not exactly Ray-Bans, per se, but a remarkably close facsimile, even if they did come from China. They even offered "VU protection").

Not wanting to appear anything less than the entrepreneur he assured everyone back home that he was, he had indeed bought a suit from Markhams on lay-by for his older sister's wedding in 2003, but he still owed thirteen instalments on the purchase and the business of being a mobile purveyor of sunglasses and fashionable timepieces saw stiff competition from other merchants. What he needed, he decided, was to find a gap in the market; get the right opportunity, a foothold onto greater security and wealth. And the only place to do that was in the city!

In the hostel at which he roomed in Broad Street (it wasn't the house of which he dreamed, it was true, but it was cheap, close to work and he shared his quarters with lots of his friends of a similar age), he would sit round a primus stove in the evening, discussing the state of the world with his colleagues.

The root of the problem, they concluded, lay not in a saturated marketplace or indeed in a lack of commercial scope for Chinese imports of questionable quality, but lay firmly at the feet of the fascist, neo-colonialist imperialists. *And* with the Xhosa, who were just as bad and sought to dominate and oppress the Zulus (who far outnumbered them anyway, so how come they were running the show in a so-called democracy?). If only he had been older when The Struggle was at it apex, mused Alpheus, then he could have made a real contribution to the cause! As it was, he decided, the real struggle was *now*, when free from the draconian laws that had bound his forefathers, a man had to make his way in a dog-eat-dog world of apparent equals.

Alpheus started to formulate a plan of action. The first part involved what he referred to as the Re-establishment of Cultural Identity, which necessitated him eschewing his "neo-colonialist" name, Alpheus (it didn't matter that his was a biblical name; this was a matter of cultural heritage!), and taking up his Zulu name, Mhlangana kaMthethwa. Alpheus was dead; long live Mhlangana!

The second, and trickier, part of his two-tiered plan involved redressing various wrongs, these being 1) his lack of equity and Bavarian transport and 2) the aforementioned marginalization of his people by Xhosa and colonial forces. In the past, his grandfather had told him when Alpheus was just a boy, if one tribe came and stole cattle from yours, the young men of the village would sneak into the kraal of the villainous tribe and steal the cattle right back. Alpheus' Plan B involved a modernized version of this very strategy. He was sure his grandfather wouldn't see his modifications of the tactic in quite the same way, however, but the man was old and trapped in the outmoded philosophies of a bygone era.

At eleven o'clock at night on a sweltering Saturday evening in January, Mhlangana kaMthethwa, political visionary and tycoon-in-the-making, and his friend Godfrey (he hadn't got around to calling himself by his Zulu name just yet) Makhatini, sought to redistribute some of the misappropriated wealth of the country and acquire a BMW in the process. Strolling nonchalantly along the promenade at Whilson's Wharf, they quickly ascertained that the car guard was fast asleep and got to work with stealth and speed. Sweating more from anxiety than from the stifling humidity, they browsed the vehicles assembled in the parking lot, debating the merits of this one over that, before finally settling on an out-of-the-box, cobalt-blue BMW seven-series, Mhlangana's vehicle of choice. Every vehicle in the parking lot was owned, he reasoned, by somebody who was at that very moment dining in a restaurant on the quayside, and if you could dine in such a restaurant and drive such a car you were either a neo-colonialist imperialist or a Xhosa. Either way the planned manoeuvre was justified.

Struggling with the locks on the sleek and shiny vehicle, this being their first-ever attempt at such an endeavour, they had just managed to prise open the driver's side door (chipping the paintwork in the process) when a car alarm to raise the dead started to shriek, waking the car guard from his repose and causing Mhlangana kaMthethwa to wet himself, something he was fairly sure his forefathers had never done while engaged in the business of repossession.

The car guard turned out to be a security guard from one of the larger companies (complete with uniform and a very real-looking gun) who set off, weapon raised, in the direction of the car alarm. Mhlangana and Godfrey, in turn, set off with haste in opposite directions and the car guard was forced to choose which of the two he would pursue. Fortunately for Mhlangana it was Godfrey's unlucky day, and the last thing he saw while glancing back as he charged off down Victoria Embankment was Godfrey stopping and raising his arms as he turned slowly round.

"Mhlangana, you bastard," he heard Godfrey shout out. But sorry as he was that his friend had been apprehended, Mhlangana had his own matters of self-preservation to attend to. You cannot win a war without casualties; that much he knew.

Sitting on his bunk bed in the relative safety of his rooming house in Broad Street, Mhlangana caught his breath and took stock of the situation. Three things were clear, the first being that Godfrey would not go quietly; the second was that within minutes (or hours at least) police would come to the hostel looking for somebody called Mhlangana; and the third was that he suddenly needed to take a break and go home for a bit. Return to his roots, as it were.

After three bus trips and one hair-raising journey in Philemon Nthuli's death-trap of a minibus up the Valleikloof Pass, Alpheus Mhlangana Senzangakona Mthethwa arrived home unannounced on Sunday evening to the complete surprise and utter delight of his grandparents, and the barely concealed suspicion of his younger sister, Sylvia.

"Grandfather," he said with solemnity, "I have come home to take care of you."

"But why?" said Oubaas, entirely confused at this turn of events. "I am not sick."

"But you are old," countered Alpheus, "and grandmother is old, too. You need a strong young man in the house to take care of both of you, and Sylvia too."

His sister smirked; she had a very good job as a waitress at the Hillman Ale & Arms and took home at least R200 every week. Sylvia was perfectly capable of taking care of herself.

"What about your business in the big city?" said Oubaas.

"Grandfather," he said sagely, "there are some things more important than making money."

"Indeed there are, my boy," his grandfather replied. "Indeed there are."

Reaching into his bag, Alpheus produced gifts for his family: a 22ct gold "Pattek Philip" watch for his grandfather, a "Tag Haur" for his sister, and a nice, dainty "Rollex" for his grandmother. Plus each of them got a pair of sunglasses and a Nokia phone charger. It really was too bad that Vodacom had given everyone Motorola phones.

Aggripina beamed with pride. Clearly her grandson had done well for himself, but it was good to have him home, too, where he belonged.

"And grandfather," the younger man added casually, "if anyone should happen to ask for a Mhlangana kaMthethwa, you should tell them there is no such man on this mountain. Alpheus is a good name, a Bible name. It is my name."

Oubaas nodded quietly. The time for questions would come later, he decided. For the moment the youngster needed the solace of his family, the wisdom and guidance of his grandfather and the protection that only this village in the mountain could provide. That night Alpheus Mthethwa ate his first decent meal in months and slept soundly on clean sheets in the house of his birth, the sweet smell of pine needles and the sighing of the forest lulling him into the best sleep he had had since leaving for Durban almost six years previously.

On Monday morning, while his grandson slept on, Oubaas put on his Sunday jacket, donned his hat with the feather in it, affixed the Ray-Bans to his face and, strapping on his new watch, took the short walk down the main road to see Pompies.

Seeing the old man walking down the street wearing his new dark sunglasses and with his walking stick one pace ahead of him, Doffie left the petrol pump and ran up the street.

"Oubaas!" he cried. "What's wrong, man? Have you gone blind?"

"No," chuckled Oubaas. "My grandson has returned home. He

brought me presents," he said proudly, brandishing his watch.

"Sjoe! That's a luck, hey!" said Doffie. "For a minute there I thought I'd have to use sign language or something."

"Sign language is for deaf people," said Oubaas.

"Oh, ja! I forgot," said Doffie. "What I *meant* to say was that I thought you might need Eskom as a guide dog or something."

Oubaas shook his head and sighed. There simply wasn't enough time to indulge in idle banter today. He had Important Business to discuss.

"Is your father in the store today?" asked Oubaas.

"Ja, oom," said Doffie. "But he doesn't want to be," he added as an afterthought. "Mrs Gericke's making pampoenkoekies this morning."

"Perfect!" said Oubaas.

"*Jaaa* ..." nodded Doffie, his mind transported to the magical world that was Mrs Gericke's kitchen. "She never uses too much cinnamon."

The bell sounded over the door as Oubaas stepped into the cool, dark interior of the General Co-op. For as long as he could remember the shop had smelled of furniture polish, fresh vegetables, paraffin and Sunlight Soap. The floor was always polished and the shelves tidy and well stocked. The counter, too, was always clean and shiny, on top of which stood the very same cash register that had rung up his purchases when he was a child. The minus button had broken off some years ago, but Pompies reckoned that very few people ever changed their mind about what they were buying anyway.

"When the plus sign goes, it goes," said Pompies. "Not before." It was as sound an economic policy as any Oubaas had heard.

Oubaas had known three generations of De Wets, good men all and hardworking too, but none particularly sharp or academically inclined.

Pompies looked up from the coins he was sorting into plastic bags.

"Oubaas!" he cried. "What's wrong, man? Have you gone blind?"

With that Oubaas removed his sunglasses and pocketed them, deciding that the infernal eyewear would cause more confusion than was tolerable for the time being.

"No, no, Mr de Wet," he sighed. (He always called Pompies by his surname, not out of deference but simply because he couldn't bring himself to call a grown man "Pompies".) "My grandson Alpheus came home with presents for his old grandfather."

"Sjoe! That's a luck, hey," said Pompies. "I thought for a minute there you might need a wheelchair or something."

Oubaas straightened himself up and took a deep breath.

"My grandson has come home to stay for a while," he said. "He needs work, responsibility, discipline and a firm hand. I was wondering if perhaps you had a job for him here?"

"In the store?" said Pompies.

"Yes, perhaps, or in the petrol station."

Pompies' mind raced ahead. He couldn't depose Doffie from his position as manager of the petrol station; the lad would be crushed. He had only recently mastered the finer points of how to fill a radiator after several less-than-successful efforts over the years, which had resulted in second-degree burns to his hands and at least one cracked radiator. Reginald Robinson had sworn never to use the petrol station again, but with very little option available to him he had grudgingly returned four days later, his bakkie having been fixed in Estcourt.

On the other hand, Pompies knew Alpheus was a hard worker and smart with numbers; creative, too. One school holiday he had even done a stocktake, moving older cans to the front of the shelves, which was something Pompies had never thought to do. Until then he simply cast a glance over the shelves and made a mental note of what was looking low, before climbing into his Nissan and racing off to Harrismith or Maritzburg to replenish his supplies. If he forgot something, which wasn't often admittedly, there was always next time.

Then there were Mrs Gericke's pampoenkoekies, which he knew would be coming out of the oven in around twenty minutes. He could just about put up with a discussion about the Annual Needlepoint Workshop for a plateful of piping-hot pampoenkoekies washed down with freshly brewed coffee.

"Can he start this morning?" said Pompies. Making split-second decisions of commercial importance was something the mayor of a town needed to be able to do.

"Of course!" said Oubaas.

And with that the deal was made. Whether or not Alpheus had wanted it that way was never under discussion, but he was pleased at the opportunity to earn a steady salary while laying low until the whole beastly business of mistaken identity blew over in Durban. After that, he decided—telling no one of his plans—he would return to Ethekwini, using his experience at the co-op to garner himself a job at the big OK in West Street. The way forward was clear.

The contender

Alpheus had been working at the Hillman Co-op for four months and Pompies was pleased with how hard the boy worked and with the new-found freedom that his appointment of an "associate" offered him. At last Pompies' business was expanding, and at the age of fifty-eight he could finally afford to take a few hours off here and there to sample, at a more leisurely pace, the epicurean treats that were on offer in the kitchens of various widows and singletons around the mountain.

In those four months Alpheus applied himself well and made a few significant changes that did not go unnoticed by Pompies. He started by replacing the duplicate roll in the cash register so that Pompies could keep a track of the day's sales versus receipts. (Actually, Alpheus did that, but Pompies took a look at it every day and was surprised to learn what his turnover was.) He also replaced the gas canister in the cold-drinks fridge, so now the Coca-Cola, Sprite and Mirinda was actually cold, as opposed to the room-temperature beverages that had been stocked in a previously whining fridge. Alpheus also undertook to do home deliveries on his bicycle (for a small fee, of course), the added convenience of which saw Pompies' stock with the townsfolk go up tenfold; and he moved the KitKats and Chocolate Logs into the fridge with the polony and cheese, so now they didn't melt in the summer months.

The residents had never had cause to complain about the Hillman General Co-op, aside from the one particularly bitter winter when Pompies ran out of candles and paraffin at the same time that the electricity supply to the town was interrupted for over twenty-four hours, but the new, improved features contributed immeasurably to the townsfolk's enhanced shopping experience. Everyone was happy.

On Thursday the 11th of May, Alpheus was busy arranging that week's special (Selati Sugar; 1kg for just R11.99) on the new "Specials Display Shelf", when Mrs van Vouw came in to buy eggs and self-raising flour. She also bought two kilos of sugar.

"Impulse purchasing," Alpheus had said, when explaining to Pompies his theory behind a weekly special. "Added value to your basic supply and demand."

"Ja, boet," Pompies had said, scratching his head. "But it doesn't matter how much you supply; they still demand, demand, demand."

Alpheus' specials were a great hit and they were also excellent for disposing of old stock, too, like cans of corned meat or chakalaka that were approaching their sell-by date.

"Morning, Alpheus," said Mrs van Vouw. "Next week put condensed milk on special please. I'm making lemon meringue pie for the Needlepoint Workshop."

"I'll try, Mrs van Vouw," said Alpheus, "or you could buy in bulk to qualify for our discount." Mrs van Vouw looked perplexed at all this newfangled, big-city talk; if you were going to buy in bulk you went to the Checkers in Harrismith. Everyone knew that!

"Pompies," she said, moving right along, a new conspiratorial note entering her voice, "isn't it about time for the election?"

Mrs van Vouw had a shrewd head for dates and knew exactly what was happening in Hillman at any given time. She made it her business to keep track of other people's business and she wanted to be certain that the position of mayor would not be vacant any time soon.

"Bliksem!" said Pompies. "I almost forgot! Has it been four years already?"

"It has," she said, very matter-of-fact. "The Hillman Arms on Saturday at three, then? I'm making koeksisters ..."

"Ja-nee," said Pompies, "Why not, hey? I never miss my own election!"

"Or my koeksisters," said Mrs van Vouw, who knew that with creativity, sugar and a deep fat fryer, most men could be convinced to do just about anything.

Entirely satisfied with the outcome of her shopping trip, Mrs van Vouw left the shop and squeezed her ample derrière into her powder-blue bakkie with the hand-embroidered seat-backs, lace-trimmed steering wheel cover and broderie anglaise tissue box. Mr van Vouw, she knew, would be attending an auction of his Merinos on Saturday in Martizburg, and wouldn't be home until late. Far too late to contest the election, anyway.

The issue had never raised its ugly head since the Three-Chocolate Threat of 2002, but it was best to keep these matters in check long before they became an issue, she thought.

Alpheus stopped stacking sugar for a moment and asked pensively, "What election is this, boss?"

"Ag, nothing, man. It's just the election for mayor. We do it every four years. It's just a ... whatyoucallit ... a formality. Then everyone gets babelaas and we all go home."

Pompies chuckled heartily at fond memories of elections past.

Alpheus could scarcely believe his ears. Here was the very opportunity he'd been looking for all this time; a chance to depose the colonialists and put a Zulu back in his rightful place at the top of the mountain. The head honcho. The main man. The mayor! And the very man for the job was his esteemed grandfather, Oubaas.

Alpheus could hardly think straight for the rest of the afternoon. By mistake he put one kilo of Selati on top of Mrs Gilmore's extra-large eggs, breaking every one of them, and he charged Mrs Kloppers the normal price for the six packs of sugar she had bought on special. For the first time ever Pompies found he had need of the minus sign on his cash register.

"What the donder is the matter with you, Alpheus?" he asked. "You sick or something?"

"No, boss," said Alpheus. "Sorry, boss." In truth, Alpheus had never felt better!

At 6pm sharp, Alpheus turned the sign to "Closed/Toe" and literally ran home. Bursting through the door without even greeting his grandmother, he blurted out, "There's going to be an election, baba!"

"An election?" the old man said, "When?"

"Saturday. At the imperialist shebeen."

It took Oubaas a minute to figure out what on earth Alpheus was prattling on about.

"Oh, *that*," said Oubaas. "That's nothing. It's just a bunch of crazy white men looking for an excuse to get drunk," he said. "They do it every four years. The election part, anyway. The drunk thing they do every week at least. It's all a load of nothing."

Alpheus was incredulous.

"Nothing? What do you mean 'nothing'? The election of a mayor is definitely not 'nothing'!"

Oubaas laughed out loud.

"It's not an official election, my boy," he said. "It's not even an official position."

Alpheus could feel his blood rising. "Our forefathers died for the freedom to vote," he stated with as much drama as he could invest in the moment, "and if people are gathering in a public place to vote for mayor of this town, then that's just about as official as it needs to be. And what's more, *you* have to run for mayor. It is your *duty* to our ancestors!"

Oubaas burst out laughing. Whatever had gotten into the boy? Now he was just talking crazy!

"I don't think much of elections, child," he said. Since receiving his ID in January 1999, just six years after applying for it, he had voted in two general elections at the Hillman Town Hall. On each occasion every eligible resident of Hillman had turned out to vote and there were queues lasting at least twenty minutes on each voting day. In 2003, he also had to help Josephina Nguni with her ballot paper because it was the first time she was voting and she wasn't sure what to do. In the end she put an "X" next to all the names, "to give everyone a fair chance" she said.

At the end of both general elections, however, despite his votes to the contrary, a Xhosa had retained the presidency, so to Oubaas the whole thing was a bit of a con anyway. A bit like his new Nokia phone charger: very nice to have, but virtually useless to him. He had once entertained high hopes for Zuma to be the first Zulu to lead the country, but since the former deputy president's lamentable involvement with his friends Schabir and Chippy it was frankly all looking a little shaky for poor Jacob these days. Not to mention the embarrassing business about taking a shower to "prevent AIDS". Hah! That was just plain umbhedo! Everyone knew that's what a diet of garlic, beetroot, lemons and African potato was for!

Besides, in the seventy-odd years Oubaas had lived on this hilltop (his ID book said he was born in 1936, but that was only because that was the year in which he *said* he was born. Rather like Hillman, however, his exact date of establishment in this world could not hold up to much scrutiny) no politician had ever been to visit the place. Even when the queen came to the Drakensberg in 1947 she had gone straight to the Royal Natal National Park and never even so much as popped her head into the Hillman Ale & Arms for a cup of tea. Everyone at the time had thought that pretty poor form, especially as the town had just established its very first post office in time for her visit. Perhaps she didn't send postcards when she went on holiday, they wondered?

In 1994, before The Election (capitalized in Oubaas' mind because that was the real milestone in the country's history), campaigners had come to Hillman from both the IFP and the ANC, the former receiving a noticeably warmer welcome than the latter, he noted, perhaps because they gave out free T-shirts that day, but not a single politician from any camp had ever made the journey up the Valleikloof Pass. It was almost, he thought, as though Hillman didn't matter. It was only at Pompies' insistence that the town had gotten its own polling booth; until one week before the big day the Election Commission had suggested that the townsfolk double up in bakkies and Philemon's minibus and go to Underberg to vote.

And now here was his impassioned grandson foaming at the mouth about some fictitious election that didn't even require an ID book.

"Grandfather," continued Alpheus, "our family has been on this mountain since before you were born. Mthethwas have lived on this hill since before a single white man ever set foot on this land. It is your rightful place; by *rights* you are the only official leader of this village."

That night Oubaas thought long and hard about what Alpheus had said. It was true that Mthethwas had lived here since before even old man Van Vouw set up house down the hill. There were probably, he mused, Mthethwas here or hereabouts since the dawn of time. But what could be gained from running for mayor? It didn't pay anything and, from what he could see, the job was far more hassle than it was worth. He didn't want to listen to a bunch of white ladies moaning about sewing and baking and women's stuff. So what could be gained by such a ridiculous notion?

He hardly touched his pigs' trotters that evening, even though Aggripina had cooked them in oil with plenty of onions, just the way he liked them, and after that he cut a solitary figure, sitting in his yard and contemplating the past and the future.

"Why didn't you eat?" she had chided him at bedtime. "You better not be dying on me, old man."

Oubaas smiled. Far from it! For the first time in a long time, maybe, he felt the stirrings of mischief. For the first time in a long time he was going to have a little fun!

Since retiring from his position as farm manager for Kobus van Vouw ten years previously, having worked at De Leeuk all his life (first for the father and then for the son), he had enjoyed the benefits to be reaped after a life of hard work. His children had scattered to the far corners of the country in search of work, it was true, but he had his wife, his grandchildren, his great-grandchildren, his own herd of sheep and goats, and a nice house from which to look out over the valley of an evening. He had a good pension; he ate well; he was seldom sick. All in all life was good. If a little dull.

That night he kept asking himself the question he had asked Alpheus several times that evening when the boy had insisted that he run for mayor: "Why?"

And then in the early hours of Friday morning the answer came to him, straight from the words of the mayor himself: "Why not?"

A few hours later Oubaas washed his face with Lifebuoy soap, put on his Sunday jacket, donned his hat with the feather in it, left the Ray-Bans on the shelf next to Stephina's wedding photo and the Nokia charger and, strapping on his gold watch, took the short walk down the main road to the post office.

Watching her husband set off for the town centre, Aggripina shook her head with resignation.

"Crazy old fool," she muttered before returning her attentions to her laundry. Why were women the only sensible people in any place? You didn't see white *women* running for mayor, either! But she knew it would do no good to dissuade her husband from his chosen path, and besides, it was good to have him out from under her feet for a little while so she could clean the linoleum.

As Oubaas walked down the hill, his entire carriage and bearing had the air of a Man on a Matter of Great Importance. Even Alpheus, looking out from the co-op, could see him striding with purpose towards the post office and felt a frisson of excitement that set him all aquiver ...

Although the Hillman Town Hall serves as the meeting place for official town gatherings, weddings, the Hillman Primary Annual Prizegiving, and occasional market days when the weather is bad, it also hosts the Ladies Auxiliary Club on a Tuesday and Needlepoint on a Thursday. It is *not*, however, the place to which one goes on any official town business. For that one goes either to the General Co-op or (after hours) to the Hillman Ale & Arms to find the mayor. For all other matters one reports to the post office, the seat of all knowledge and learning in a town the size of Hillman.

The post office in Hillman is nestled between the Hillman Town Hall and the Hillman General Co-op on the right-hand side of Main Street and opposite the Hillman Ale & Arms, in a neat, white, gabled building with a green corrugated roof, a polished wooden counter, a black and white tiled floor and a bright red post box outside. When it was built in 1947, the stonemasons had sculpted into the gable the words: "The Royal Hillman Queen Elizabeth II Post Office", these letters bring filled in with glossy black paint. But when it became apparent that the town had been snubbed by the royal party the words "Royal" and "Queen Elizabeth II" were hastily painted over in white so that since November 1947 it has read:

"The   Hillman   Post Office"

Everybody knows it is the post office, however, so it doesn't really matter what it says on the front.

Tienkie Groenewald was flustered that morning. After a bad night's sleep in which she had been tormented by dreams of misdirected mail, which could only be interpreted as a portent of an ill wind blowing her way, she had arrived to the post office to find no fewer than two people already waiting for her, and the non-stop flow of human traffic had shown no let-up since that inauspicious start to the day.

By the time Oubaas came in (followed immediately by his agitated grandson, Alpheus), she was helping Farmer Robinson send a particularly bulky package to Vryheid and had Lady Lambert-Lansdowne waiting in line to post her annual subscription to *Fair Lady*.

"Good morning, Lady," Oubaas said to Eleanor Lambert-Lansdowne as he entered, doffing his cap respectfully.

"Good morning to you, Mr Mthethwa," she replied primly. When she said his name it always came out "ma-tet-wah". She also referred to the president as "Ma-bay-ki". It was her way.

"Sawubona, Nomsa Lambert," said Alpheus, stoically.

Lady Lambert-Lansdowne eyed the boy quizzically. Was it Foreign Languages Day in Hillman, she wondered? What fun! She knew that modern schools were very progressive these days and were offering all sorts of exciting programmes and activities; why not join in the spirit of the occasion!

"Bonjour, Alpheus," she countered. "Ça va aujourd'hui?"

Alpheus stared back at her, completely nonplussed.

Tienkie looked up from Mr Robinson's parcel, saw Oubaas standing there with nothing but his cane in his hands and said "Môre, Oubaas. Did you forget your letter?"

Oubaas looked perplexed.

"I'm not posting a letter today, Miss Groenewald."

"Oh? Then how can I help you?"

"I need the application form, please," he said.

"Which form is that, Oubaas? You already got your ID book al lankal. You getting a driver's licence now, too?"

"No, no, the form for the mayor. For the election. I am applying to run for office."

With that, Tienkie dropped Farmer Robinson's parcel on the floor, smashing the contents, and Lady Lambert-Lansdowne fainted straight into the arms of Alpheus.

Oubaas grinned. The fun was just beginning.

A call to arms

By 9.25 that morning the only residents of Hillman who had not heard about the unprecedented turn of events were Dominee van Vouw, who had his hands full, quite literally, with a sheep suffering from bloat, and the teacher and pupils of Hillman Primary. In a desperate attempt at damage-control, Tienkie Groenewald—for the first time since becoming postal mistress in 1979—closed the post office during office hours and put a sign on the door saying "Back in 15 minnits", which was something she only ever did on weekends and public holidays.

Having arrived in Hillman in December 1978 at the age of nineteen, Miss Groenewald was the town's newest resident. Still regarded by some (namely Dominee van Vouw) as a buitelander, hailing as she did from the nether regions of Vereeniging, she was proud of her status as a "foreigner". It gave her a certain exotic cachet and imbued her with an air of worldliness and sophistication which put her in much the same league as Lady Lambert-Lansdowne (who had moved to Hillman from Tongaat, which was only marginally better than Vereeniging because at least she came from Natal). And like Lady Eleanor, she too had a title: "Miss Pasture Cattle Feed, Vereeniging", a title which had come with a crown, a sceptre and a full scholarship to attend a one-month typing and shorthand course at the Tip Top Typing School and Secretarial College. She also had her picture on the front page of the local chronicle and was invited to cut the ribbon at the grand opening of the "Vark en Vleis Slagtery" with Joggie Steenkamp who was captain of the Vereeniging Rugby Club that year. The months after winning the title were a giddy whirlwind of social events and pressing engagements and she would tell anyone who asked that she had emigrated to Hillman simply to escape the incessant harassment by members of the press that fame and fortune had brought her. But nobody—not even Mayor de Wet, with whom she was often in close consultation over the years—knew exactly how it was that she had ended up in Hillman of all places.

But come she had, in a yellow Volkswagen Beetle with a "Love is ..." sticker on the back window. In Hillman she had found a home and a purpose, if not a husband. Positively smitten with widower De Wet since the day she had arrived, she was certain that it was only a matter of time before the poor man overcame his crippling shyness where matters of the heart were concerned and made an honest woman of her. She had waited twenty-seven years, as long as Mandela was in prison, so she figured that Pompies would make up his mind any day now. Her Long Walk to Wedlock was, she was sure, almost at an end.

Tienkie was happy in Hillman. She had a lovely cottage with a neat and tidy garden complete with two plaster garden gnomes; her trusty (if rusty) Beetle; and—more importantly, as befits a person with a title—she also had a realm, a domain of which she was the sole empress and over which she had complete control: her post office. Following the timely death of the previous postal mistress, Doris Snodgrass, whose predilection for licking the stamps eventually got the better of her at age eighty, Tienkie was promoted from postal clerk to postal mistress. She was a natural choice for the job: she was bilingual, had typing skills, one year's post-office experience, and—coming from the Transvaal—was more au fait with foreign place names like Klerksdorp and Fish Hoek than native Hillman-ites.

In the role of postal mistress, Tienkie Groenewald found her true calling. The position commanded respect, demanded efficiency and reliability, and gave her an enviable opportunity to snoop on the affairs of the townsfolk of Hillman. She knew, for example, that

Koekie van Vouw was corresponding with a certain young gentleman in Pietermartizburg, which correspondence was reciprocated with letters sent on sky-blue stationery with hearts and XXs drawn on the back. Tienkie would keep these missives to one side for Koekie, for which small discretion Koekie was eternally grateful. Tienkie also knew that Koekie's father's sheep farming business wasn't doing as well as he said it was on account of the number of letters he received with the words "Final Demand" stamped on the front, and that he sometimes just didn't pay his bills even though he continued to buy things for himself even when he said he was "short". She also knew that young Neels van Vouw had a subscription to *Cosmopolitan*, and that Farmer Robinson also had a subscription to a publication, which was sent to him monthly in a plain brown wrapper. Knowledge, as Tienkie was keenly aware, was power. And she had plenty of inside knowledge ...

Following the alarming developments of Friday the 12th of May she knew she had to act fast. There was no time to lose because a post-traumatic Lady Lambert-Lansdowne would tell Dotty Gilmore, who would tell Esmé Gericke, who would tell Brumilda van Vouw, and before you knew it there would be talk of a collapse of government, mass hysteria and general anarchy in the village. And over her dead body would she let that happen to Pompies.

While Oubaas could still be seen walking sedately and regally back up the hill from whence he came, Tienkie locked the post office and scuttled furtively over to the petrol station, crouching low behind the pump so that Alpheus couldn't see her from behind the counter of the co-op.

"Doffie," she whispered, "*Doffie!*"

Doffie was under the hood of his father's bakkie, trying to locate the chewing gum he'd dropped somewhere in the engine while changing the oil.

"Pssst! Haai! Doffie!" she said in a stage whisper so loud it could be heard in the inner sanctum of the co-op.

Doffie looked up sharply, banging his head on the bonnet.

"*Ei-na!* Blerrie bliksemse genade! O, hallo, tannie. Wat maak tannie daar agter?"

"No time to explain, Doffie. Go get your father. Tell him to meet me at the Ale & Arms. *Now!* Go, GO!" And with that she took off in the direction of the local imbibing emporium, looking left and right and for all the world like a woman possessed.

Doffie rubbed his head where he'd banged it on the metal. Life in the post office must be getting very stressful for Tannie Groenewald if she was starting to dop so early in the day. He was glad he was no longer a postman and that his father had saved him from the corporate world before it got to him, too.

Six minutes later, Pompies entered the Ale & Arms looking very confused.

"Wat die donder is going on today?" he said to Tienkie, who was trying with little success to drink a cup of coffee with hands that wouldn't stop shaking. "First Alpheus disappears. Then he comes back five minutes later and starts all this Zulu-talk. And then Lady Lambert comes in all pale and shaking and asking if we have smelling salts or lavender oil. So I tell her we only have Cerebos table salt and sunflower oil and what in the hell *is* smelling salts anyway? And the next thing Alpheus greets her in Zulu and she goes and faints right there on my floor!

"So *she's* all passed out on a bag of mielie-meal and Doffie comes in, bleeding on the back of his head, and says Tannie Groenewald has lost her mind and is hiding in the bar. What the bliksem is going on in hierdie donderse dorp, Tienkie?"

"You'd better sit down, Dewaldt," she said quietly but firmly.

Pompies sat immediately, the colour draining from his face. If Tienkie was calling him Dewaldt then whatever was coming next was very bad news indeed. In those interminable seconds between sitting down and hearing what the Very Bad News was, Pompies' mind was spinning and he could feel prickles of cold sweat forming at the collar of his nice checked shirt. Maybe Dominee had finally taken delivery of those tungsten darts with the brass tips from America. The bastard! It was tantamount to cheating! How can it be a fair fight if one of you is using equipment that comes from a country that makes heat-seeking missiles? And there was Pompies with darts that had feathers missing, for Piet's sake! Next time he went to Maritzburg, he vowed, he would buy those darts he'd seen in the window of Cash Converters. No question!

Or perhaps, Pompies thought, he *hadn't* been selected for the annual Drakensberg Fly Fishing Contest in Himeville this year. Those buggers were always trying some angle or other to only include the ouks from the bigger towns. It wasn't right! Hillman was in the Drakensberg, too!

Or had the postal authority finally made good on their threat to close the Hillman post office once and for all? That *must* be it! Surely only news of such grievous import could lure Tienkie away from her counter at this hour of the day. Oh, boy! *Now* there would be snot en trane.

Tienkie looked around to make sure that Sylvia wasn't lurking in the shadows. Oubaas had spies everywhere: one grandchild in the co-op, another in the Ale & Arms. The old man already had a network of operatives and the news wasn't even half an hour old! They couldn't have met in Copper Kettle Coffee Shop and Tuisnywerheid, however, because Mesdames van Vouw, Gericke or Gilmore would be there setting up for the day and who knows what scandal a rendezvous à deux in the Copper Kettle at 9.20 on a weekday morning would provoke. Fortunately, however, Sylvia–having brought Tienkie's tea–was holed up in the kitchen of the Ale & Arms polishing off last night's beesstert for breakfast and didn't give a damn what the old white folk were nattering about anyway.

"Dewaldt, it's about the election," she said gravely.

Relief washed over Pompies like Eskom's tongue on his face after a bowl of milk.

"Ag, Tienkie, don't worry so much. I keep telling you there's *plennnnty* of time to get all the ballot papers by 2008. And this time Dorf won't get anywhere near them, I promise. True's Bob!"

What a fuss about nothing, thought Pompies. OK, so the ballot papers had been mailed to Bulwer by mistake in 2003 and they had to go all the way over there to pick them up. What a carry-on by Tienkie there was *then* about the new postal service and "why-doesn't-anyone-use-the-right-postal-codes-anymore"! And then there was all the kafuffle when Doffie got bored in the back of the bakkie and made paper aeroplanes out of one stack of ballot papers. But they'd still had plenty left over and they were only twenty minutes late for the official start of the election anyway. It was no big deal.

"Not *that* election, Pompies. YOUR election. For mayor. We have a ... a problem ..."

Pompies stared at her blankly and blinked. Tienkie sighed; this was going to be harder than she thought.

"It's not just you in the running anymore. There is ... another ... candidate."

Another candidate? What was the woman on about? Nobody else wanted the job! In twenty-four years not a single person had ever so much as even considered coming forward. Not one! What 'nother candidate? Was this Van Vouw's idea of a joke? Or was this one of those times where you started to get all cross because somebody told you Eskom had been run over and then they said "April Fool!" and everybody appeared from behind the bar and packed up laughing? Pompies made a mental scan of the calendar; he wasn't falling for *that* old trick again!

Tienkie decided to cut to the chase.

"It's Oubaas, Pompies."

Pompies burst out laughing. It *was* a joke! Oubaas Mthethwa? Never! The man had to be a hundred if he was a day. Still, it *was* funnier than telling him Eskom was under the wheels of Robinson's tractor.

"It's no joke, Pompies. He really *is* running for mayor."

Pompies stopped laughing. Oubaas? Really? The sly old bugger. And what a cunningly conceived plan, too. He'd probably set Alpheus up in the co-op all along to get inside information about the machinations of being a mayor and decided he wanted a slice of the pampoenkoekie for himself. Well, I'll be ... thought Pompies.

It was almost like the coups de tats Pompies liked to read about in *Soldier of Fortune* magazine. Betrayal from within the ranks! Right under his very nose! There he was thinking Alpheus was just a polite young man doing a splendid job, when all the while he'd been a covert agent for the vaulting ambitions of one Ephraim Oubaas Mthethwa. He could scarcely believe it.

Still, it did present an unusual dilemma. With the election on Saturday, less than thirty-six hours away, Pompies knew that statistically the odds would be stacked against him. In the last population census the results had come back showing that the town had two hundred and thirty-seven residents (although really there were two hundred and thirty-eight), of which one hundred and twenty-three were Zulus—and many of them Mthethwas at that—giving Oubaas a slim majority of eight should every one of his kinfolk turn up to vote for him tomorrow. But a majority was a majority, and a democracy was a democracy, and Pompies knew—as surely as he knew that Dominee cheated at darts—that every single Zulu *would* turn up to vote for Oubaas tomorrow. You can't not have the vote for more than three centuries or whatever and then *not* turn up for an election; that's just crazy talk. Hell, if they held an election about what item to put on special at the co-op that week, Pompies was pretty certain all of Mthethwa's kinfolk would turn up for that, too! Not only that, but he was sure that several of Oubaas' grandchildren or great-grandchildren were now over eighteen, which they had not been at the time of the last census. Added to which, most of Hillman's adult sons and daughters whose mother tongues were English or Afrikaans had moved away to the bright lights of Estcourt and Harrismith, reducing his average even more. The situation looked grim and there was simply too much at stake to sit idly by, adopting a wait-and-see attitude about the outcome of this truly startling revelation.

Sitting there by a cold fireplace in the empty lounge of the Ale & Arms Ladies' Bar, Pompies' cellphone started to ring. And ring. And ring. And ring. Most of the time nobody ever switched the damn things on, but today of all days they all decide they know how to use them. Typical! First Klippies phoned from the feed store wanting to know if it was true. Pompies said ja, as far as he knew, it was. To which Klippies said, "O, OK."

Then Petronella Stevens phoned all the way from the tack shop in Himeville to say she'd heard from Brumilda van Vouw who'd been told by Esmé Gericke who had an SMS from Dotty Gilmore who was with Lady Lambert-Lansdowne at the time, and was what she heard really true?

Pompies sighed.

"Ag, I dunno, Petronella, what *have* you heard?"

"That Oubaas is running for president and that every white person in Hillman will have their farm repossessed as part of his land reform policy. We're very worried that this whole thing will spread to Himeville, you know, Pompies. This is how it starts; just look at Zimbabwe."

"No, Petronella, that's *not* what's happened. Nobody's getting kicked out of anywhere and Oubaas isn't running for president; he's running for mayor of Hillman."

Pompies heard a saddle fall to the ground followed by the hasty beep-beep-beep of an SMS being stabbed into Petronella's cellphone, which would doubtless spread the message to every corner of every town in the shadow of the Amphitheatre even as he was on the phone to her. And today had started out so nicely, what with the medal 'n all. Ja, swaer ...

The last straw came when Lynette Butler, principal and lone teacher at Hillman Primary, popped her ashen face around the door and said she'd closed the school early that day because she'd had an SMS from the principal of the school in Bulwer about potential riots in Hillman and would the children be safe going home?

Enough was enough, said Pompies. He needed to go home and think. With that, Pompies left a stricken Tienkie to her coffee and, without even telling Alpheus that he wouldn't be back for the rest of the day, he went straight home to Think The Whole Thing Through. What had started out as such a promising day had been ruined and it wasn't even ten o'clock yet. Even Eskom wasn't there to greet him when he got back. Abandoned by his bullmastiff in his hour of need! Treachery, treachery, everywhere treachery.

A world-weary Pompies removed his vellies, turned off his cellphone, lay down on his bed and began to devise his battle plan. That's what he needed: a *plan*!

Issuing forth

After staring bleakly at the wallpaper in his bedroom for over two hours with not a single useful idea rattling around his cranium, Pompies' head started to hurt.

The De Wet family home was a large, white-washed farmhouse typical of 1930s South Africa, with a green corrugated roof, a broad red verandah that ran around the building on three sides, and large, low windows with breathtaking views of the Valleikloof Pass to the south and the impressive panorama of the Amphitheatre to the east. The master bedroom, however, was somewhat less typical of the period.

Pompies' house had last been decorated when his beloved Maria was still alive. In the full flush of post-nuptial bliss, the young Mrs de Wet had decided to update the house in line with the latest trends as tabled in the *Your Family* magazine of August 1970, and had hung in the bedroom wallpaper that featured an epilepsy-inducing array of symmetrical squares in different sizes and shades of brown (with curtains to match), partnered with a chocolate-brown carpet (laid over the original yellowwood floors), which had a crazy-paving pattern of caramel and white geometric swirls woven into the pile. This symphony of brown, taupe and beige geometry was the reason that Pompies slept on the La-Z-Boy in the lounge on those nights when he sampled the various lagers on offer at the Ale & Arms. Not just once in the past three decades had Pompies woken up in his bedroom thinking he was cocooned in some frightening sphincter, the walls and floors "alive" and encroaching on him menacingly.

Maria had also painted the bedroom cupboards with a brown

"eggs hell" enamel onto which she had stuck mirror tiles at regular intervals, the nett result of which was that not since the mirror-mosaic was completed shortly before Dorf was born had Pompies seen his full reflection.

The De Wet's new décor had caused a huge stir in Hillman the year Maria turned the erstwhile traditional bedroom into a celebration of brown. Nobody had ever seen anything like it! Farmers' wives came from across the Valleikloof and beyond to see what décor anarchist, Maria de Wet, had done with her late mother-in-law's formerly spartan boudoir. And it *was* revolutionary for its place and time, futuristic, even; although chocolate brown was the new white in the fashionable salons of London and New York in 1970, it would be twenty-four long years before the trend would really catch on in South Africa.

In the three and a half decades since Maria's bold statement debuted on his bedroom walls, floors and windows, Pompies had not sought to change one thing about the room. He told anyone who asked (Tienkie, Esmé Gericke and Mrs van Vouw) that this was because he didn't know "the first blerrie thing about daa'ie decoration se nonsens", but in truth it was because his bedroom, brown as it was, was the last tangible vestige of Maria that he had left.

Sadly, poor Maria never did get to export her fashion statement to the other rooms of the house. This, however, proved rather more fortunate for the widower De Wet, for had she done so he would have been in quite a predicament about where to sleep on Darts League evenings. As it was he had five other rooms to choose from, all of which were decorated in his mother's ubiquitous style, which could best be described as Calvinist Chic.

On Black Friday, however, as he now decided this May day would be known, a forlorn Pompies wanted to be around the essence of his beloved Maria. Had she been alive she would have known exactly what to do about this whole unsavoury situation. But after hours of staring at the wallpaper without any epiphanies (just a headache that warranted two Grandpa Headache Powders), he decided to go into the kitchen and organize a snack.

"Organizing a snack" entailed delegation, to whit asking Josephina to make it for him, which she grudgingly did.

Josephina Nguni had worked for Pompies since he and Maria married in 1969. A broad, capable woman with six children and several grandchildren of her own, a big heart and an even bigger a behind (that Doffie swore one could balance a tea-tray on; a theory he did actually try to prove one day), she was ever-practical, unfailingly loyal, and fussed over Pompies and Doffie in a brusque, good-natured, matronly fashion. Though no party had ever expressed it in as many words, the three of them were family: she the matriarch, and the two De Wet men her hapless, surrogate children.

"Why aren't you at work today?" she chided. "Are you sick?"

"Nee, man," said Pompies, sitting down at the Formica kitchen table with a weary sigh.

Josephina pursed her lips and raised one eyebrow. She had heard what had happened long before Pompies' bakkie had turned down the gravel path to the house. Aggripina Mthethwa had told Beatrice Ndlovu, who'd told Patience Makathini, who simultaneously SMSed Josephina and Florence Dlamini, who was making Lady Lambert-Lansdowne's bed at the time. Plunging a carving knife into a side of biltong Josephina began sawing through the meat with a good deal of aggression.

"Haibo! You should be at work," she scolded. "Only Zulu men can sit under the trees all day. You should be at your shop. What about your customers? It won't do you any good sitting here!"

Josephina had said the same thing to her employer many times in the weeks and months after Maria died. Back then she had said it because she knew it to be true, and because it broke her heart to see him in such a state of despair. Now, however, she said it because she didn't want to miss *Days of Our Lives*, which she most definitely would if Pompies was moping around the house all day.

Josephina never missed an episode of *Days*; in fact, she loved *all* American comedies: *The Bold and the Beautiful*; *Jerry Springer*; *Santa Barbara*; *Dynasty*; all of them. There really was nothing funnier than white people getting all dressed up with the shoulder pads and the big hair and lots of make-up just to throw each other into a swimming pool or smash things in their big houses. No self-respecting Zulu would ever do that! You can smash an empty bottle of Black Label over the head of your neighbour if he pinches your goat, but why on earth would you tear your nice Sunday shirt or smash things in your own home like they do in *Dallas*? And all because JR was with another woman? Aikona! When Mr Nguni was with another woman, Josephina called it a holiday! Even if he made her *very* cross (which he sometimes did when he spent all her housekeeping money at the shebeen), she could never imagine throwing her gold clock with the inlaid plastic roses at him. And he'd have to do something really bad for her to smash the melamine plate with the picture of the praying hands on it. Eish! White people: they kill each other to get the nice cars and the nice houses, and then as soon as they have them they crash the cars and smash the houses. Hilarious!

But today Josephina's clucking went unnoticed by Pompies, as did her martyred air when it became apparent that she wasn't going to find out what happened to the evil twin who had returned from the dead in the previous episode.

Pompies took his biltong sandwich and a cold beer and went dejectedly out to the front stoep. Josephina may be getting on in years, he thought, but she still made the meanest biltong sandwich this side of the Vodacom tower. (Prudence Robinson lived on the other side of the tower, and he had to say her biltong sandwiches were pretty good, too.)

Unequivocally, this was a situation which called for biltong sandwiches. In life, there were some crises that only the combined medicaments of desiccated, salted kudu rump and the chilled essence of fermented hops could remedy. And this was most definitely one of them.

Next to Pompies' chair on the front stoep was a small occasional table. He often wondered why they called it an occasional table when he used it every day. On top of the table was a pile of intellectual reading matter. Pompies leafed idly through an old copy *Soldier of Fortune* magazine, but the words and the pictures swam before his eyes nonsensically. Even reading about the war in Afghanistan just wasn't any fun today. And his spirits were far too low to enjoy the nice article on that little skirmish up there by Darfur (even if they did spell "daarvoor" funny, which usually made him laugh).

Pompies gazed disconsolately out over the valley. Three things were now clear in his mind, the first being that he needed to win votes on both sides of the fence in order to win the election; the second was that the only way to do that was to find an "Issue" that would win the support of the majority of the people in Hillman, both white and black; and the third was that Pompies had only twenty-nine hours in which to divine what this Issue would be, and then exploit said Issue in such a way that it ensured he wasn't deposed any time soon.

Pompies was an educated man: he'd watched *Carte Blanche* and the e.tv news enough times to know that politicians were always tripping each other up on the issue of Issues. He had heard the phrase "Yes, but what is your policy on ..." often enough to know that that's what he needed: a policy. A strategy. Some catchy, current concern that Mthethwa would never have conceived of, which would expose the old man as being ill-prepared for the fast-paced world of governance at a local level.

But what?

Education was hardly an issue. The primary school had an excellent teacher and each child shared a desk with only one other pupil. There were forty-six scholars at Hillman Primary, all of whom were passing their subjects, even if Lynette Butler did sometimes give them extra marks for neatness of handwriting in order to ensure that they squeezed through. Yes, the Hillman Agricultural and Domestic Science College had closed down, but the government had assured them that there was no funding available to reopen the institution any time soon, what with so many fine secondary schools in nearby Harrismith and only thirty-four students of high-school age in Hillman.

Health was also not an issue that could swing the vote. Dr Miller's mobile clinic on a Thursday was very popular and Mrs Ethel Coleman, who assisted him, had actually completed a first aid course in Kokstad in 1985, so one couldn't argue that there was a skills shortage. Pompies had campaigned to get a permanent clinic in Hillman in 1998, but again the powers that be in the provincial legislature had argued that a town with only two hundred and thirty-seven residents did not warrant the budgetary expenditure that this would entail. And it was true that most people went to the hospitals in the bigger towns to treat maladies of a more serious nature. Either that or they gave birth in their own houses.

In fact, the last recorded medical "emergency" was in 1986, when Klippies Klopper had his foot crushed under a tractor which his father was reversing at the time. Had there been a hospital in Hillman that day, Klippies would probably not have lost his foot, it was true, but the hospital in Pietermaritzburg had given him a very nice prosthetic so it all turned out OK in the end and they all laughed about it now.

Even Transportation wasn't a thorny issue. Everyone either had their own bakkie or availed themselves of Philemon Nthuli's daily taxi service to and from the village. Admittedly, the road up the Valleikloof Pass had once become a subject of some discussion after two citizens had gone to meet their maker in separate accidents in the same week over the side of the mountain. That week prompted many debates in the Hillman Ale & Arms (now minus its proprietor and one of its regulars), about whether or not the road should finally be tarred. However, in the end the general consensus was that it *had* been a week with unusually high rainfall and that they would all rather club together and buy a big-screen TV for the pub so that everyone could watch the rugby. This was eventually the route that was taken, and heads were bowed for a full minute before the start of play between the Waratahs and the Sharks in honour of their fallen landlord, Kobie Gericke, and the late Nigel Dingle.

Crime was also never going to win the day. The only incidents that happened in Hillman on a regular basis were beer bottles getting smashed over the heads of some of the dorp's citizens when they tried to steal a goat from their neighbour, and these were usually resolved quite amicably by the smashee giving the purloined goat back to the smasher and then popping into Dr Miller's clinic the next Thursday to make sure there was no permanent damage. In fact, the last reported incident of any Serious Crime was a case of automobile theft, which happened the same day that Klippies Klopper lost his foot. Upon returning from Pietermaritzburg, Mr Klopper senior had discovered that the tractor which caused all the bother had disappeared from his barn. But it turned out that Farmer Robinson, who had heard about the accident from Dominee van Vouw, who'd been told by Reg Parkinson, who'd had a visit from Jeremy Lowell, who was with Klippies Klopper at the time, had just decided to borrow the tractor for the rest of the day, seeing as how it wasn't being used 'n all. He returned the tractor the very next morning, with a basket of fairy-cakes that his wife Prudence had made as a thank-you for the loan.

The only contentious issue in recent years had concerned the erection of the Vodacom cell tower at the very top of Hillman Mountain in 2000. At first, opinion had been greatly divided: it would look like a "blerrie Krismis tree" said Dominee van Vouw, who resented the fact that Vodacom had not requested to put it on his land. Mrs Gericke said that she had heard from her sister Agnes that people who lived too close to cell towers got Bilharzia or somesuch; she wasn't sure who Bill Harzia was, she said, but he sounded German and she definitely didn't want him in her house! Lady Lambert-Lansdowne thought it would be "just lovely"; she had no idea what a cell tower was exactly, but thought that perhaps it might be like the Eiffel Tower, and Lord knows they could use a little culture around here!

Aggripina Mthethwa, whose house was right next to the tower, didn't mind the structure at all as it gave her a new place on which to hang laundry after her windy-dry broke when the grandchildren tried to swing on it. And Farmer Robinson, on whose land Vodacom ultimately placed the tower, had resented the idea from the start until Vodacom told him what they would offer him in rent for the very small piece of real estate on which they were to raise the tower.

However, when the unstintingly cheerful Vodacom representative had phoned Mr Robinson to discuss the terms of the lease she had said very chirpily, "We are offering you a monthly figure, as previously discussed, or would you like every resident to get a cell phone and a starter pack?" Robinson had not heard the "or" part of the clause and said, "Sure, why not?" And so it was that every resident in Hillman got a brand new Motorola cell phone, a starter pack, and a R29 phone voucher, while Robinson got not a cent in monthly rental. From that day forth, he refused to buy any more raffle tickets for the Hillman Primary annual fundraiser, saying that he had done all the charitable work and community service he was ever going to do for Hillman. Nobody minded, though; they all now had cell phones so no one had anything to grumble about. Everybody bar Robinson was happy.

So what der duiwel was the winning issue, if none of the above, thought Pompies? Reclining in his chair he put his bare feet up on the occasional table, knocking off the *Soldier of Fortune*, a *Landbou*

Weekblad and a back-issue of *Guns & Ammo*, July 2005, beneath which lay a folded edition of *The Mercury* from three days previously. The headline caught the mayor's eye. In bold letters, two-inches high, the banner headline read: "Sutcliffe in Name Debate Row".

Three minutes later, having read the copy, Pompies at last had his Issue.

The gathering of the clan

By 2pm on what turned out to be a balmy Saturday afternoon, the Hillman Ale & Arms had already drawn a sizable crowd, most of whom were not there simply to witness some bulls and cheetahs chase a ball around the Absa Stadium. Not since Dominee van Vouw's prize Merino won Best of Breed at the Pietermaritzburg Agricultural Show had there been such a turnout at the Arms, and for the first time in its existence what looked like the very impi of Shaka himself had camped out on the bowling green in front of the little hostelry, waiting for their de facto leader to arrive: mothers with babies strapped firmly to their backs or clamped to ample breasts; barefoot children jumping cheerfully on the begonias; and groups of men standing stoically at a distance in the shade of the flamboyant trees. The only white face in the gardens of the hotel was red, as Neels van Vouw (maître d'hôtel of the Hillman Ale & Arms) ran around the garden with a clipboard shooing children off the flowerbeds like so many flies.

"Damn pansies," snapped Farmer Robinson at Neels as he entered the Ale & Arms.

"No, it's the begonias!" countered an exasperated Neels as he chased off another cluster of imps who were about to violate his rockery.

The air was alive with expectation.

Even Lady Lambert-Lansdowne had Phineas drive her down to the Arms that day so that she could cast her all-important vote. Ordinarily she would have abhorred being in a place so full of smoke, loud noise and distasteful furniture, but having recovered sufficiently from the shock of yesterday's extraordinary events, she too had done the arithmetic and felt it incumbent upon her to make the effort and endure the assault on her sensibilities in order to help preserve the status quo. Sitting stiffly on a wing-backed chair in the bar lounge, under a veritable canopy of a hat and with gloved hands folded delicately in her lap like a cat, she smiled tightly at the rest of the beer-addled throng and hoped fervently that the whole bally business would be concluded swiftly so that she could forget the entire episode and have a nice nap before bridge that evening.

Everyone in Hillman was there that afternoon, with the exception of the two mayoral candidates themselves. Even Dominee van Vouw, fearful that the apocalypse he had predicted in 1994 was finally at his doorstep, had curtailed his attendance of the sheep auction that day in order to see what the outcome of the election would be. And the *actual* "dominee", Anglican vicar Cedric Parsons, also came from his permanent parish in Underberg to bless the day's proceedings on this "most joyous of days". Dominee eyed the vicar suspiciously; one, a man of the cloth; the other, a man of the wool. The vicar thinking this was all the work of God; Dominee quite certain that the devil was in the details.

Mrs van Vouw, fearful of all outcomes save that which saw Pompies retain his mayoral seat, had come fully prepared for any eventuality, with a basket of koeksisters clasped firmly in one hand and a shaker of white pepper in the other. She had heard all about the uprisings elsewhere in the country throughout the tumultuous 70s and 80s and knew that pepper-spray was a proven antidote to any antagonistic crowd. However, with no access in Hillman to whatever pepper-spray the SAP had used in such situations, she reasoned that the condiment in its undiluted form would be as effective, if not more so, should the need arise.

Reginald Robinson had broken with anti-social tradition and was nursing a Jameson's in taciturn silence at the far end of the bar. His chief concern was that if Mthethwa was elected that day he might get lofty ideas about land reclamation, starting with the property adjacent to the house in which he lived, that being Robinson's farm. Prudence Robinson sat quietly by the fireplace with the rest of the ladies of the HLANC, crocheting furiously lest trembling hands betray the anxiety she felt. Last night, the Robinsons had actually locked the back door before they went to bed! Already they were having to make too many adjustments to their routine ...

Aside from the Ale & Arms, all other businesses in Hillman had closed early, which actually was the normal order of things for a Saturday, so at least that didn't cause too much disruption to the ordinary flow of commerce. But the throng of people assembled at the Ale & Arms was simply unheard of.

Neels was in his element. Weaving his way through sweaty bodies Neels marshalled the crowds, shrilling, "Scuse me. 'Skuus. 'Scuse me. 'Skuus. Ex*cuse* me!" as he went.

Dominee watched his younger son. If the boy had shown even the vaguest interest in the family business he'd have made a brilliant shepherd, but it wasn't to be. Although he knew that Kerneels was somewhat "saggeaard", he couldn't quite put his finger on the exact nature of Neels' peculiarities. He was just "different", somehow. It really was very queer.

Neels' real talents, however, lay with a needle and thread, as his mother knew. Some day he'd make his bride the *most* fabulous wedding dress, she had told the ladies at the Needlepoint Club one Thursday afternoon, and as he was twenty-five now, that happy day must surely be imminent. The ladies were engrossed in their tapestries, however, and made no comment (although Dotty Gilmore did make a choking noise, but said that she had swallowed her thimble by mistake).

At 2.25pm Pompies turned up in his bakkie to a resounding cheer from the patrons inside the establishment, and to a somewhat more muted reception from the party assembled on the bowling green out front. In his hand he held a piece of paper, which he affixed to the front door of the tavern before getting back in his bakkie without a word (to the utter astonishment of all present) and driving across the road. In an instant everyone crowded around the notice, which read: "Mayor Eleksion Meeting: Hillman Town Hall. 3pm. Sharp".

Outside the pub the Zulus all high-fived each other and said "sharp" several times.

A chorus of dissent went up inside the bar. At least if they were at the Arms they could have a pint no matter which way the result went, and also the wrestling was going to be on straight after the rugby; this new agenda was most inconvenient. However, fricasseed as their faculties may have been after two hours of concentrated imbibing (Neels van Vouw and the gentle ladies of the HLANC excluded, of course), the party gathered *inside* the pub knew instinctively that if they didn't make the short expedition across the road, then the party presently assembled *outside* on the lawn would undoubtedly win the day.

It wasn't so much a case of anybody harbouring any ill-will towards Oubaas Mthethwa, per se, as much as it was a case of wanting to keep things exactly as they were. In a town like Hillman, and in Hillman specifically, change of any description was regarded much like a new Sunday suit: uncomfortable, somewhat painful in the groin area, and generally best put off in the acquisition thereof until it was absolutely unavoidable.

Once everyone had read and discussed Pompies' cryptic notice, however, Hillman then bore witness to the exceptional sight of its entire cadre of citizens disgorging themselves from the pub and its grounds and trundling across the road to the Town Hall twenty feet away. The Zulu mothers gathered up their blankets, unclamped their infants—transferring them to their backs—and ambled over the dirt road at a leisurely pace. Their menfolk strolled over casually as a united group, some of the younger members of their number dribbling a football backwards and forwards across the high street. Every Zulu who owned an ID book held it in plain sight, like invitations to a ball.

Farmers in the universal farmers' uniform of long socks, veldskoens, very short shorts and checked shirts that all seemed to have been sourced from the same outfitter, sauntered over the road with a beer in one hand and a back-up in the other, singing *We are the Champions* loudly, off-key, and far too early in the game. Those who still had hair wore it short and greased about the head, and trimmed and moustachioed about the facial area, and everyone except rail-thin Reginald Robinson and Dennis Bagshaw had matching beer-bellies.

The farmers were trailed by a nervous twitter of pastel-clad wives carrying baskets of baked goods, knitting, and flasks of KoolAid; and wide-eyed children attired in their Sunday best. The whole occasion had an air of church-fair festivity about it that belied the sense of uneasy anticipation that each group felt. Only the teenagers from both camps looked like they'd rather be anywhere but there that day.

At the door of the Town Hall stood Tienkie Groenewald, who had been apprised of Pompies' plans the night before. Together the pair of conspirators had gone through the schematics with a fine-tooth comb, and Tienkie was now exactly where she wanted to be: controlling the proceedings at the side of the mayor.

Dressed smartly in a no-nonsense black trouser-suit with a daffodil-yellow cardigan and matching daffodil-yellow pumps (too progressive for Hillman, the whole pants thing, Mrs van Vouw sniffed disapprovingly), Tienkie adopted the manner of a garden-party hostess, greeting everyone with her most winning Miss Pasture Cattle Feed smile. Aware that there weren't too many opportunities to play First Lady of Hillman, she milked it for all it was worth.

"Good afternoon. Goeiemiddag. Sawubona," she chanted sweetly, regardless of who she was greeting at any particular moment.

"Welcome. Welkom. Siyanemukela," she said through a Botox-defying smile.

"How are you? Hoe gaan dit? Gungane?"

People passed through the door with expressions of bewilderment etched onto their faces. If the postal mistress was doing Zulu-talk now, what on earth did the rest of the afternoon hold in store?

Doffie had been given the role of usher for the afternoon's meeting, which Pompies knew he could pull off without too much catastrophe, as he'd been doing the same thing at the Hillman Anglican Church every Sunday since he was in high school. He now almost never put any old people or pregnant ladies too far away from the toilets.

Doffie's only moment of confusion and panic when seating everyone arose when it became clear that the Town Hall didn't have sufficient seats for everybody. As if sensing poor Doffie's dilemma and his complete inability to handle it, several Zulu ladies quietly unpacked their infants from their backs, smoothed out their blankets on the floor, and sat down around the periphery of the Town Hall, to the visible relief of poor Doffie.

How Neels would have loved to have MC'd this event! He was never happier than when he was running the show ... or starring in it. The last time such an opportunity had presented itself was the year his sister Koekie was crowned Miss Hillman, but back then he'd had to choose between staging the pageant or making Koekie's ballgown for the event. The frock had won.

But *there* was Tienkie, officiating like a queen bee. She was even *dressed* like one in that *hide*ous black-and-yellow ensemble! Oh yes, Neels knew a queen when he saw one, alright! And *there* was the idiot son of the mayor, shepherding people around with absolutely no style or finesse. Hopeless! Neels had once called Doffie the "Hillman Hillbilly" to his face, but Doffie had just looked at him blankly and said, "But my name is Dorf, not Billy." And that was that.

He really was an oaf, mused Neels, watching Doffie seat Lady

Lambert in the middle of the third row. Lady Lambert's hat was so wide (and so *fê-bulous*, thought Neels) that nobody could use the seats on either side, in front or directly behind her, which was probably her avowed intention all along. Four perfectly good seats wasted, spat Neels, and all because Doffie was a primate.

"Doffie!" hissed Neels when Dorf knocked him as he bulldozed past.

"Moffie!" said Dorf, without a pause.

And that was that.

A rose by any other name ...

By 2.50pm the Town Hall was packed to capacity; only the stars of the show were conspicuous by their absence. The crowd was subdued but restless in their seats and only the smaller children forgot that they were supposed to remain in their invisibly demarcated camps on each side of the hall, and ended up playing with their Zulu, English or Afrikaans school friends to pass the time.

At 2.55pm, however, the doors opened once more and in came Alpheus, wearing his Ray-Bans and his suit from Markhams and adopting the solemn air of a CIA bodyguard. Behind him, as per protocol, stood Oubaas Mthethwa, framed in the doorway with a halo of sunlight behind him, resplendent in the shiny polyester suit he had worn for Stephina's wedding in 2003, and with his hat-with-the-feather-in-it, his gold watch and his cane in his right hand. It was an impressive entrance and was greeted by the resounding ululations of more than one hundred and forty Zulu voices of all ages. The Mthethwa faction spontaneously broke into song, bodies swaying and clapping in unison, and it was to this chorus of joyful support that Oubaas made his way with the bearing of a regent to his front-row seat next to Aggripina.

In the mens' urinal of the Town Hall, Pompies de Wet washed his face and stared at his reflection. He could hear the reception that Oubaas had received. Hell, he was pretty damn sure they could hear it in Underberg! As the strains of *Shosholoza* echoed all around the gaping porcelain maws, Pompies felt something he hadn't felt ... well *ever*, really; he felt nervous!

"Ja, jong," Pompies said to the weary face that stared back at him.

Part of him worried that the battle was already lost, but another part of him knew that he had a battle-plan that was failsafe, watertight, bulletproof. Even Tienkie had agreed that his strategy was guaranteed to win.

In the newspaper the previous day, Pompies had read about Durban City Manager, Mike Sutcliffe, who in 2005 had "spearheaded a campaign to transform the city's image to comprehensively reflect the country's political and historical past". A past, which magically no longer seemed to include people like Dick King, Paul Kruger or Cecil John Rhodes, as far as Pompies could tell. The article hinted that Sutcliffe now had plans to change all the street names in Durban and many of the buildings, too. Durban itself was being referred to these days as the metropolitan area of Ethekwini, which always made Pompies collapse with laughter; everyone who knew even the most rudimentary Zulu knew that Ethekwini meant "bulls' testicles". This new government really was a riot, thought Pompies!

He read on: Despite being white, Sutcliff had won huge amounts of praise (within the ANC at least) for his progressive vision and foresight. But he also read that the city manager had failed to win the support of many of the Zulu-speakers (or the English, for that matter) in Durban because of the names themselves proposed by Sutcliff.

So, thought Pompies: here was both a solution and a warning. He had at last found his Issue, the pivot on which his election could be swayed in his favour, but he needed to be extra careful about its application. He wouldn't be caught napping like poor old Mike Sutcliffe when it came to his electorate; he would be vigilant, savvy; cunning, even.

With one hundred and twenty-three Zulus to Hillman's one hundred and fifteen citizens of English or Afrikaans extraction, Pompies needed the votes of just five Zulus in order to attain the majority. What he also needed to do was ensure that his voters, his party faithful, remained true to Pompies when it came to the ballot.

Late into the night on Black Friday, Pompies and Tienkie pored over the mildewed copies of the *Encyclopaedia Britannica* that Pompies had always used to keep the doors to the front verandah open on those nights when he slept in the lounge after Darts League. There he rediscovered a forgotten world of Zulu kings and intrepid warriors that he had last heard about in Standard Four at Hillman Primary. The legendary names of warlords and famous battles came back to him, echoing down the ages from decades and centuries past: Dingaan, Shaka, Rorke's Drift. Pompies was entranced! Barefoot men in leopard-skin skirts and headbands, armed with nothing more than assegais, shields and a fearless fighting spirit, who struck terror into the very hearts of the British as they stood sweating their gatte off in their woollen jackets on the fields of Isandlwana. (Only the stupid Poms, he thought, would wear red on the battlefields of Africa.)

What he actually said was: "Blerrie rooinekke in hul rooi jasse! Hell, it's like strapping a man to a dartboard and saying: 'give it your best shot, my *boet*'. Hey, Tienkie?"

Tienkie had agreed. But then if Pompies had said that the British were the smartest fighting force in the world ever, *especially* on the battlefields of Africa, she would probably have agreed to that, too. She didn't care for the Ingelse too much, what with their cups of tea and their goodness-gracious and their cucumber sandwiches, but what Pompies said was gospel, either way.

Once she and Pompies had decided on the right course of action, they worked on his election speech. And now, as Pompies stood in the urinal of the Town Hall, saying the words over and over again as he had last done the day he got married to Maria, he ran through his oration one last time. Too much was riding on his speech today so he couldn't afford a repeat of his wedding day when he had forgotten what he was supposed to say when the vicar asked him all the damn questions. Despite saying "I do" into the bathroom mirror about twenty-five times before he left for the church, the only thing he could think of saying when the preacher started with his whole "Do you Dewaldt Stephanus Christiaan de Wet ..." inquisition was "Sure, why not, hey?"

At last he combed his hair, said a quick prayer to the God of all that is good and just, took a deep breath, and went into the Town Hall. Two hundred and twenty necks craned to watch him walk down the central aisle and all the farmers stood up, raising their beers in a salute of solidarity, shouting "Pompies! Mayor! Pompies! Mayor!" and stamping their vellies on the parquet floor in time as they intoned their leader.

It didn't have nearly the same ring to it as Oubaas' entry, he knew, especially as Klippies, too full of beer to stand on ceremony, let forth a resounding belch at the end of the last "Mayor!" All the farmers cheered. Pompies looked witheringly at his brothers-in-Ale-&-Arms. Evidently, the extreme gravity of the situation was lost on some of his less sophisticated voters.

Climbing up to the small stage usually reserved for Hillman Primary Prizegivings, the Miss Hillman Pageant and the occasional auction of sheep and goats in inclement weather, Pompies took to the small wooden lectern and a hushed silence descended over the entire gathering.

"Ladies and gentlemen. Dames en here. Manene namanenekazi," said Pompies in a voice usually reserved for dealing with people at the municipal offices in Pietermartizburg.

Oh, thought Lady Lambert, so it *was* Foreign Languages Day in Hillman after all! How very quaint! Things were looking up.

'We stand on the threshold of change," said Pompies dramatically.

Pompies liked that word "threshold"; it sounded grand. He'd worked very hard on his opening statement and had spent hours tweaking it until he achieved the perfect balance. It had to sound positive yet ominous; united, yet divided; evocative of progress, but with an augury of menace. Tienkie had told him that that type of thing was called a "peroxide" when it was two different things at the same time. So, after trying out several different opening statements, they had finally decided on the one that had just the right amount of built-in peroxide: "We stand on the threshold of change."

"Speak up!" yelled Robinson.

"*What* did he say?" said Dominee van Vouw.

"He said '*we stand on the thresher of grain*'," said Klippies helpfully.

Pompies stood dumbfounded. Here they were about to lose their farms, their land, their homes (because it was true what Petronella Stevens had said; Robert Mugabe *had* started out all friendly and nice and let's-all-be-friends, and now see what kak was happening up north!), and there were his friends acting like it was 80s Quiz Night at the Arms, while their wives sat there knitting and passing around the vetkoek! The Zulus, however, were sitting perfectly still throughout and being thoroughly well behaved, polite and respectful. Even the Zulu children sat quietly, cross-legged in their mothers' laps. Pompies was ashamed of his friends in a way that burned right to the very soles of his Grasshoppers!

He started again, louder this time, "We stand on the threshold of change. Hillman has been lost in the mists of time. Snubbed first by the queen in 1947, we have been overlooked by the provincial legislature, dismissed by our neighbouring towns, disregarded by the Drakensberg Fly-Fishing and Angling Association, and ignored by the departments of Roads and Transportation, Forestry and Agriculture. Even the regional Darts League has refused to recognize Hillman as a town worthy of inclusion in its league tables."

He'd saved the most damning indictment for last, knowing that he had to hit the Afrikaners and the Englishmen where it hurt most: on the dartboard. So far so good. He at last had the attention of the farmers and even the women had put down their knitting for the time being.

"We need to reclaim our rightful place in the mapbooks of South Africa. We need to move with the times. We need, ladies and gentlemen, to transform the image of Hillman in a way that reflects our town's own political and historical past."

He had poached the phrase wholesale from the article in *The Mercury*, but it had sounded so impressive when he read it that it just demanded incorporation into his speech, with a few minor tweaks here and there to localize the content. Furthermore, he was fairly sure that the only person who may have read the article in *The Mercury* was Lady Lambert-Lansdowne, but she always said she went straight to the "Tonight" section because she couldn't bear to read about all the depressing things that happened to poor people. If only everyone would paint their rooms in soothing hues of peppermint green and lavender, she said, they'd all feel a whole lot better about life and stop being silly. Pompies glanced at Lady Lambert to see if he'd been caught in the act of burglary of prose, but her face registered no recognition of the phrase whatsoever and the woman was completely engrossed at that moment in trying to extricate her hat from the French knot (or "Chelsea Bun" as Doffie always called it) of Prudence Robinson's hair, in which it was snared.

"We need to refine who we are; *define* who we are. We need, fellow citizens of Hillman, to *change*."

Pompies didn't know what half of this nonsense meant, he just knew that politicians said this type of drivel on the e.tv news every day, so people must 1) know what it meant and 2) like the sound of it. And "change"? Well, "change" was the mot juste. "Change" was a bankable currency in the New South Africa! "Change" was the thing that got you hired, elected, re-elected, canonized! In years gone by, mothers would tell their children that the secret to happiness was not "having what you want, but wanting what you have". It seemed to Pompies now, however, that latterly in the New South Africa the secret lay in *taking* what you want, and if you still don't like it, then *change*! Change was everywhere. Magazines imparted secrets on how to "change your look", implored you to "change your attitude", "change jobs", "change your kitchen", "change your future". Change was where it was at!

Hitherto, the only change Pompies had ever been comfortable around was the stuff he sorted into the little plastic sakkies every Saturday afternoon after the co-op shut for the week, but he knew that he had to make all the right noises today or it would be curtains for Pompies, and not the kind with the brown squares and circles on them.

"Before this election was tabled, I consulted with my colleagues in the provincial administration and we feel that the time is right is for Hillman to fall in line with the rest of South Africa, which has been undergoing a process of evolution since 1994."

Instead of "evolution" Pompies had wanted to use the word "metamorphosis", which he had also read in *The Mercury* article and which sounded really posh, but after several attempts at the word it always came out as "met-a-form-e-six" so he and Tienkie had decided to go for another word that meant the same thing but didn't pose the same linguistic challenges. "Evolution" was a gamble; it was a little too close to "revolution" for comfort, and he also knew that both Dominee and Esmé Gericke said that evolution was anti-Christian and a word of the devil, but he hoped they would take it in the context in which he meant it today.

The entire statement was also a lie, of course, and he hoped that God and Doffie wouldn't mind too much and would realize that he was saying these untruths for the greater good. He knew that politicians, as leaders of the people, had to set an infallible example and could therefore never lie, steal, commit adultery, or get drunk, but he also knew that he needed the implication of a little governmental muscle in order to expedite the whole business at hand, hence the whole "I consulted with my colleagues ..." fabrication.

"We need to embrace the past and look to the future, and we need to do this bearing in mind the history of *all* of our brothers and sisters." He looked to the Zulus on the left side of the Town Hall in order to emphasize the statement and hoped that the familial phrase "brothers and sisters" had worked the magic that was intended. But they all looked a little nervous, frankly, as though they knew *exactly* who their brothers and sisters were (Millicent, Philomena, Joseph, Portia; there they were, right there) and this funny white man wasn't one of them.

Pompies continued, "As mayor of this town I have sought an application for Hillman to join the process of change, as is the current policy elsewhere throughout South Africa."

This was another lie, he'd sought no such thing, but he'd sort that out with God later once this was all over. Damn, but his mother was right! "Lies," she had said when he was little, "have to breed like rats in order to survive." He hadn't known what that meant then, but he sure understood it now!

"Ladies and gentlemen, I am spearheading a campaign for Hillman to change its name."

Pompies looked at the Zulus again. He had deliberately pilfered the word "spearheading" from *The Mercury* because he thought the Zulus would like it; it would remind them of assegais and Shaka and the rest of his merry men. A gasp went up in the crowd. Pompies assumed that he had achieved his aim.

"And the name that I propose is ..." (dramatic pause here to allow the moment to gather momentum before the big flourish) "... Dingaan Berg!"

This was the point at which, in Pompies' imaginings since he had first conceived of this plan, the crowd would leap to their feet and start cheering unabashedly. Thunderous applause would ring out across the Valleikloof and the Mthethwa clan would completely forget all about Oubaas' ridiculous pretensions to the throne of mayor. What could the old man possibly bring to party as an encore after *that?* Nothing! The Zulus would hug the English, the English would hug the Zulus, and the Afrikaners would hug each other, because *here* was a visionary, a man truly of the people. In Pompies they would recognize a leader who saw both sides of the coin; well, three sides of the same coin, in all actuality: one who embraced the sensitivities of the Zulu, the Afrikaner and the Englishman simultaneously.

The name itself had been carefully selected. In "Dingaan Berg" he had chosen a great Zulu warrior first, possibly the greatest Zulu warrior of them all. And "Berg"; well "berg" was Afrikaans for mountain. It was simple: the mountain of Hillman could become Dingaan's Mountain, but "Afrikaans-icized" said Pompies to Tienkie, as he explained the philosophy behind it all. She thought it was a stellar idea.

Plus Berg was a famous English name. So many English had "berg" in their name: Spielberg, Ingrid Bergman; Bloomberg; they were all English, weren't they? OK, maybe American or some other funny European, but it was all the same thing at the end of the day.

Mathematically he couldn't lose. Each party won fifty percent of the name: the Zulus with their Dingaan chap, and the Afrikaners and Poms with their interpretations of Berg respectively.

"Dingaan Berg": it just sounded so New South Africa; so progressive; so *right*, didn't it?

Pompies got his answer just three scant seconds after he had made the pitch. But it wasn't at all the response he had imagined as he drifted off to sleep the night before ...

The Battle of Hillman

What happened next, Pompies would later recall, was precisely what it must have been like at the Battle of Waterloo exactly three seconds after Napoleon yelled, "Chargez vous!"

Almighty hell broke loose! To the right of the hall the farmers rose to their feet and started firing a barrage of projectiles and virulent abuse all at once. Missiles whizzed past Pompies' ears: one entire koeksister, a quarter of a naartjie, and—more sinisterly—an almost full bottle of Castle Lager, which shattered on the wall behind his head, sending glass and amber liquid spraying out like so much shrapnel. Terrified farmers' wives started throwing knitting and Tupperware back into their baskets in readiness for a hasty exit, and their children, alarmed by the sudden explosion in noise, burst into tears and clambered screaming over chairs and startled individuals to get to their mothers.

Lady Lambert-Lansdowne summarily fainted in her seat on hearing Pompies' proclamation, and all he could see was the collapsed mushroom of her enormous hat, underneath which, he assumed, the inert form of Eleanor Lambert-Lansdowne must be lying on the parquet floor.

Neels van Vouw was cowering for protection along with the rest of the farmers' children, shrieking all the while in unison with their petrified squeals, and Tienkie Groenewald sat rooted to the spot in her seat, gazing about her with the same stupefied expression of disbelief that Pompies had plastered on his bewildered countenance.

A similarly confused Doffie ran up and down the aisles yelling, "Please sit down. Please sit down. Please sit down," as though saying it enough times could restore order to what had in one horrifying instant dissolved into utter chaos.

The only discernible words in the midst of this melee were "jou moer", "bliksem", "bedonder" and "traitor", plus a few more unsavoury epithets that Pompies had last heard directed at him the winter his co-op ran out of candles and paraffin.

Over these invectives and more, sounded the hysterical wails of Neels who kept screaming "Not the face! Not the face!" over and over like an air-raid siren. The terrified maître d' had by now taken refuge beneath the sanctity of Lady Lambert's hat and had armed himself with both of Mrs Gilmore's knitting needles, stabbing frantically at the air to ward off potential attacks on his person.

Mrs van Vouw, who had come to the meeting properly armed and prepared for such warfare, was furiously shaking pepper at anything that moved, and the rest of the ladies of the HLANC who didn't have children clinging to them, held out their tapestries like floral shields against a hostile invasion. At some point in the midst of all this calamity, Neels finally succumbed to the horror of it all and passed out right next to Lady Eleanor.

To the left of the hall, however, the Zulus were falling about the place laughing, to the complete astonishment of Pompies. It was as though he had just delivered the punchline of a tremendously funny anecdote that he didn't quite understand. Even Oubaas and Alpheus lost their steely reserve and were chortling heartily with the rest of them, while Aggripina was reduced to a virtual jelly of jollity, every ounce of her generous bosom positively shaking with laughter. And, in what Pompies viewed as the ultimate act of treason, there sat Josephina Nguni in the fourth row, holding onto her doek in case it fell off because she was laughing so hard.

Pompies stood there completely at a loss for words. The right side of the hall was a burgeoning uprising of farmers, the like of which was probably last seen when Piet Retief was alive, with the men forming a corpulent lager of antagonism around a cluster of terrified women, children and Neels van Vouw, necks straining at their collars like the entire Springbok scrum; while the left side of the hall resembled a gathering of people who were watching *Nommer Asseblief* for the first time, everyone clutching their sides lest their innards spill out in all the hilarity. It really couldn't get more bizarre, thought Pompies, surmising shrewdly that the situation demanded a speedy resolution and an assertion of authority before things got even more out of hand.

"Be quiet!" he threw out into the mix, his words instantly drowned out by the deafening clamour. "Quiet!" he said, louder this time. Nothing.

"ONE ... AT ... A ... *TIIIIIIIME!*" yelled Tienkie at the top of her voice, reverting in her panic to the phrase she used most often when dealing with those interminable queues of three or more on busy days at the Hillman post office. An instant hush fell over the hall and everyone sat down again in orderly fashion.

"Now, nice and calm," said Pompies, "can you please tell me, like Tienkie said, one at a time, exactly what the blerrie hell is wrong with you blerrie people?" At once thirty hands shot up in the crowd.

"OK, Oubaas, as you are running for mayor also, let's start with you."

Oubaas rose to his feet, using a hankie to wipe tears of laughter from his eyes.

"You can't call Hillman 'Dingaan' anything, Mister de Wet," he said.

"Well why the blerrie hell not?" said Pompies.

"Well, for one thing, Dingaan never came here. Not even once. Everyone knows that. It was a bit like your Queen Elizabeth," he said. (OK, so Pompies wasn't English, perhaps, but English, Afrikaans, Dutch, German, or some other funny European; it was all the same thing at the end of the day.) "He snubbed the area, Mr de Wet;

thought our little mountain wasn't worthy of inclusion in his army. He recruited warriors from all around the place, but never here. And for a lot of the time he was over there by the place your people called Stanger. If you are going to change things to reflect our 'historical past', it should at least be accurate. Do you not read history, Mr de Wet?"

Pompies was incensed. Of course he bloody read history! What do you think he had spent all of last night blerrie well doing!

"Not only that," said Oubaas, "but Dingaan wasn't an Mthethwa man. Dingiswayo was. And worst of all Dingaan was a very violent man; very cruel. He didn't at all have the same military and leadership skills of his brother, Shaka; a much finer man, a finer solider, who died at Dingaan's very own hands. We are a peaceful group here in Hillman, Mr de Wet; pacifists, if you will. We wouldn't want any association with Dingaan's sort of violence. I am very surprised that you do."

Wild applause and ululations all round to the left of the hall. Women and children danced and spun around in circles, stamping their feet in rhythm. Oubaas held up his hand and order instantly returned. Pompies' mind was racing. He didn't understand; they were *miles* from the Pacific! And how come he'd missed that nugget of information about Dingaan in the *Encyclopaedia Britannica*? He *knew* he should have read the entry more carefully, not just looked at the pictures, and at the very least he should have turned over the page! With despair he looked at the forest of hands all waving in the air, each waiting their turn.

"And you, Dominee, what's up with you? Just the other day at the Feed Store you said that you wished that Hillman would 'get its shit together and get with the programme'. Hey sorry man, vicar, ladies," he said to an aghast Vicar Parsons and an open-mouthed gaggle of the HLANC on realizing that he'd vloeked in a public place. He really was going to have some explaining to do to God at the end of the day. "Now you're throwing me with a koeksister? Wat gaan aan, man?"

Dominee raised himself to every inch of his formidable six feet and sucked in his belly.

"In the first place, Pompies, I was talking about the Sheep Handlers Institute of Technology's programme for farm workers. What I actually said was that I wanted to get SHIT together and get into the programme. Second of all, you can't just go changing the name of the town without asking anyone, Pompies. It's not constipational, or whatever it is. And it's sure as bliksem not demographic. If you're going to go changing the name of Hillman, we at least all deserve a say in the matter. And I'm not voting in any bakgat election until I do!"

Enthusiastic applause and shouts of "Vrystaat!" (from Klippies) and "Uitsa!" to the right of the hall. Women and children clasped each other tight and Eskom ran around in circles, chasing his tail. Tienkie made a karate-chop motion and order was restored.

At the back of the hall were Lady Lambert-Lansdowne and Neels van Vouw, both of whom—in the midst of the fracas—had been laid out by Dr Miller on the trestle tables that were normally used for the Hillman Primary Cake Sale on the first Friday of every term. The two individuals in question had now revived sufficiently from their respective ordeals to rejoin the rest of the column on the right, but remained visibly pale and shaken by the frightening outburst. However, without even waiting to be selected by the mayor, Lady Eleanor stood up, inhaled deeply and addressed the throng, her now-crumpled Durban July hat sitting akilter atop a birds-nest of lacquered silver-mauve hair.

"Mister de Wet," she said icily, the name coming out "dee-wet", as in water, as it always did. "One completely concurs with what Mr de Vouw [dee vow] has said," she stated, resorting to speech in the third person as she knew was proper when addressing people of lesser standing than oneself. "You simply cannot make unilateral changes to anything in this village without consulting those of us who live in it. You are not a sovereign here, Mr de Wet; you are an elected representative, and even that in only the vaguest of senses; a servant of the citizenry; something you seem to have forgotten. Not only that, but did it ever occur to you that there may be many of us here who do not *want* the good name of Hillman to be changed?

"Whatever is wrong with Hillman?" she went on indignantly. "It's a perfectly good name; a fine name; a name that offends no one; a name we have used for over a hundred years with not so much as a hint of dissension from anyone until now. One deserves a say in this matter, Mr de Wet, and one is not voting for you or anybody else in any bally election until one gets it!"

Dignified applause from every English-speaker in the crowd, plus subdued utterances of "Hear, hear!" and "Bravo!" and one enthusiastic cry of "*Div-ine!*" from Neels, who really did think that Lady Lambert's choice of cashmere and raw silk was an inspired one that day.

In the fourth row on the left side of the hall, Josephina was enjoying herself immensely. She'd had no idea that today was going to be as entertaining as it was proving to be. Already things had been thrown and she wondered when they would start pushing each other into the pond out the back of the hall. It was a shame they were all being so ugly to her boss, though, she thought, especially as he never stole goats from anyone, but it was all very amusing nonetheless. She thought of starting a Mexican wave, but knew that not everyone had DStv like Pompies did, so they probably didn't all watch Jerry Springer on a Tuesday morning. So instead she moved to sit next to Beatrice Ndlovu along the wall at the front of the hall in order to get a better view of the spectacle, setting to work on a mango while the white people all yelled at each other.

"So what the bliksem do you want me to do?" said a dejected

Pompies, on whom it was swiftly dawning that the victory he should have been celebrating by now with Tienkie and a nice brandewyn over at the Ale & Arms was but a distant and rapidly dwindling hope.

This prompted a flurry of suggestions, which included, but were not limited to, Farmer Robinson shooting Pompies for being "plain bloody stupid" and Van Vouw seconding his suggestion on the grounds that Pompies was clearly a closet ANC sympathizer and agitator (the words he actually used being unprintable in a book with any sense of gentility).

As this was going on, a huddle formed around Oubaas on the left side of the hall, with all the men clustered around their leader-in-waiting, each whispering their suggestions to Oubaas as to the way forward under these extraordinary circumstances. Oubaas listened to each one in turn, nodding quietly as he considered every proposition. They had started the day with a numerical advantage, they knew, but with these exceptional developments they would win by a landslide. The time to strike was now, said Alpheus. Divide and conquer. Pull the rug from under their veldskoen-clad feet as they threw deep-fried dough at each other. The men all nodded in agreement, retrieving ID books from under woollen caps and back pockets in readiness for asserting their democratic rights. But Oubaas sat where he was, thinking for a minute. He knew something of the human heart, did Oubaas, and knew what it is like to have no voice or at least for people not to listen to it. Besides, he thought to himself, it would be a terrible shame to finish this all so quickly, especially when the fun was only just beginning.

It was then that Oubaas stood up and addressed the crowd with all the dignity and humility of Nelson Mandela, even if Mandela was a Xhosa.

"Ladies and gentlemen," he said. "We all came here today to decide on a mayor, but in truth there seems to be a bigger issue at stake.

You have all made good points today: Mr de Wet, Mr de Vouw and Lady Lambert. Do we move with these modern times and change our name? And if so, to what? And who decides what that name will be? Or do we keep our name and keep our mayor, or keep our name and change our mayor? There are too many things to decide today.

"It is my suggestion that we go away and think about all of these things in our own homes, and anyone who wants to make a stand as far as Hillman and its name is concerned must make their application to Miss Groenewald at the post office on Monday. We should then all come back here at the end of June, and whoever wins the most votes on this issue of name changing will become the mayor of Hillman, or whatever it is that we decide we will be called, for the next four years."

For the first time that day, everybody cheered in unison and, with a show of hands, Oubaas' proposition was approved. Dominee and Mrs van Vouw looked at each other in surprise; who would have thought that the only reasonable suggestion of the day would come from Oubaas, who had worked with sheep on their farm all his life? Imagine! But Dominee was satisfied because now he had a good reason to raise the Vierkleur and stir up some national pride among his fellow Boers, who'd all gone a bit soft around the edges of late.

Lady Lambert-Lansdowne thought the outcome acceptable because it gave her a chance to stir up some media interest in the "proper press" of the "free world". She would contact that friend of hers who had worked as a columnist for *The Times of London* in 1969. It was high time that people in England became aware of just what was going on in Her Majesty's Last Outpost and the level of the disintegration of law, order and propriety. People there were would be outraged to learn that in South Africa place names were being changed willy-nilly to completely foreign and utterly unpronounceable mumbo-jumbo. And, by Jove, learn they would!

Neels was delighted because with six weeks' notice he could put together a *faaa*-bulous Election Day; he could even decorate the hall! He'd liven up that über-tatty lectern and the re-*volting* stage with some swags of colour and a floral arrangement or two. It would be stunning!

Even Pompies clapped enthusiastically at Oubaas' proposal, because at least it gave him some time to fine-tune his original plan which now seemed to have some unforeseen flaws that needed ironing out. And Tienkie was relieved because, whatever happened, Pompies would be mayor for another six weeks and in that time she'd help him sort out what needed to be done, just like she'd done in Vereeniging in 1978. All was not lost.

And the Zulus were happy because whatever happened six weeks hence they still had the statistical advantage and knew that Oubaas would win. It would just be a bit of fun, really, to watch the whites battle it out even as the impi closed in on them, quietly, stealthily, democratically.

Everyone started filing out of the hall: the Zulus all went back to their respective homes to have dinner with their families and relive the incredible scenes they had witnessed that day.

Neels and the farmers crossed the road to the Ale & Arms, the former to have a nice stiff something-or-other to help him recuperate, the latter to watch the wrestling, drink as much beer as could reasonably be downed before dinnertime, and everyone to talk about the day's incredible events; Lady Lambert-Lansdowne would repair to her lavender boudoir where she would sip a restorative and try and have a nap before bridge that evening; and the farmers' wives would take their children home where they would immediately make notes on what needed to be stockpiled in the larder in the event of a siege or any other threat of invasion.

In the end only a forlorn group of Pompies, Tienkie and Doffie remained, Eskom having reverted to treacherous form by disappearing in hot pursuit of Lady Lambert-Lansdowne's poodle, Lavinia.

Pompies shook his head. How had it all gone so spectacularly wrong? And *why*? He didn't understand. Last night it had all seemed so perfectly clear and now it was ruined. His perfectly conceived plan was reduced to ashes and his role as mayor hung very much in the balance. All of this was lost on poor Doffie, however, who'd spent much of the afternoon just trying to keep people in their seats, like he was supposed to. Having stacked the chairs neatly at the back of the hall he came over to his father and said, "So did you win, pa?"

"No, son, not today," said Pompies.

"O, OK," said Doffie. "Never mind. We'll try again next week."

"Moenie worry, Pompies, ou man," said Tienkie quietly, her eyes narrowing. "I have a plan ..."

Castles, Laagers and Voortrekkers

Dominee returned straight home on the Saturday evening after stopping in at the Ale & Arms for a few hours where, he knew cognitively, there would be plenty of bottles of beer in the hands of plenty of angry farmers, and where, as a result, he would feel entirely comfortable.

"Dingaan Berg?" he'd boomed out across the bar as he crossed the threshold of the AA, as everyone who drank there regularly called their local. "What the hell kind of blerrie schupid name is Dingaan Berg?" Twenty beer-sozzled farmers all grunted in agreement, some even belching their concurrence with enthusiasm, and Dominee—with uncharacteristic generosity—immediately ordered another round "for everyone that isn't a whipping-dog of the blerrie ANC". Most of the barflies that were there could barely comprehend the sentiment by that stage, but if *not* being whatever it was Dominee didn't want you to be got you free dop, then hell, they definitely weren't!

"Dingaan? Jislaaik! He chooses some barefoot ouk in a leopard-skin skirt and a headband, armed with nothing more than an assegai and a shield, mind you, and Pompies thinks this guy is some kind of hero just because he frightened a few Poms! Well, boet, let me tell you: when my great-great-grandfather Van Vouw went to war against those same blerrie rooinekke, at least he put some blerrie pants on!" More grunts of drunken agreement, and Klippies (who was good friends with Pompies, but terrified of Dominee) said, "Ja, you mos need to wear pants, hey?" because he couldn't think of what else to say.

"And 'Berg'?" Dominee sallied forth. "Pompies doesn't mean no berg, berg. I know *exactly* what he means, and he means that blerrie Duitse skelm, Günter Sibelius Berg what stole three—*three!*—sheep from my great-great-grandfather, Jacobus Johannes Ezekiel van Vouw, in 1901. Ja, and see what happened to *him*! Fell on a pitchfork while lying down; ag, sjeim. My groot-oupagrootjie sorted him out one-time, finish en klaar; my great-great-grandfather what *started* this town; brought three sheep here first, before anyone else, and started the whole thing! You ask Brumilda, she'll tell you: no Van Vouws, no Hillman; true's Bob. And Pompies thinks I'd forget a thing like that whole German nonsens. Hah! Uh-uh," he said, tapping the side of his head as he vented forth. "Us Van Vouws, we got it *alllll* going on up here." Everyone nodded vigorously.

"The whole blerrie country's gone soft, man," continued Dominee, throwing darts at the dartboard with so much venom that Jossie Vermeulen nearly lost an eye on his way to the toilet. As it was he just bled a little on the side of his head, but no more so than was usual for a Saturday night. "What we need, mense, is to reclaim what is ours. Take back what our forefathers fought for and died for. We need to stand up as a united volk and say, 'Luister, my broe! We is also Africans. This is our land also!'" Muted grunts at this declaration, because nobody felt particularly able to stand at all.

At this point, however, poor Klippies got so caught up in the moment that he blurted out, "Ja, but isn't that the same as what the blacks was doing before '94?"

Dominee van Vouw stopped stabbing the dartboard and took Klippies by the scruff of the neck. "Are you going soft on me, too, Klippies? Your people were Voortrekkers also, jong, and sheepfarmers, nogal. The day you forget *that* is the day you forget where you came from." Klippies assured him fervently that he never forgot where he came from (how could he? He still lived in the same house he was born in!), but then he'd have said just about anything to get Dominee to let go of his collar, especially while the man was holding what appeared to be six very sharp darts.

"It's like these people want to rewrite the whole damn history so that the Afrikaner just disappears; like we did nothing here; never existed," Dominee fumed.

"These people" evidently included anyone who wasn't of egte, suiwer, boere extraction. It didn't occur to him that those who held the paintbrush in the halls of government were also painting over the existence of Cecil John Rhodes, Dick King, Queen Victoria, and a whole host of Anglophiles whose own histories were inextricably intertwined with South Africa in antiquity, like it or not. It also never even entered his mind that there were those long before him, before Jacobus Johannes Ezekiel van Vouw and his three sheep ever came to Hillman, whose existences had *never* been mapped on the landscape of South Africa. No, at this particular point there were just two sides to Dominee's argument: that of all "these people" and the absolute, inviolate truth!

"So you tell me, hey: what's the point of all of this? What's in it for *us*, hey?" asked Dominee.

The barflies wondered if perhaps this was like Quiz Night, where you have to give an answer quickly, and if yours is right then you get more free dop or a nice Castle Lager cap. The answers came thick and fast from all sides of the bar; *everyone* wanted a free Castle Lager cap.

"Well, we would get new roadsigns." (Lots of agreement there, and Jossie Vermeulen said that when his sister came from Howick they always missed the turnoff because of the roadsign.)

"And perhaps the CNA will give out T-shirts again?" said Klippies, keen to get the answer right. "Or pens, maybe?" He sat there thinking about why the same people who ran the country also sold so many books and pens. Didn't they have enough to do? Or perhaps they need the extra income to pay all their fancy new politicians ...

"And it could be a lag and a half when 2010 comes round, eh?" said

Stoffie de Villiers. "We change the name of the town, change all the maps, change everything, and then just before 2010 we change all the signs back to Hillman again. Then we can go and park our tractors at the foot of the Valleikloof Pass and watch the Poms driving up and down, up and down, because 'Hillman' isn't on their map and they may well be 'lorst' on their way to Wherever." Everybody laughed heartily at that. There weren't too many weekend sports in Hillman, but tourist-baiting was an old favourite that never lost its appeal.

Dominee then rounded on poor Doffie, who had spent Van Vouw's entire diatribe trying to prove whether or not it was actually possible to balance a bottle of Castle on your nose. "What the hell's wrong with your father?" Dominee spat at Doffie. "What's he doing this all for anyway?"

The bottle that had been trying to stay aloft Doffie's nose crashed to the ground and he looked at Dominee as though he couldn't believe he had asked him such a stupid question.

"For the pampoenkoekies," he replied, amazed that there could be any other reason.

Dominee looked at him blankly. There really was no point in picking a fight with a half-wit, and even that was being generous.

Dominee knew why Pompies was doing this, of course: he just couldn't bear it that even with his fancy mayor title and his very own co-op and his petrol garage he had still lost to Dominee in the Darts League final in 2003. He just couldn't let it be, could he? Well, Dominee would show him!

"We are all boere!" Dominee bellowed. Twenty beer bottles were raised. "This ... Is ... Who ... We ... Are!" Twenty cheers. "Are you with me, or are you against me?"

In the fervour of the moment everybody decided they were most definitely with Dominee, but even the most inebriated of Hillmen knew better than to disagree with an irate six-foot man wielding a fistful of literal and figuratively pointed barbs.

Dominee was a bully, like his father before him and his grandfather before that. Even his great-great-grandfather, the much-vaunted Jacobus Johannes Ezekiel van Vouw of three-sheep fame, had been a bully and a cheat and, although the annals of history had no documentation to attest to the fact, the truth was that it had been Jacobus van Vouw who had pinched three of Günther Berg's sheep from the German's farm in Bulwer in 1901, and it was when the hapless farmer came to reclaim his belongings, not steal them, that Van Vouw had dispatched of Berg in a two-pronged attack.

In reality, however, and unbeknownst to everyone else, Dominee van Vouw's fierce demeanour belied a crippling sense of inadequacy that stemmed from being bliksemmed once too often by his tyrant of a father if the young Kobus couldn't shear a sheep in under five minutes by the time he was eight, or down a beer in one go by the age of ten. But he'd turned out all right in the end, thought Dominee, so when the time came he used the exact same school of parenting with his own three children and for his pains got an elder son who was a true chip off the old block; a younger son who was a little queer and couldn't shear a sheep, but who showed enormous promise in other trades; and a beautiful, if none-too-bright daughter who was as pure as the driven snow. Job done!

Dominee prided himself on being "opreg" as a farmer, a husband, a father, and a citizen. He never ever missed church, not even if the Springboks were playing somewhere funny where they played rugby at four o'clock in the morning (that always amazed Dominee; why play rugby at four in the morning? Nobody's awake and you have to get up early just to watch the television. It was baffling! They should play at two o'clock in the afternoon like normal people, blerrie buitelanders!).

It was because of this very fastidiousness when it came to church attendance that Kobus van Vouw had earned the moniker "Dominee"; that and his ability to recite entire Bible passages verbatim from a very early age (you really *do* get to know them when your father makes you say each one out loud fifty times in a row just because you're too "soft" to extract a black mamba from a dark attic when you're eleven years old). And he liked the name, too. In fact, if he hadn't gone into the family business (or indeed if he'd had any option at all), he would have gone to Bible College and become a dominee for real. Then he could have shown everyone what Christianity was *actually* about, and it sure as bliksem wasn't all that "blessed are the meek" nonsens that Cedric Parsons like to natter on about on Sundays. No point in being meek in this world. You can't be a moffie when you're in the business of sheep farming (a fact that dear Neels knew only too well). Besides, what did Cedric know about anything? He kept going on about "shepherds" and "watching your flocks by night" and being "a lamb", but the man knew nothing about sheep farming, nothing! So who the donder was he to start giving advice, farming or otherwise, to anyone, hey?

Dominee drank up and left the Ale & Arms. Tomorrow was Sunday and there'd be church, during which he'd have to keep tjoep-stil and be polite because God would be angry with you if you *weren't* on a Sunday. What Dominee was also hoping for was that Cedric Parsons had paid close attention to what had transpired today and that he would somehow use his speech to tell people that they must stand up to the mayor for the sake of moral rectitude, because he really was being a doos. And after that; well, after that the Van Vouw Family Battle Plan would take shape in earnest, Sunday or no. "There are no days off in wartime," grandpa Van Vouw had been fond of saying; "No rest for the righteous." Or even those to the right of righteous.

In God's house there are many pews

On Sunday morning, Pompies woke in his lounge in the same rumpled clothes he'd been wearing the day before, but with a brand-new and altogether cerebellum-splitting headache. He'd returned home the previous evening without stopping in at the Ale & Arms where, he knew cognitively, there would be far too many bottles of beer in the hands of far too many angry farmers for him to feel at all comfortable. Instead, he had gone home tout seule to a cold meal of leftover bobotie and buttermilk rusks. Tienkie had offered to cook for him ("ietsie special", she'd promised). But he wanted to be alone that evening, he'd replied, to figure things out. Besides, it didn't feel like a special occasion; just a disastrous one. He wondered if perhaps there were meals you cooked just for catastrophes.

He noticed that Mrs Gericke hadn't offered to cook for him that evening. Perhaps she, too, now thought some of those vloekwoorde that had been hurled at him that day. And why not; everybody else did! The day before he was everybody's friend; today, with the exception of Tienkie and Doffie, he felt like he didn't have a friend in the world. Even Eskom had deserted him.

Having dined despondently in his sunshine-yellow all-Formica kitchen, Pompies went to what had been a wall-to-wall bookshelf when his mother was alive and retrieved a bottle of Southern Comfort from the second shelf next to a copy of *Volk en Vaderland: Die Boer se Stryd*. It was just what he needed (the bottle, that is, not the book; he'd had enough damn stryd from Boers for one day), and he hoped he would find the promised comfort south of the neck of the bottle if he looked for it hard enough. Taking a tumbler from the shelf below, next to *God se Doel vir die Afrikaner*, he went out onto his verandah and sat staring into the gathering gloom. It was the middle of May now and bitterly cold on the mountain at night, but Pompies just sat there, quietly nursing his Southern Comfort until the cold no longer seemed so cold, and the day not quite as disastrous as it had been.

At some point, however, he must have got up and stumbled into the lounge, because that is where he awoke the next morning, on his La-Z-Boy, with his head pounding, stomach heaving, throat burning and body aching. That was the thing about dop, thought Pompies; it truly made you aware that you were alive the next day; every aching inch of you.

He was late getting ready for church, but he knew that he couldn't leave his house and go to God's one in his present state. What he needed was a palliative for the overwhelming nausea he felt in the abdominal area and the skull-crushing pain he felt in the cranial area. His liver and kidneys had apparently also not found the litre of neat spirit aperitif he'd ingested quite as comforting as Pompies himself had the night before, and much like the rest of the country both were threatening to go on strike. If only Eskom was here he could try that "hair of the dog" thing that Reginald Robinson was always going on about. Then again, Eskom was a bullmastiff and therefore shorthaired, whereas Farmer Robinson had a border collie, which had much longer hair, so perhaps it wouldn't work so well.

Drinking nearly a litre of water with a Listerine chaser in the futile hope that the peppermint liquid would refresh his intestines, Pompies dressed slowly in his Sunday suit and headed wearily for the Hillman Anglican Church at the top of the mountain. For the first time in a very long time, though, Pompies was actually looking forward to going to church. Normally, he found it difficult to stay awake while Vicar Parsons went on about "eternal damnation" blah, blah, blah, and "blessed are the meek" yadda, yadda, yadda (especially if he had been at the Ale & Arms the night before), but he figured that Vicar Parsons only had to work one day a week so he probably wanted to show everyone that even though he didn't work very often at least he worked hard, so they should still all give money when the plate went around. Perhaps he also gave such long sermons to show off that he could still remember passages from the Bible, even if he only used them on a Sunday and cheated a bit because he wrote all the stuff down on pieces of paper. Pompies wondered what Vicar Parsons did on the other six days of the week over there by Underberg? With all that time off the man really should be playing darts; that's what Pompies would do if he had six days a week to practise.

Today, though, he was looking forward to church and even to Vicar Parsons' long speech in the middle. At least at church everybody was always well-behaved and friendly, because God would be angry with you if you *weren't* on a Sunday, and he knew that nobody would vloek him or throw anything at him because you can't even take koeksisters into God's house, much less throw them.

At church everyone always sat together and smiled when the time came to shake hands with the person next to you, even if they worked on your farm, and afterwards there was always tea and coffee in the garden and nice cakes that the ladies of the HLANC made. In fact, he was sure that most people really came for the cakes. Pompies knew in his heart that *he* did, although he usually said sorry to God afterwards. And anyway, just the thought of Mrs Gilmore's Caramel Treat sponge cake was making him feel sick, but still he was going to church so God couldn't be cross with him today.

What Pompies was also hoping for was that Cedric Parsons had paid close attention to what had transpired yesterday and that he would somehow use his speech to tell people that they must be nice to the mayor because he really was trying his best. People always listened to a minister, thought Pompies, because 1) he knew the whole Bible so he must be very smart and 2) anyone who only has to work one day a week is obviously doing something right.

The Hillman Anglican Church is at the very top of Hillman Mountain, a short walk from Oubaas Mthethwa's house and at the very end of the single dirt road into and out of Hillman. Built in 1903 by the founding fathers of the town, it is a round stone chapel with a thatched roof set in a beautiful garden under a canopy of old oak trees. The garden is tended by Jeremiah Buthelezi, who also polishes the wooden pews and the organ, and flower arranging is done by the ladies of the HLANC in rotation. At the back of the chapel is the little cemetery in which most of the town's residents eventually seek their eternal rest, except for those who cannot be retrieved from the foot of the Valleikloof Pass.

It had been twenty-five years since Hillman had its own resident minister. The previous vicar, Percival Pearce, who had lived in Hillman since 1962, had been rushing to give a service in Himeville when the minister there had gastroenteritis, and had misnegotiated one of the notorious bends on the Pass. Not even divine intervention could prevent poor Percival from going to join those of the faithful who had preceded him, and it had been ever such a business to find a minister to officiate for his funeral, especially as the minister in Himeville had particularly bad gastroenteritis and wasn't able to perform any official duties whatsoever.

Since that time, the town had enjoyed the services of a roving minister, Cedric Parsons, who was based in Underberg but ministered in three other parishes, including Hillman. But because Hillman was the poor relation of Bulwer, Himeville and Underberg, its church service was always the first of the day at 7am sharp, prompting Pompies to question how come the Bible said Sunday was a day of rest if you still had to get up at the same time as you normally did every other day of the week?

Ordinarily Pompies arrived at 6.55am for church, just late enough so that most people would already be there, but still in plenty of time to take his favourite seat, which Doffie always kept for him in the front row on the left. You could sit where you liked in the Hillman chapel, but after so many years most people had established their "usual" seats and that way at least everyone could see at a glance who was there and who was missing, who had a new Sunday hat, and who was dozing off during the long speech in the middle.

"Morning, vicar," Pompies would say to Cedric when he arrived for the service.

"Morning, mayor," the vicar would reply.

And then the two men would nod at each other and shake hands and it was all very civilized.

Today, however, Pompies arrived at one minute past seven and already the congregation was into verse two of *I Know that My Redeemer Lives* when he closed the bakkie door and hurried down the path, straightening his tie.

When he entered the church, he saw Doffie shrug at him in an apologetic "what-can-I-do?" sort of way and instantly Pompies saw exactly why that was. Nobody was where they normally sat! The Van Vouw clan were camped in Pompies' usual spot; Koekie van Vouw was home from college in Martizburg and they'd managed to find some extra Van Vouw reinforcements from somewhere, too. Each of them was dressed in orange, white and blue (except for Neels, who wore a plain blue suit with a white handkerchief in the pocket, knowing as he surely did that orange went with nothing at all).

On the right were the Mthethwas, from the eldest to the youngest, all beautifully turned out in suits and frocks, hats and gloves. Even Alpheus was there, despite having said in matric that he wouldn't go to the Hillman Anglican Church anymore because the stained glass windows had pictures that depicted Jesus and all of his followers as being white.

Most of the Zulus normally went to the church in the veld where, they said, the songs were much better and you could dance and be happy in the presence of God. The Anglican Church, they claimed, was much too boring and church there was a very quiet affair, almost like people were ashamed of being Christians. But not today! Today the entire right side of the Hillman chapel was taken up by Mthethwas of every age, as well as many of the other Zulus, including Florence Dlamini and Josephina Nguni and her whole family, who also usually went to the veld church where you could wear colourful clothes and make a joyful noise unto the Lord. Oubaas had said to his family that everyone everywhere has the same God so it doesn't matter where you go to church. Alpheus replied that this may be true, but at least in the veld church God allowed you to turn up the volume a little.

Behind the Van Vouws sat Lady Lambert-Lansdowne, Farmer and Mrs Robinson, Dotty Gilmore, Dr and Mrs Miller, Mrs Coleman, the Forresters and most of the English-speaking residents of Hillman, an entire empty pew separating them and the Van Vouws. They were all dressed in their usual Sunday finery, except for Lady Lambert-Lansdowne, who was dressed like a Union Jack in a new navy blue and white ensemble with a red pillarbox hat and matching gloves. Political affiliation in Hillman, it seemed, was evidently still very much on the basis of colour.

And relegated to the back, again separated by an entire empty bench, were Doffie de Wet, Tienkie Groenewald, Klippies Klopper, Esmé Gericke and some of the other folks who were either the mayor's close friends or who weren't sure where their allegiance lay.

As Pompies entered the chapel, all heads turned, hats bobbing like summer blossoms caught in a breeze, and then returned to the hymn, but not before many of the congregation glared fiercely at the mayor, who slunk into a seat next to Klippies.

Pompies could barely concentrate on the first part of the service. Obviously, battle lines were already being drawn, even on holy ground! Whoever heard of politics and religion combining forces to prove a point? That was just madness! Despite it being May and already freezing cold, Pompies started to sweat in his suit. He had hoped that this being the Sabbath everyone would forgive and forget yesterday's messy business in the Town Hall and that they'd all be friends again, but evidently there was still some residual ill-will in the air. Hopefully, Vicar Parsons' sermon would make everyone rethink the situation.

At around half past seven, after an awful lot of blah, blah, blah, Cedric Parsons took to the lectern. Even *he* seemed different today, as though he knew that all eyes would be on him, as God's emissary in Hillman, to tell them what to do next. He began his oration:

"A reading from the Gospel of Matthew: 'But Jesus called them together and said: You know that in this world kings are tyrants, and officials lord it over the people beneath them. But among you it should be quite different. Whoever wants to be a leader among you must be your servant, and whoever wants to be first must become your slave. For even I, the Son of God, came here not to be served but to serve others, and to give my life as a ransom for many.'"

Nobody heard a word that came after that, even though poor Cedric had worked very hard on this particular sermon and wanted to use it as a vehicle for his beleaguered flock to make judicious decisions in the leadership of their little village. Mrs van Vouw was horrified at his choice of Bible passage; she definitely didn't want Patience getting any ideas about who was a servant and who wasn't. If she came home tomorrow to find that no dusting had been done, Vicar Parsons was going to have to answer directly to her! Dominee saw the Bible passage as proof positive that Vicar Parsons was indeed one of those bleeding-heart liberals he always thought he was; it really was a crying shame that there wasn't an NGK closer to home, but in a town like Hillman you had to be whatever religion happened to be there, even if it was Englikaans. It wasn't like in the big city where there were all sorts of different religions to choose from and you could just pick and choose the God that suited you best, and even change from one week to the next if you got bored. If you lived in Hillman, you were Anglican. And that was that.

Lady Lambert-Lansdowne had missed much of what was being said. She'd had one too many gin fizzes last night over bridge and was still wondering how on earth she had lost to Dotty Gilmore and Margaret Dawson when her cards had been so much better. She perked up at the mention of slaves, however. How sagacious of Vicar Parsons; it was high time somebody made the case for a return to old-fashioned values. She hoped that Florence and Phineas were paying close attention in their seats on the right of the chapel.

In his pew on the left, Pompies fumed quietly. In an age of hijackings it was foolish in the extreme to start sending out messages about ransoms and such; this may be Hillman but it's never too late to start with all that big-city nonsens. And was he *actually* saying that Pompies was "lording it over the people"? He was doing no such thing! Stupid Cedric Parsons had missed the whole blerrie point (sorry, God), but then what can you expect from a man who is virtually unemployed and has to hand around a plate once a week in order to put food on his table?

Oubaas Mthethwa was the only person who listened to the sermon in its entirety. There really was an answer to everything in the Good Book, thought Oubaas. You just had to know where to look …

At some point Cedric stopped talking and the very plate that Pompies had been thinking about was handed around. Reaching into his pocket, Pompies grudgingly got out a ten-rand note and saw another note lying on the plate, in handwriting he couldn't quite place. It read: "For the faithful only. Not for traitors". Pompies went scarlet but the plate was taken out of his hands before he could look at the note again, and the time had come for everyone to shake hands as they normally did and say, "Peace be with you". Today, however, with all the empty pews, you could only shake hands with the people next to you, and it seemed as if everyone was only looking for peace in their own camps and voetsak to the rest of them (sorry, God). It really was most disconcerting. Finally, it was time for the recessional hymn, *Onward Christian Soldiers*, and for the first time in a very long time Van Vouw's rich baritone could be heard over everyone else, especially when it came to the bit "marching as to war". Normally, Dominee just mumbled through the hymn and looked forward to taking off his tie and eating a nice skaapboud for lunch, but today he made sure that everyone knew that there *was* a war, and that he was the Veld-Marshall for the side of right. Or rather, for all that which was to the right of right.

After the hymn, everyone filed out into the little tea garden to the side, where the ladies of the HLANC had set up their tables. But today, instead of there being one table for tea and coffee and one for cakes, there were four tables: one for tea and coffee, one with Mrs van Vouw's cakes on it, one with Lady Lambert-Lansdowne's cakes on it (well, the cakes that Florence had made the day before), and one with Esmé Gericke's cakes on it. It was clear that you had to choose your confection according to your political allegiance, and instead of the normal, happy bird-chatter of post-church exchange everyone stood in their respective corners and nibbled away in virtual silence.

Pompies went to get a cup of coffee and Dotty Gilmore asked him how he took it.

"White, please, Mrs Gilmore," said Pompies, smiling a little too brightly.

"Are you quite *sure* about that, mayor?" she said through a brittle smile, passing him a cup that had not a drop of milk in it.

The only folk who had no trouble at all with eating cakes from any and all of the tables were the Zulu children, who had never seen so much free food and were happy to fill pockets and hats with slices of Victoria sponge and little almond Florentines. The veld church may be more fun and God may be much happier there, but at least the God at Hillman Anglican had cake! It was, they supposed, some small compensation for having to be quiet and sad for a full hour.

It was Lady Lambert-Lansdowne herself who, in a rare moment of Christian charity, had looked at the little scamps and said, "Oh, let them eat cake ..."

Finally an olive-branch of peace came from Brumilda van Vouw who said loudly across the courtyard, "Piece of cake for you, mayor?"

Pompies exhaled with relief, but then Brumilda said snidely, "I have both of your favourites, *mayor*: Black Forest and Devil's Food Cake."

If he wasn't there already, Monday was going to be hell.

The lady in bed

Lady Lambert-Lansdowne had taken to her bed directly after church on Sunday, citing a splitting headache and a definite case of the antisocials. The headache, she was sure, was provoked not by the gin fizzes the night before, nor by those infernal hat pins in her lovely new pillarbox hat, but from sheer exhaustion following her proximity to working-class people wearing polyester and all the resultant beastliness the previous day. When people were horrid and improperly attired, it just made one feel utterly wretched. And Dotty Gilmore had even had the temerity to tell her that she looked a bit "peaky" after church and then offered her a few drops of her "Rescue Remedy"!

"What the bally dickens is that?" said Lady Lambert, one eyebrow raised indignantly. It sounded like the beverage of ambulance drivers.

"Oh, it's frightfully good stuff, Ellie. Perks you right up," Dotty had enthused. Dorothy Gilmore was the only person in Hillman permitted to be thus familiar with Lady Lambert-Lansdowne. "It's made by Lennon; jolly tasty, too."

The rejoinder was waspish: "You must be *utterly* dotty!" (and indeed she was); "I'm not ingesting anything made by any bally Communist!" On this point, and others, Lady Lambert and Dominee van Vouw would prove to be unlikely and unwitting allies.

Returning to a freezing Grasscroft ("Why oh *why* can they not get up just that bit earlier to attend to the heating, hmm?"), Lady Lambert got Phineas to light a fire in her study and asked Florence to tell anyone who called that Miss Lambert regrets she's unable to lunch today, madam, but when Clarice Bagshaw phoned to enquire after the mistress of the house she was told that "Missy Lambert is unbearable for lunch today, meddem." And indeed she was.

It really had been altogether too much excitement for one weekend. What she needed now was a little peace and quiet, a nice pre-lunch libation with a slice of lemon, and then an afternoon of quiet contemplation in order to formulate her plan.

While Lady Lambert reclined in the sunroom observing the day of rest and self-medicating with three mint juleps in quick succession, Florence prepared a lovely bouillabaisse ("Something light, Florence; nothing that's too much fuss" had been the luncheon instruction), which was to have been followed by a steamed winter pudding to warm the cockles. It took Florence a good hour to prepare the dessert to meddem's very specific specifications, but only five seconds for Lady Lambert to wave it away from her dismissively, saying she didn't feel like any spotted dick today after all.

Repairing to her study, Lady Lambert went to her escritoire and withdrew two sheets of hand-pressed, monogrammed vellum, her Mont Blanc pen and her address book. Now was the time for all good friends to come to her aid in the country ...

She sighed. This was going to be so wearisome, this little skirmish, but hopefully with dashed good common sense and a sensible plan it could all be over by dinnertime, or at least in time for the Durban July. In twenty-two years she had never missed out on having a flutter on the gee-gees and a few Martinis with Dinky and Badger Babcock and all her fun friends, and she wasn't about to start now because some fatheaded oaf suffering from foot-in-mouth disease wanted to upset the applecart.

She so missed her dear friends in her self-imposed exile, she lamented, but the country air was far more agreeable, the servants much more pliable, and at least she had the July to look forward to. She would also do a little light shopping then (for a new hat, if nothing else), heavy-duty shopping being reserved strictly for London, and take in a lovely opera if one was available. Something jolly, like Wagner, perhaps. God knows they seemed to have abolished all the beautiful arts at The Playhouse lately in favour of gumboot dancing and mass displays of Irish people bouncing around a stage with metal stuck to their shoes. If they couldn't afford proper footwear they had no business being on a professional stage!

And the plays! Dear God, the positively awful plays! She'd nearly had apoplexy the day she opened the "Tonight" and read a review of something frightful called *The Vagina Monologues*. Whatever next! If you couldn't stage a nice cheerful *Hamlet* once a year then the whole bally country was disappearing down the drain.

In Tongaat she had been a patron of the Arts Society and had positively revelled in the role. Of course, Lady Lambert-Lansdowne was no stranger to the performing arts herself, although the full biography of the lady in question was something of a closely guarded secret …

Born in 1927 (a fact which would have been successfully expunged save for the petty bureaucrats who insisted on their ghastly little ID books and passports that were designed to keep the proletariat in check but which were of no good use whatsoever to people of any refinement and class), Lady Eleanor Lambert-Lansdowne had actually started life as Ellen Mavis Perkins—not in Harrow or Belgravia, but in Scunthorpe—in a terraced council house she shared with her mother and her Aunt Maude. At the end of the war (the proper one, not *this* testy little fracas), she had been eighteen and socially determined, but with little opportunity and even fewer means. She would like to have been able to say that it was the war that had interrupted her dreams of becoming the next Anna Pavlova, but in truth mother Perkins (*Mister* Perkins having absconded early in Ellen's childhood) had no disposable capital available for the young Ellen to pursue her lofty ambitions and had encouraged her daughter to join her at the assembly plant where there "was good wages". Ellen would do no such thing. Blessed with a fine physique and no qualms about putting it on display, Ellen Perkins took to the stage … the stage at the CoCo Club in Soho, where she performed nightly under her professional name, "Ginger", for gentlemen of varying ages and girths but, more crucially, of consistent wealth. It was there that she met Rupert St John Lambert-Lansdowne, fifteen years her senior and an ex-Etonian with a very British fondness for crumpet and an insatiable appetite to go with it. Ellen had been a very creative girl in her youth, both on the dance floor and off it, and having seen much of her wares on artistic display in a professional capacity, Rupert decided he'd like to see the rest.

He'd married at the very beginning of the war, while on a furlough, at the insistence of his father who urged him to do the right thing and produce an heir forthwith, just in case the dastardly Huns got the better of their only son while he was over there helping the French overcome their spinelessness. It had been a hasty wedding to Daphne Edwards-Fitzgerald, a homely girl but at least one of suitable stock and appropriate lineage, followed by an even hastier and altogether lacklustre consummation of the nuptials, which produced—to Rupert's immense relief—no immediate heir. Upon return from the war, having escaped Jerry on the battlefield, Rupert found he enjoyed no such respite from the whinings of a rapacious wife whom he barely knew. The only solution was to take comfort where comfort was offered, namely in the gentlemen's clubs of Soho, and subsequently in the bespangled arms of "Ginger" Perkins.

Ellen was shrewd, however: while her fellow danseuses were content with a bauble here and a trinket there from the patrons of their little burlesques, Ellen kept her eye on the prize. Although the other girls would give it away for a tennis bracelet or a nice brooch, Ellen drew Rupert out until the poor man was half-crazed with desire. Using her mother's oft-used adage, she told Rupert that "nobody wanted soiled goods" and said that if he wanted to see the rest of the show, including the reveal, then (somewhat paradoxically) he'd need to make an honest woman of her. And indeed he did.

Mrs Lambert-Lansdowne the First was summarily dispatched and Ellen Mavis Perkins became Eleanor Lambert-Lansdowne, according to the marriage certificate issued at Marylebone on the 18th of February, 1947. Having unseated the former mistress of the house, Eleanor set about doing a little additional personal housekeeping (which was the last time she did housekeeping of any description) and began by dispensing with her erstwhile accent, wardrobe, family history, and even her family itself. The last Mildred Perkins ever heard of her daughter was a postcard from the Union Castle which read: "Orf to Africa with Rupert, Mummy. Will write. Ta-ta, Eleanor LL".

South Africa had been the logical place to go. Well, it was either that or Kenya, but Kenya was already full. Having scandalized his family, not by divorcing and remarrying, but by marrying a person of such dubious and lowly origin, Rupert did what all idle, wayward Brits did at the time: he left the country and went elsewhere, elsewhere *sunny*, to take in all the delights the colonies had to offer.

When Rupert's father died (of shame, his mother said) seven months after the Lambert-Lansdownes arrived in Durban, Rupert— who was starting to get just the teensiest bit bored of croquet and polo; endless parties; wayward totty and Eleanor's reproachful glances re the same—decided that he'd invest some of his inheritance and do something useful during the day for a change of pace. So he laid down a fraction of Papa's bequest in exchange for an enormous sugar cane farm in Tongaat because ... well, because sugar cane farming sounded like a bit of a lark, really. He quickly discovered, however, that he knew nothing at all about cane, except that it was a drink best served with orange juice. And, being savvy enough to recognize his own shortcomings, he hired a farm manager who did it all for him so he could return to the polo, the croquet, the endless parties and the fillies of questionable virtue, because, as it turned out, all that *was* much more fun than working for a living. The lark of it all, really, was that he ended up making an absolute fortune, and far more than he would have had he decided to persevere with being an actual sugar cane farmer himself. This way he could *say* he was doing x, y and z without *actually* doing it. Splendid!

Everything all went along swimmingly for a score and two: Rupert followed his passions, all of them (as did Eleanor, with binoculars if necessary). His young wife in turn completely reinvented herself in Africa and spent her days in a giddying whirlwind of shopping, canasta, bridge, Mah Jong, and ladies' teas. Which is exactly how she wanted it and exactly why she tolerated Rupert's indiscretions along the way. Her affectations might belie her rather more humble beginnings, she knew, but that was all "so lorng ago" and one had acquired a certain je ne sais quoi in the interim. She also became an avid supporter of the arts, and was behind at least two successful productions of *The Importance of Being Earnest* and a stellar musical revue celebrating the combined genius of Messrs Gilbert & Sullivan.

The Lambert-Lansdownes had a magnificent mansion on the sugar cane estate itself with tennis courts, a croquet lawn, stables, a swimming pool and hot and cold running servants; a grand pied-a-terre on Durban's tony Berea, and a country seat in the highlands of Natal which she had hitherto never visited on account of there being no polo, no bridge, no shops, no theatres, no parties, and basically bally sod-all to do there. Rupert had only bought the pile in Hillman on a whim because his uncle Rufus had been stationed in the area during the Boer War and had said that there were some "bloody good chaps there, what".

They were regular fixtures on the society pages of Natal's newspapers: polo events, gala theatrical performances, horseracing, in fact any event that involved high jinx and neat spirits, they were there. It was all a smashing wheeze!

Then came 1969: the age of Aquarius, free-love and all the other liberal cant that spoiled the party and heralded the dawning of the age of Poor Taste. It wasn't the fact that some appalling little hack at some tawdry little newspaper had caught (on camera!) Rupert LL, pillar of the community and charitable benefactor of many deserving causes, in the act of dispensing a little bit of personal charity of his own to an impoverished young performer at the GoGo Club in Durban's Point Road (the girl was so poor she had virtually no clothes on!); what *really* stuck in Eleanor's craw was when the same meddling hack decided to "profile" Rupert and dig around into his past, and—more devastatingly—that of his wife. Eleanor Lambert-Lansdowne nearly died on the spot the day *The Daily News* ran a cover story that featured a current picture of her brandishing an ice-pick at the photographer from the ghastly little rag, and—to her eternal mortification—a picture of her in a state of undress, taken at the CoCo Gentleman's Lounge in 1946. The headline read: "Ginger Snaps!" They even had the effrontery to print her date of birth, the hateful bounders! It was absolutely insupportable!

Without waiting to see just how shattering the fallout from that exposé would be, the Lambert-Lansdownes upped sticks and headed directly for the country, where they decided to lay low for a little while until it blew over. At least nobody even knew that the Lamberts had a country pile in Hillman, or indeed where the hell Hillman was, and the road was virtually impassable (even the Bentley struggled with it) so it was unlikely that any tatty shutter-bugs would turn up to gloat or spread their vile sensationalism. The Lamberts needn't have worried: unbeknownst to them the story was bumped two days later in favour of a little story about men landing on the moon. ("Of all the daft places to go! Anyone with any sense summers in Monte Carlo," posited Betsy Parker-Ross.)

It was only when Rupert passed on, fifteen years later (after watching a vigorous display of Zulu maidens at some tribal festival that had excited his heart to complete stoppage), that Eleanor felt she could once again dabble her toes in the refreshing waters of civilized society. Nobody would dare victimize a grieving widow, she thought, but she also took the added precaution of only visiting Durban for short periods of time, and never in the silly season. That way she didn't run the risk of anyone unearthing the story and persecuting her all over again. She needn't have worried: by 1984 nobody cared.

In Hillman, however, she found vestiges of a kinder, gentler time. The folk were rough-hewn, perhaps, and wantonly primitive, but they all minded their own business and were generally polite, discreet and suitably deferential. There was a very pleasant Ladies' Auxiliary Club of which she was, with all her sophistication and glamour, the undisputed queen, and the domestic help had none of the newfangled ideas that seemed to be polluting the minds of the serving classes in the coastal towns. After a rude introduction to the merchandise available (or not) in Hillman, and once the niceties of providing the basic essentials had therefore been ironed out (Phineas drove to Durban every fortnight and stockpiled supplies of imported foie gras, camembert, grouse, Bolly, and other basic staples at Stuttafords in West Street), life in Hillman became very agreeable indeed.

In fact (and this, too, was a closely guarded secret, which Eleanor hoped had been consigned to the dustbin of forgotten memories), it had only been as a result of her first shopping expedition upon arrival in Hillman that Eleanor Lambert-Lansdowne became a lady. She had been attempting to acquire a certain condiment at the co-op ("What do you mean you don't stock HP Sauce? That's absurd!") and had left her hat on the counter as she marched out in high dudgeon. Just before she got to the door, old man De Wet shouted out after her: "Hey lady, you forgot your hat." Seizing the opportunity gifted to her she fixed a frosty stare on the man and said, "If you're going to call me lady, at least call me lady Lambert-Lansdowne."

The other people who were in the store that day told others of the extraordinary exchange and in the telling and retelling over dinner tables all over Hillman, and without another word from the chief protagonist herself, the former Ellen "Ginger" Perkins of Scunthorpe moved up a notch in the social standings from a simple Mrs to the far loftier and noble rank of Lady.

And that was that.

Flock and vaderland

Dominee wasted no time in drawing up his battle plan either. 'n Boer, as he knew only too well, maak altyd 'n plan, but *his* plan was going to be the first plan thought out on such a scale; bigger and better than any plan that had gone before. Ever.

On Saturday evening, having recruited the footsoldiers of his army, Dominee had returned home to De Leeuk and announced to his wife that they were officially at war. She had astutely surmised as much during the whole uncivil unrest at the Town Hall that day and had immediately returned home to make notes on what—aside from pepper—needed to be stockpiled in the larder in the event of a siege, which same list had to be revised later in the evening because she used most of the raisins and all of the sugar to make cakes for church on Sunday. This prompted Dominee to remind her that it didn't matter if Selati was on special, there'd be no more shopping at the commie co-op until there had been a successful coup de tit. They would stockpile at the Checkers in Harrismith on a weekly basis and fill up at the petrol station in Himeville, and other than that they'd simply have to weather the storm.

Straight after church on Sunday, the Van Vouws had returned home, and while a nice skaapboud was cooking in the oven they all sat around the dining room table with an exam pad on which Dominee outlined his campaign.

Koekie had been summoned home the day before from college in Pietermartizburg (much against her will and with loud remonstrations of protest including the fact that she was twenty-two and didn't *have to* do anything anybody told her to anymore; by law!), and promptly shut herself in her bedroom to sulk. It was only when Neels came in with "troos geskenkies" of last month's *Cosmo* and a Ricky Martin CD that she began to feel even the teensiest bit better about being exiled to the sticks. She was, however, still the reigning Miss Hillman, Neels had reminded her gravely, and her place was here, among her subjects. "Once a queen, always a queen, dear ..." he said knowingly.

Wessel, Dominee's firstborn, at thirty years of age, was five years older than Neels. He had returned to the fatherland without provocation and entirely of his own volition on Sunday morning, with wife Lientjie and son Ronan in tow (Lientjie had been a big fan of Boyzone the year he was born). Wessel was a Van Vouw through and through: built with the density of a Bratislavan shot-putter (but none of the charm), he was always up for a fight if someone so much as threatened the family in any way. And what bigger threat could there possibly be than the impending oblivion they all faced if Pompies' or Oubaas' dastardly plans actually came to fruition?

Dominee so regretted that his eldest had left the family homestead to seek his fortune in the wide world, but that's how it was nowadays. Very few young people remained in Hillman when there was so much excitement and opportunity to be had elsewhere, but at least he had still gone into the family business and in any case, Underberg wasn't *that* far away.

The Van Vouw Battle Plan was code-named Operation *Volk en Vaderland*. Simple and brilliantly conceived, it included seven main points of action which were, in no particular order:

1) Reclaim dorp
2) Strategy
3) Uniform ✓
4) Logo dinges
5) Reinforcements
6) Boycott
7) Staff

As far as the first point of action went, the only obvious choice was to rename Hillman after the family patriarch, Jacobus van Vouw the First, who had, as had been so eloquently stated the previous evening, founded the town with his three sheep. In fact, said Dominee, Pompies may actually have done everyone a favour because at long last the town would be named after its rightful founder. Nobody had ever heard of this Hillman bloke, who must have just been standing around with a cup of tea and a pole saying, "One names this town Hillman ..." on a day when Jacobus van Vouw was otherwise engaged with his sheep, like any decent, God-fearing man would be of a weekday. He'd never liked the name Hillman anyway; it sounded too much like mayonnaise; the condiment of moffies. Application would be made the day after election victory, said Dominee, to change the name of Hillman to Jacobusville. In fact, directly after putting his name on the mayor form thingy at the post office he would set about phoning the provincial administration or even those other shysters, the ANC, and see how one went about it. It was probably a very simple matter. Twenty rand under the counter; something like that ...

Strategy was also a piece of spons-koek. The overall goal was to change the name of Hillman to Jacobusville and assume the role of mayor upon election, whereupon Dominee would bring back good, old-fashioned values like a night-time curfew for everyone who wasn't in the Ale & Arms and the abolition of the minimum wage. What did people need all that money for anyway? They'd only spend it in the shebeen after work.

The minutiae regarding strategy involved presenting a united front (see Reinforcements) and subtleties of innuendo. In other words, "If you vote for Pompies or that other communist, Mthethwa, I'll break your legs"; that type of thing. That way no *actual* violence would have to be used and there would be far fewer casualties than is usual in conventional warfare. The whole transition would be very peaceful indeed and not a single commandment of the original ten

(Dominee had added a few of his own over the years) would need to be broken. Every farmer would also put signs with "Jacobusville" on their bakkies, tractors and cars, and that would literally drive the message home. De Leeuk would be reinforced with sandbags, and two guards (Wilson and the improbably named Perseverance, who normally cleaned out the sheds) would be on rotational lookout from the water tower. The two gentlemen in question thought this a grand idea when they were told of their new duties because it gave them twelve hours each to catch up on a nice little bit of shut-eye.

Reinforcements would be a doddle. They had the whole Van Vouw family to hand ("onder andere: Wessels, Neels, Koekie ens") and a veritable legion of troops in their fellow farmers, all of whom had signed up to the cause the night before and none of whom, said Dominee, wanted any of this progressive, left-wing nonsense to visit the hills of their peaceful village. United they would paint the town orange, white and blue again, unlike those other two traitors who wanted to paint it red, the colour of comrades and communists, who were all cut from the same cloth anyway.

Neels perked up at the mention of cloth; *finally*, something he could relate to! All this talk of "volk en vaderland" blah, blah, blah, had bored him to tears, as it had done Koekie, who sat at the table painting her nails green and wondering how long this war would last. Neels took the opportunity to interject that he was very sorry but he'd have to take a neutral stance on this whole oorloggie thing because he was, after all, maître d' of the only hotel in Hillman and it wouldn't behove him to be seen to be taking sides. A discussion was held on this point between the senior Van Vouw men and it was decided that Neels could sit this one out.

Nobody had said so in so many words, but the boy would actually be more of a liability if it came to actual combat (as evidenced by the embarrassing episode in the Town Hall on Saturday) and he could probably be of more use as a mole in the Ale & Arms, which is where Koekie would be planted, too. Dominee knew that Pompies was a sucker for a pretty face, so perhaps she could be like that Martha Harry chic who'd done all the damage back in toeka se tyd. Using Koekie for intelligence-gathering, however, might prove a little redundant; what the good Lord had so abundantly given Koekie van Vouw in aesthetic appeal was matched in equal measure by what, in His infinite wisdom, He had held back on in terms of cerebellum. Many of her peers had often wondered how on earth the girl had passed matric and got into secretarial college, but Koekie knew that she had more assets than simple charm alone, and she also knew how to use them.

"Uniform" was checked off on the list even before they started. The Van Vouw men and women already had khaki uniforms aplenty left over from previous preparations for siege/invasion/national collapse, circa 1993/4. They had just been waiting for the right opportunity to bring them out of mothballs again; it had simply been a matter of time. Everyone bar Neels and Koekie had expanded a smidge around the waist, perhaps, but Brumilda was excellent with a needle and thread and could let them out a bit here and there. Neels could have done that, too, but he said it infringed his human rights to make him work with khaki. Everyone knew that, even with the best intentions, there wasn't a single colour you could dress it up with, and no amount of accessorizing could rescue what was just plain h-i-d-e-hideous! Koekie said she also wasn't wearing it, citing the Miss Hillman title holder's Terms & Conditions, and Brumilda knew in her heart of hearts that donning the uniform made her look like a Bavarian prison warden. Lientjie said she had low blood pressure so she couldn't wear the uniform on medical grounds, and in the end it was just Dominee, Wessel and little Ronan who would don the khaki. Dominee was confident that the other farmers would too, however, especially when they saw the Van Vouw clan cutting a dashing trio about town, and if necessary Dominee knew some people in Pietersburg who had khaki uniforms left over from another little organization that had sadly fallen from grace when its leader fell from his horse.

The Van Vouw "logo dinges" referred to the family crest for this particular conflict and was of critical importance. It had to embrace at once the pioneering spirit of the Voortrekkers as well as conveying the Van Vouw family values. In the end it was Neels' creativity that came to the fore and he designed for his father a natty emblem that looked a bit like an ossewa wheel if you used your imagination a little, and encompassed the four crucial Vs: "Van Vouw: Volk en Vaderland". This crest would be hand-embroidered by Brumilda on her embroidery machine, in shiny black thread and set on a bright-red armband or hatband, as the case may be ("Net 'n effensie splash of colour, pa," Neels said), and attached by velcro so that Patience could wash them easily.

The only remaining items on the battle plan agenda were "Boycott" and "Staff" so at one o'clock they broke for grace followed by a nice rack of Sunday lamb, after which Patience cleaned up the kitchen

and the mess in the lounge because it was a day of rest so nobody could do any work. And then, having had a nice nap, they returned to business.

The "Boycott" entailed making sure that every self-respecting Boer boycotted any commie sympathizers and their retail outlets, specifically the co-op and petrol station and possibly the Farm &

Feed Store if Klippies didn't pick a side, and the right one, quick-smart. The Tuisnywerheid was jointly run by the ladies of the HLANC so at least Mrs van Vouw could keep an eye on things and take care to sell baked goods only to those whose sympathies were in concord with theirs. The Ale & Arms had been owned by Esmé Gericke since her husband's demise and Dominee was aware that Pompies had been known to share a pampoenkoekie with the Widow Gericke on occasion, but (and this was NOT a double standard at all, he was at pains to point out) there was no point in boycotting the Ale & Arms when 1) Neels and Koekie would be doing intelligence reconnaissance there; 2) so many of the troops would rendezvous there for the sake of convenience; and 3) there was nowhere else to get a cold beer in town after a hard day in the fields.

All farm staff would need to be informed that their very livelihoods depended on them doing the same in terms of boycotting and that if they did not comply then all parties in charge of Operation *Volk en Vaderland* were to revert to clause 2, vis-à-vis implicit breaking of legs etc.

Everybody agreed that tactically it was a magnificent plan and agreed to call the meeting closed: Koekie and Lientjie because they both wanted to go and watch *Sewende Laan*; Brumilda because she needed to go and sew armbands and hat badges; Neels because he wanted to go and rehearse for *Idols* (he'd heard a rumour that they were going to hold auditions in Underberg); and the two senior Van Vouw men because they thought that it was a magnificent plan, plotted to perfection.

Dominee had nothing against Oubaas, as such—he was a fine man and had been a very reliable worker in his day—but let's face it, he knew nothing about governance or cultural pride; the man had worked with sheep, for goodness sake! His candidacy was just ludicrous.

Lambert-Lansdowne wasn't an issue either. For a start, she was a woman, couldn't speak a work of Afrikaans, and couldn't even drive a car herself. Beside, she had to be a hundred if she was a day! All she had was money, and that never influenced anything in the real world. What you needed were connections and supporters, and you can't buy those!

It was the upstart Pompies that was the dark horse, with his clandestine associations within the provincial administration and his dangerous philosophies about "progress" and "moving forward" and all that other left-wing fancy-talk he'd used on Saturday. Ja, Pompies would need to learn the hard way about Christian values, starting with his livelihood ...

The wisdom of Winston

Lady Lambert-Lansdowne had a battle plan of her own by the time Florence brought in her tea on Monday morning. In her flowing script were listed the following points on a sheet of vellum which had LL embossed daintily in the top right corner. Her list included, inter alia:

- Hillman—history et al
- *The Times of London*
- Reinforcements
- Dinner Party
- Flag
- Swizzle sticks (She'd meant to put that on the second sheet of paper, which was Phineas' shopping list for Woolworths, which was now much more sensibly located on the Berea since the centre of Durban had been left for dead by once-thriving enterprises heading for the safety of the hills and suburbs.)

All Eleanor Lambert-Lansdowne knew was that she had to preserve the name of Hillman at all costs. The rest of the country might be going to hell in a picnic basket all around them, but Hillman had always remained impervious to the slings and arrows of "change". Indeed, it was one of the things that Eleanor loved best about Hillman; the fact that nothing ever changed. And everybody liked it that way, until that pompous oaf of a mayor had stirred up all the discord on Saturday. Hillman was a fine name; a pleasant name, evocative of green valleys and bracing, mountain air; a name redolent of all that is solid and agreeable. Eleanor's first car had been a Hillman and it was a fine and reliable machine: not too racy or sleek of form, but eminently dependable and always did exactly what you expected of it. Just like Hillman. No, no; to go messing about with the name of Hillman was to mess about with all that was reliable in the world and Eleanor Lambert-Lansdowne was not going to put up with that at all! And besides, in a country gone quite mad with this disease of "change" surely some vestige of a kinder, gentler time could remain untouched? Lady Lambert had no designs whatsoever on the mayoral role itself, but then again Maggie Thatcher had done such a magnificent job with teaching another little community a lesson in manners when they'd started all their nonsense in the Falklands, so perhaps it wasn't such a bad idea.

On Sunday, Eleanor got to work in earnest; day of rest be damned. She began, after a nice post-luncheon nap, by consulting that absolutely indispensable volume in which is contained all knowledge and worldly wisdom: *The Life and Times of Winston Churchill*. In this compendium of rare insight and erudition were included the great man's pithy observations on every subject from Afrikaners and Arabs to Xenophobia and Zionism and she had consulted it several times over the years, including during "Gingergate", as she came to think of 1969, and that time after a little soirée held at Grasscroft in 1982, when Prudence Robinson had made a case for the "rights of the native" and had all but welcomed the winds of change that were fairly gusting down the valleys in that turbulent decade. "I do not agree that the dog in a manger has the final right to the manger even though he may have lain there for a very long time" had been Churchill's astute observation on a similar matter, and she had taken this quotation to Prudence and said that if this was the viewpoint of the man who had single-handedly saved the world from the hateful Hun, then who was she to counter it? Prudence had backed down at once and said not another word, but Eleanor swore she caught the vaguest whiff of triumph about the woman the day the new flag was raised in Hillman. She remembered that Prudence had even talked at some point in the 80s about becoming a member of something called the "Black Sash" movement, which sounded fun and stylish and even a little bit cocktail-dress-ish around the edges, but it turned out to be something tedious and v-v-boring and Eleanor lost interest in the matter very swiftly. Still, Prudence was English-speaking and she needed her on her side now, so she'd let that little peccadillo slide for the time being. Besides, Prudence had had a complete about-turn on all her liberal nonsense ever since she heard that there were plans afoot to change NMR Avenue in Durban to Masabalala Yengwa Avenue. Her father had been in the Mounted Rifles and Prudence took this planned change as a deliberate and personal sleight on her family, her father's wartime efforts, and all those who had fought to prevent the world from speaking German as a mother-tongue.

Lady Lambert leafed through her favourite tome, hoping that the way forward would be made clear to her from beyond the grave. Winston had never yet failed her and she was sure he would not now, in her hour of greatest need. Any man who supported compulsory sterilization of the "the feeble-minded and insane" was not only politically correct, he was bally spot on! Mind you, if that plan had come to fruition there would only be a very small group of people left on the planet … but at least all of them would be English.

Her spirits perked up a little when she read about his advocacy of the use of poisoned gas. "I am strongly in favour of using poisoned gas against uncivilized tribes" was Winston's standpoint. Now there was a thought! That might eradicate both the "feeble-minded" and the "insane" of Hillman—who were legion, as it turned out—for whom sterilization was already too late. But then again, it *was* winter and she needed all the gas canisters for heating the upstairs bedroom and study. One could not be without heating in Hillman in the chilly months. No, there had to be another way …

For the first time ever, Lady Lambert-Lansdowne thought she may need the assistance of Dotty, or more specifically, Dotty and her blasted computer. The bally woman had nattered on for months about "email" this and "internet" that and it had bored Eleanor to distraction.

Computers were so bourgeois, requiring neither style nor penmanship, and all the talk of "firewalls" and "viruses" convinced her that not only were computers dull, dull, dull, but that the strange, intangible world of the world-wide-wotsit was clearly a perilous place to inhabit. Still, Dotty *had* managed to look up her entire family tree on the daft contraption (Eleanor had been tremendously surprised and relieved to find out that Dotty's family tree was not a baobab and that the woman was descended from proper English stock), so perhaps they were of some use after all. If that buffoon of a mayor (what was it the prols called him? "Pampers"? Something to do with cat food or nappies, anyway ...) was going to blather on ad nauseam about the "historical past" of Hillman, then Eleanor Lambert-Lansdowne wanted to know as much about the original Hillman as she could.

Nobody could ever say why the town was called Hillman and the origin of the name had never been even the slightest point of curiosity for the town's residents. It was just how it was, which was a prevailing attitude in Hillman that both frustrated Lady Lambert and pleased her. She wanted people to just accept things on the surface if those things pertained to her, but a little spirit of enquiry and lively interest would not go amiss when it came to other matters. But if anyone had ever known the origin of the naming of Hillman, those records that may have existed had disappeared with all the other archive material when the Town Hall went up in flames in 1919.

Eleanor phoned Dotty at once and in a brusque, businesslike fashion explained to Dotty what her mission was to be (it was best to appear purposeful about these things so that people understood the gravity of the situation). Dotty was only too happy to accept the task, and within minutes she was back on the phone with the answer. Dotty may be a tad dull, thought Eleanor, but she was terrifically industrious and resourceful.

"I have *tremendously* exciting news, Ellie," said Dotty, breathless with excitement.

"Oh?" Lady Lambert thought that perhaps there was going to be a White Sale at Stuttafords. That was usually Dotty's idea of "tremendously exciting". She couldn't possibly be phoning about the Hillman request; they'd only been talking about it fifteen minutes ago.

"Yes! There *was* a Hillman! And he *was* stationed here in the Boer War in 1899!"

Eleanor was amazed. Dotty must be smarter that she had assumed; you can't just get information like that in an instant. Well, well ...

A creeping fear pricked the back of Eleanor's neck that if Dotty could find information that dated back one hundred and seven years in an instant, what in the name of all that is just could she unearth from the archives of that annus horribilis, 1969 ...? Eleanor remembered that Dotty kept talking about the emails she received from her daughter in Australia, which she got "within seconds" of Cassandra sending them, but Eleanor had been deeply suspicious of all of that; Australia was even more full of expatriate renegades than South Africa and all Australians drank like Irishmen, so there was just no way that this "email" thing could possibly be delivered within seconds like Dotty claimed, especially as Australia was eight hours ahead of South Africa and nobody delivered mail at night, not even in England. Nonetheless, Lady Lambert made a mental note to find out all she could about this "internet" business once the Hillman thing blew over. I mean, it couldn't be so that you could just look up any old thing like you would in a library, could it? Impossible, surely!

"Apparently there was a 'W. A. Hillman' in the Royal Engineers stationed in the area; hailed from Chatham in Kent," Dotty continued, without pausing for breath. "Poor chap died in the war."

Well, now, that was a spot of good news! How perfectly lovely! And he'd died! How utterly marvellous! It was almost poetic. Here was an intrepid chap, obviously full of moral fibre and courage, who came to pastures foreign and hostile to protect Her Majesty's possessions from the savagery of the Boers. He'd perished on a green hill far away (well, right here in fact) and this town had preserved his name for time immemorial. It was perfect! There was the mayor's "political and historical past" right there on a plate! How was it not? The Boer War had been very definitely "political" and it was certainly a war of "historical" significance; entire books had been written about the subject, for crying out loud! So how would that *not* fit in to all this liberal, left-wing, "embrace the past" piffle? The name Hillman didn't just embrace the past, it was the absolute living embodiment of it.

"Jolly good, Dotty! Bravo!"

Every now and then Eleanor permitted herself to get carried away just a smidge and drop her cool reserve. On the other end of the line, Dotty blushed crimson, thrilled that she'd done something right and aware that her research had great significance for whatever it was that was going on in Hillman.

Eleanor said her goodbyes and got on with her list. "Dinner party" and "Reinforcements" were inextricably linked. It was Eleanor's avowed belief that if all the leaders of the world got together around a handsomely laid dinner table and there was a sufficient flow of good quality aperitifs beforehand (not that domestic nonsense, which was guaranteed to provoke a quarrel), then there would be no war or cross-border carping. Ever. Her plan was not to get the mayor to her dinner table, however (dear God, the man drank *beer*, for heaven's sake!), it was to get every decent—and therefore English-speaking—resident of the village to invite to their homes every member of their immediate and extended families for the weekend of the election, the pretext of which would be a fabulous dinner party that Eleanor would host the night before the election. The thought was that everyone at her little gathering would be 1) utterly sozzled and therefore 2) getting on so famously that they would all be up for the election the following day. There was nothing to say that the election was for *permanent* residents only and here Eleanor believed she had hit on an election loophole. With a riveting speech and sufficient numbers of sensible folk in place, they were bound to win the day. "Plans," Winston Churchill had written, "are of little importance, but planning is essential." So planning was what she would do; *party* planning for the most political of parties! And she would have in her arsenal of weapons that most potent of persuasives: imported, vintage wine and lots of bubbly!

The Union Jack (which was so much more elegant than this festival of vulgarity that was the new South African flag) would be raised forthwith aloft Grasscroft, and Lady Lambert would also be flying a miniature version of it on her Bentley. Every English-speaker was to put discreet, tastefully signwritten banners saying "Hillman" on their cars, tractors and other vehicular conveyances, and that, she said, would literally drive the message home.

Dotty had also come up with the inspired suggestion of printing out a Hillman bulletin on her computer on a weekly basis in the run-up to the election. In it, she and Eleanor would run a carefully crafted and edited selection of articles which would win the hearts and minds of the citizens of Hillman in the most subtle way. It really was an idea of astonishing brilliance on Dotty's part. Whoever would have thought to use the printed word as a form of political propaganda? Astonishing insight, really; that Dotty was a dark horse and perhaps not so aptly named after all. Hillman had no newspaper of its own, and aside from *The Mercury*, which was brought in specially for Lady Lambert and Lady Lambert alone, nobody read newspapers of any description in Hillman, as far as she knew. It did occur to Eleanor that perhaps the people of Hillman couldn't read; in fact, she had rather counted on it in 1969, but in case there were those that *could*, it was worth using this bulletin idea as a vehicle of subtle manipulation.

The last item of business Eleanor attended to before retiring on Sunday night, was to pen an artfully worded letter to the editor of *The Times of London*. She had thought of writing to Buckingham Palace as well but decided that she didn't want to cause Her Majesty any unnecessary alarm when she was so awfully busy cutting ribbons and attending other events of tremendous importance, especially as there was every possibility that this whole mess could be sorted out through diplomacy alone. She had not even entertained the notion of writing to Downing Street because that Labour upstart, the rapscallion Blair, was in residence and as he was a warmonger of considerable renown there was no point in appealing to the finer sensibilities of a man who clearly had none.

She opened her letter to the editor of *The Times* by stating that she was an old friend of Lord Roderick Hawthorne (that should stir his interest; there was nothing people liked better than knowing they were dealing with a person who was "in the fray", so to speak), and that there was a frightful business afoot in the colonies of which she thought he had better be apprised tout suite. Britons would be horrified, she wrote, to know just what was going on and how this threatened the Commonwealth. She mentioned the gumboot dancing and the Irish people with the bottle-tops on their shoes and the fact that Winston Churchill's advice, while brilliant, was sadly not practicable at this time, what with it being winter and all, and that perhaps Her Majesty should consider sending troops to Hillman, now that the whole beastly Iraq business seemed to have been dealt with.

As missives go, it was a masterpiece! She was absolutely certain this was front-page, banner-headline material, guaranteed to stir the soul of every God-fearing patriot in England. Satisfied with her epistle, she addressed an envelope to "The Editor, *The Times of London*, London, Greatest Britain" (it would get there even sans postcode, she was certain; *everyone* knew The Times!) and as her final flourish she closed the envelope and affixed her seal into blood-red sealing wax on the back. It was a marvellous seal, designed for her as a gift by Klaus von Reiniger, an old friend of Rupert and Eleanor Lambert-Lansdowne, who had left South Africa rather abruptly for South America in the early 1970s. Klaus *was* a character! And a man with a particular gift for creative flair and style. Some said he had once been an art director for Leni Riefenstahl, but he always said no, no, he was just a simple farmer from Henley-on-Klip who'd never done anything worth mentioning. This had endeared him to Eleanor instantly and she'd asked him when they hosted their regatta as she'd just *love* to attend! What fun! So sad that she never got to go; he'd disappeared off to Brazil before she could badger him about it. Still, Klaus was the only man of German descent that Eleanor could tolerate and, good heavens, he could hold his schnapps! How she missed him at her dinner parties! For all her kindness, he wrote in his card, and because he recognized in her "something of himself" Klaus had very kindly created and sent to Eleanor as a gift her very owl seal, which combined the four initials of her name, Lady Eleanor Lambert-Lansdowne, into a symbol of flowing form and breathtaking symmetry. If this didn't impress the socks off the editor at *The Times*, then nothing would!

Business unusual

Pompies was at his co-op earlier than usual on Monday, braced for whatever ghastliness the day held in store. If Sunday had been a portent of things to come, he wanted to be prepared for any and every eventuality, and he certainly couldn't afford even the vaguest whiff of scandal because he might be kuiering over at Mrs Gericke's, having morning coffee and coconut slices. He'd learnt from Bill Clinton's mistakes and he definitely also wouldn't be having any cigars or brandewyn over at Tienkie's until this was all done and dusted. No sirree, for the time being he needed to have his wits about him and concentrate on official matters only.

His chief concern at the start of the day was how he and Alpheus were going to deal with this whole issue in the workplace, but to his immense relief, when Alpheus turned up for work (on time and seemingly ready for the day), the two men did what men the world over do whenever there is a problem: they didn't mention it at all, pretended as though nothing whatsoever had happened, and carried on completely as normal. No discussion necessary.

Tienkie was also at her station earlier than normal. She, too, wanted to be ready for the day and took preventative measures to ensure that she didn't have hoards of people filling up her post office on non-postal business like she'd had to endure on Friday. Taking a piece of paper and a ruler she made three columns down the length of the page and wrote at the top of each: "Name of Candida" (she'd been in a hurry); "Name of Dorp"; "ID Number".

Pinning the piece of paper to the noticeboard outside the post office, she stuck another to the inside of the door glass which read:

"Postal bisness ONLY. Election nonsens: see noticeboard". And that, she decided, should take care of that.

Dominee Van Vouw was also in town. In the normal scheme of things, he would be in a field from sunrise, attending to matters ovine, but today he wanted to keep a close eye on developments. He read *The Beeld* fairly often and knew just how quickly things could take a nasty turn. Just look at the Volklande or whatever that little island was there by Argentina; one minute they're on their island, minding their own business and looking after their sheep, and the next the damn Poms turn up and everyone's getting shot. Always the blerrie Poms, he thought. No, today he needed to be in town, close to the heart of the matter in case things got ugly. And besides, he had a surprise of his own up his short-sleeved shirt.

Elsewhere in Hillman, the women of the HLANC were doing what women the world over do whenever there is a problem: they talked about nothing else, pretended as though they themselves were the focus of it, and carried on as though the world itself was coming to an end. Much discussion necessary. News about the surprising turn of events had spread even faster than usual because Dotty Gilmore had sent an email to Petronella Stevens on Saturday, copying several other people on it at the same time, and Petronella had forwarded it to several of her friends in the Drakensberg and beyond, and before Mrs van Vouw could phone anyone to tell them her version of events, everyone already knew. By 6pm on Saturday, the email that was going around stated that Hillman was seeking independent republic status under a new name; that Afrikaans and English were to be abolished; and that the new republic of whatever-Hillman-would-be-called would get its own currency. *And* that Mthethwa was—as had previously been predicted—seeking to invoke the Land Reformation Act and everyone without a Zulu name was losing their farms. Someone had added a PS that perhaps Van Vouw and others should change their surnames by deed pole to Mthethwa and then nobody could do anything about it.

At Grasscroft, the country seat of Lady Lambert-Lansdowne, the lady in question was having a petit déjeuner of Eggs Benedict and stewed fruit at 8.30am on Monday morning. (One might be planning a campaign of National Importance, but one still has to be regular.) It was here that the first cracks in the Hillman domestic façade began to show. Not only did Florence show no signs of having heeded Cedric Parsons sage advice the day before, but she seemed a little more sullen than usual and Lady Eleanor could swear that boiling water had not been put in the teapot before Florence made the tea. This was how it started, she knew: first the tea, then the whole bally country would go to pot! She'd need to keep a close eye on household matters before it all got out of hand. Tiresome; so very, very tiresome ...

At the Hillman Farm & Feed Store, Klippies was surprised to see Dominee there at opening time, when he knew he should be in his fields.

"Môre, Dominee," said Klippies, "lets fout?"

"Nee, jong," said Dominee. "Just looking, thanks."

"Looking?" said Klippies, baffled. Nobody came into the feed store "just looking". This wasn't Morkels!

"Jaaa ... for ... a new ... tractor."

Klippies knew this wasn't true. Dominee had bought a very nice John Deere tractor just a few months ago at the Agricultural Show in Pietermartizburg and everyone was very envious of it. It had a leather seat, not vinyl, and a cup-holder, and was much more fuel-efficient than other models. Unless one of the farmhands had broken it, Dominee wasn't looking for a new tractor.

Dominee kicked the tyres of the tractor in the forecourt and pretended to be very engrossed with the dials on the dashboard. He did this for several minutes and kept looking at his watch, as though he was waiting for something.

"So ... you heard any more about this election business, Klippies?" Dominee finally said, trying to invest in his voice as much indifference as he could possibly muster.

"Uh-uh, oom," said Klippies, shaking his head. "Oh, but there's a dinges up by the post office. You have to put your name on it if you want to, you know, claim your steak, or whatever it is."

"Oh?" said Dominee. He knew he needed to work on sounding casual. "Casual" wasn't part of his vocabulary any day of the week. Serious farmers weren't casual. "Anybody put their name there yet?"

"Nuh-uh, oom. But it's mos early still. You want to hide here some more until somebody does? I got coffee in the back."

Dominee tried to think of a snappy retort that would save him from exposure, but in the end he just sighed and said, "Ja wat, jong. Why not, hey?" and together they went inside.

And within minutes the first official candidate did indeed turn up to "claim his steak". As current mayor, Pompies knew that it fell to him to come forward first and to put in writing that which he had set in motion on Saturday. Under "name" he wrote "Dewaldt de Wet"; under "dorp", "Dingaan Berg". (No going back now; the die was cast. And besides, he'd already told everyone that he had talked to the provincial administration about it, so he couldn't change his mind now.) And then he wrote his ID number, copying it straight from the book. For more than thirty years he'd had an ID book and still couldn't remember the number, except for the amazing coincidence that the first six numbers were exactly the same as his birthday! That done, he popped his head around the door and said hello to Tienkie, who told him that she'd keep "an eye on things" for him, and went back to the co-op.

From the Copper Kettle Coffee Shop and Tuisnywerheid three pairs of beady eyes watched the proceedings closely, as did Alpheus, who was pretending to stack boxes of cabbages in the display stand outside the co-op. Less than thirty seconds after Pompies signed his name to the board, Lady Lambert-Lansdowne, Dominee van Vouw and Oubaas Mthethwa all knew that the game was on.

As soon as Pompies had re-entered his co-op, Brumilda van Vouw sprinted over to the post office, as much as any size 20 lady in a pleated skirt and court shoes can sprint. She scrutinized the noticeboard for a minute and then entered the post office with purpose.

Smiling at Tienkie with all the warmth of a hungry hammerhead, she said, "Morning, Tienkie, did a parcel arrive for me from Martizburg by any chance?"

Tienkie was nobody's fool. "No, Mrs van Vouw. Did you get a little notice saying that it had?"

"No, but I wondered if maybe it had come in." Turquoise-painted eyes bore into Tienkie.

"Well, if you didn't get a notice, then it didn't come in, did it?" Tienkie smiled back with all the sweetness of a barracuda.

"Oh, OK then. Oh, Tienkie?" Mrs van Vouw was battling to maintain this civility. In the end she gave up the sham as easily as her husband had done, and launched forth into her diatribe with rancour: "Skaam jou for supporting Pompies with this left-wing, ANC, anti-white nonsens. You might not be from Hillman, Mejuffrou Tienkie Groenewald, but you're still a boerenooi underneath all the fancy trousers and the big career. Not only that, but have you given one single thought to what all of this is going to mean for *you* in the post office, hê?"

Tienkie had indeed given the matter a great deal of thought ever since Pompies had first mentioned the idea to her. Changing the name of Hillman could be utterly chaotic for Postal Mistress Tienkie Groenewald. Tienkie liked order. She liked a place for everything and everything in its place, and she liked things to run like clockwork every day, Monday to Friday and a half day on Saturdays. The postal world was a fast-paced one; almost every other day new mail came in and new mail went out. There was no room for error and no time to nap. In a single calendar year, Tienkie Groenewald and her postal clerk could sort literally dozens of items of mail, and Tienkie had wondered what kinds of disasters lay lurking if the name of Hillman changed. What would happen to mail that was addressed to Hillman by people who weren't aware of the change, for example? Would it be lost in some cavernous sorting office in De Aar where people would use a letter addressed to some no-longer-existent town to rest a coffee cup on?

But Tienkie had done a little research into the matter and consulted her "archives", those being the old postal code books from previous years. The postal codes for Pietersburg had remained the same, even after the town had changed its name to Polokwane, as had the codes for Krugersdorp, which was now known as Mogale City. It seemed to Tienkie that postal catastrophe could indeed be averted just as long as the postal codes remained the same, which they probably would. Added to which, she wanted to support Pompies in his campaign, as harebrained as it seemed, because she wasn't giving up the fight at this late stage having come so far and so close, Brumilda van Vouw and her seething jealousy be damned.

Looking up at Mrs van Vouw, Tienkie summoned all her professionalism and said, in as businesslike a fashion as she could when wanting to hit someone square across their fat face, "Mrs van Vouw, did you see the sign on the post office door this morning? It says that the post office is for *official postal business* only. Or perhaps I shouldn't have written it in English? If you've nothing to post, you don't need to be here. Oh, and Mrs van Vouw? Your parcel didn't arrive, but your son's *Cosmo* did. Shall I give it to you, perhaps, or deliver it as usual?"

Mrs van Vouw coloured instantly. In fact, for a brief minute Tienkie thought that the poor woman's neck was going to explode right off her beaded cardigan. But, in the end, she just inhaled sharply, pursed her thin lips, turned on her dainty pumped heels, (far too dainty to support a woman her size, thought Tienkie), and marched—fuming—out of the post office and across the road, straight past Oubaas Mthethwa who had just turned up on the verandah of the post office.

Oubaas doffed his cap at the large woman who steamed past him, and again at Tienkie inside the post office. It may be Monday, but one should always be polite. Taking a pencil from his pocket, he wrote his name in the left-hand column, and his ID number in the right-hand column, which just a few years earlier he would have been unable to do. And looking at the middle column he took a deep breath, thought about it for another minute, and then wrote: "Dingiswayo". That done, he doffed his hat once more to Tienkie without disturbing the busy postal mistress from her official duties, and walked back up the road from whence he'd come.

Inside the Copper Kettle, the same three sets of beady eyes watched what happened, but after the upset in the post office a few minutes earlier Mrs van Vouw knew she couldn't go back over there to see what Oubaas had written. After much discussion, it was decided that Dotty Gilmore should go across to see what name the old man had put down, and the door of the Copper Kettle had just opened to let Dotty out on her covert mission when Tienkie came out of the post office. Standing on the front step of the post office, she crossed her arms combatively and yelled across the street, "No, Dotty, your parcel from Pietermartizburg *didn't* arrive, and the name he's put down is Dingiswayo."

Dotty turned scarlet and scuttled back inside the Copper Kettle, while Prudence and Brumilda immediately phoned Lady Eleanor and Dominee van Vouw, respectively.

Within fifteen minutes, the Bentley of Lady Lambert-Lansdowne was purring in front of the post office, its bonnet-mounted Union Jack fluttering sedately in the breeze, as the lady herself emerged from its heated interior, looking for all the world like Queen Elizabeth, complete with a snap-shut handbag, Harris tweed skirt, and her favourite monarch's very own hairstyle. Walking smartly up to the sign on the noticeboard she took out a Mont Blanc fountain pen, wrote: "Lambert-Lansdowne, E." in flowing script; "Hillman" under "Name of Dorp" ("which *is* its name", she added underneath); and in the column marked "ID Number", she wrote: "Absolutely bally irrelevant and none of your bally business!" She then removed from the snap-shut handbag a stamped, addressed envelope with a blood-red seal on the back and deposited it into the red post-box. That done, she got back in her car, put her driving blanket across her knees, patted Lavinia on the head, and had Phineas drive her home for a nice nap before Mah Jong that afternoon.

The last to arrive was Dominee van Vouw, who had left the Hillman Farm & Feed Store with some new thresher blades, several gallons of sheep dip that he didn't need, and an entire sack of birdseed, which he certainly wouldn't use. He tried hard not to look in the direction of the Copper Kettle in case Tienkie suspected that he'd been alerted to what was going on by the ladies of the Tuisnywerheid. Nor did he cast a glance at the co-op in case Doffie or Pompies or that other ANC agitator, Alpheus, were watching. And he certainly didn't look in at the post office itself, in case Tienkie caught him looking nervous or in any way out of control. When going into battle you must never let the enemy catch you with your guard down. Or was it with your pants down? Either way, he wasn't going to let the enemy catch him at all.

Taking out a Bic pen that was a bit chewed at the top he wrote: "Kobus Johannes Ezekiel van Vouw IV" under "Candida", filled in his ID number in the right-hand column, and then, under "Name of Dorp", wrote in bold capital letters: "JACOBUSVILLE".

And with that—with not a single bugle sounding nor any formal declaration to that effect—the Battle of Hillman began in earnest.

Please hold ...

Pompies put down the receiver in his little office at the back of the co-op, quite stunned by what Tienkie had just told him. Well, well, this *was* a turn up for the books! So, Dominee van Vouw had put his name into the hat after all. Mthethwa he was prepared for, since Saturday already, and Lady Eleanor too, but Dominee? He hadn't seen *that* coming! Not only that, but Van Vouw was using this event to further his own overwhelming vanity and put a feather in his own cap. Jacobusville? How preposterous! Of all the vainglorious, self-serving, narcissistic, fatheaded names! He could have chosen anything, but no, he had to go and choose one of his *own family's* names. Even Mthethwa didn't do that, thought Pompies, and everyone knows the Mthethwas have been here far longer than any damn Van Vouw, despite whatever Dominee might say. The arrogance of the man! The pomposity! How petty. How small-minded. How blerrie typical! He thought all of these things but how they were decoded in his brain was much simpler: Blerrie Dominee! He's such a flipping doos!

Thank goodness Pompies was three years older than Dominee or else he would have had to endure him all the way through school, too, but even still Van Vouw had been a thorn in Pompies' side for the better part of forty years. Whatever Pompies did, Van Vouw would claim to have done first, better and bigger. When Pompies took Doffie on a fishing trip to Midmar one year, Dominee claimed that he'd taken both his boys there the year before and they'd all caught fish *thiiiiiis* big. Well, Pompies didn't know about any Van Vouw family fishing trip to Midmar, but he sure as bliksem knew that the only thing Neels van Vouw ever caught was a cold!

Pompies was steaming. He knew why Van Vouw was doing this, of course: he just couldn't bear it that even with his fancy darts and his very own dartboard in his bar at home he had still lost to Pompies in the Darts League Final in 2002. He just couldn't let it be, could he? Well, Pompies would show him!

The first thing he needed to do was make a truth of one of the lies he had told on Saturday. Pompies hadn't the faintest idea how one went about changing the name of a town. It would be nice if you just put up new signboards everywhere when you felt like a change and hoped that eventually the Department of Transportation and Roadworks would catch on and change the maps and the roadsigns, too, but he presumed that actually one had to go through some kind of nightmarish, bureaucratic procedure, which he was fairly certain none of the founding fathers of any towns had ever had to go through. Back in the day, you just stuck a pole in the ground, said, "I name this town Wherever" and before you knew it people were saying "Oh, you live in Wherever, do you?" and "Can I give you a lift to Wherever?" Simple. But not any more. No, he was pretty sure that nowadays there was some office somewhere in a rabbit-warren of a government building in Pietermartizburg, where an officious lady with a disapproving look would make him fill out forms in triplicate, together with certified copies of his ID book; birth, matric and marriage certificates (together with the originals); blood and urine samples; fingerprints; and a sworn, stamped and dated letter from a commissioner of oaths, before anyone would consider his application.

It was utterly pointless trying to phone the provincial administration. He'd tried that before on a different matter entirely, but no matter what button he pressed (Press "1" if you want Water & Lights; "2" if you want Vehicle Licences; "3" if you want Accounts; "4" if you want to carry on holding; "5" if you want to shoot yourself in the head; "6" if you want to start this message all over again, and "7" if you'd like to hear it in any of the other official languages), it still came back to the beginning and no human being ever answered the phone.

The article in *The Mercury* had mentioned the ANC several times, however, so he thought that perhaps he should try them first. They did run the country, after all, and they were very keen on this whole name-changing business, as far as he could tell. So he phoned directory enquiries and waited for several minutes and quite a few repeats of their doo-doo-de-doo hold music, while getting constant reassurances that his call was very important to Telkom. The lady who eventually came on the line asked which ANC office he wanted, so Pompies said "any" and she gave him a number in Johannesburg. He phoned the number and got hold music (Juluka, perhaps? Pompies wasn't sure) followed by a message asking him to carry on holding. When a lady finally answered, she said that he had the wrong number for those types of enquiries and that he should phone another number in Pretoria. He did. More hold music (Mango Groove, or something that sounded very like it. Such a pity they don't play any of the classics like Sonja Herold anymore). By this stage, Pompies was starting to feel that his calls were tremendously important to lots of people, but not enough for them to actually answer the damn phone. Eventually a lady answered (with what sounded like a mouthful of something) and said that the lady who normally dealt with enquiries of this nature was out to lunch and would he like to hold?

"Until she gets back from lunch?" said Pompies, mystified. The lady grunted something or other and he said "no thanks", so she offered to put him through to somebody else, which in fact she did without even waiting for an answer. More hold music (nothing he'd ever heard of before, but the tape sounded stretched). In the end, Pompies gave up and instead phoned Telkom again (doo-doo-de-doo again; and again, and again) and got the number for the Democratic Alliance. He didn't know what they were all about as they had never come to Hillman, not even to hand out T-shirts at election time, but the name sounded friendly and nice. Besides, in all those movies he liked to watch on M-Net, the good guys were always saying, "Just you wait until the DA hears about this" to the bad guys, so they must be pretty useful chaps.

This time he was actually humming along with the hold music (something by Marvin Gaye) when on the line came an actual, live person, who asked him to state the nature of his enquiry.

"I want to change the name of my town, please," said Pompies. It was a reasonable enough request, politely stated.

"Your town, sir?"

"Yes, my town. I'm the mayor."

Long silence. No hold music. But Pompies thought he could hear breathing on the other end.

"Hello?" said Pompies, wondering if perhaps the person had gone to the bathroom or something.

"Yes, sir, I'm here. Sir, you *do* know that all calls are recorded and monitored for quality control purposes, sir?"

"Yes, I do, but I just want to know how I change the name of my town."

Hand over the receiver. Some kind of discussion going on in the background.

"Sir, are you from 702?"

"No, I'm from Hillman." Where the hell was 702? If they were starting to rename towns with numbers now, then the country really was in far deeper kak than Pompies had assumed.

"It's in Natal," he added, in case maybe this 702 place was in the Cape. They were changing a lot of names there, he'd heard. Perhaps there were so many now they were just doing it all numerically until people decided which politicians/comrades/friends-of-the-minister they wanted to immortalize.

More discussion. A new voice came on the phone.

"Sir, the Democratic Alliance has a media department that can handle all press-related queries. However, if you are from the IFP you should know that this is the *fifth* prank call we've taken from you people this week and we are absolutely ..."

"I'm not from the press!" said Pompies, a little more stridently now. "I'm not from the IFP. I'm not from 702. I'm from Hillman. In the Underberg. And all I need to know is how I go about applying to change the name of our town to something ... [and here his mind raced frantically to retrieve from his memory banks the phrase he'd poached just two days before] ... that reflects our town's own political and historical past." Phew!

"Oh."

"So can you help?"

"No, sir, for that you need to contact your local provincial administration."

Spreading the word

By Tuesday, small changes were palpable all over Hillman. Early on Tuesday morning, Dominee, Wessel and Ronan van Vouw could be seen driving around Hillman in Dominee's bakkie, dressed like commandos in their khaki uniforms and vellies, with newly embroidered armbands strapped around their sleeves and on their epaulettes. Dotty Gilmore, who happened to be coming out of the co-op as Dominee was driving past, immediately phoned Eleanor Lambert-Lansdowne to tell her the "tremendously exciting news" that at long last the St Johns Ambulance had set up a mobile community division in Hillman; she could recognize them from the insignia, she said. Eleanor claimed it was long overdue.

Dominee also had a hat band with the VVVV logo affixed to it, and Brumilda van Vouw had used a staple gun to secure one side of the brim to the crown of his velhoed. Disaster was narrowly averted when Neels, always one with a sharp eye for detail, cautioned his father to remove his hat before his mother shot the staple into the side of the hat. "Sjoe, dit was amper, my seun," laughed Dominee, ruffling his son's head to said son's immense annoyance. He had *just* put gel on his hair and now he'd look like Lady Lambert's poodle! Genade! Does *nobody* give a damn about appearance anymore? That's what you get for being helpful: hideous, *horribal* hair!

Dominee wore his hat at a rakish angle and the overall effect was that of Michelin-man-meets-Boer-War-general. The man had all the sartorial elegance of a walrus, but to his wife he was the epitome of masculinity, virility, cultural heritage and national pride. She was tremendously proud of the end result of her handiwork and beamed like a very fat Cheshire cat.

By Monday morning, any niggling misgivings Dominee may have had about the way forward were obliterated the minute he'd heard that Mthethwa was campaigning to change Hillman to Dingiswayo. Over Dominee's cold, dead boerelyf would he let the town become the laughing stock of the Drakensberg by becoming known as "Dinges"! He had immediately put the day-to-day running of the farm in the capable hands of Godliver, Oubaas' successor, under threat of extreme bodily pain should anything go wrong, and set about implementing Operation *Volk en Vaderland* in full battle dress, and anyone who greeted the Van Vouw men as they went about their business got a snappy, unsmiling salute in return.

From Tienkie's counter in the post office, she could see Brumilda van Vouw fixing a sign of her own to the door of the coffee shop on Tuesday morning. In bold letters, six inches high, the sign read: "Right of Admission Reversed". From inside the Tuisnywerheid, Brumilda fixed her nemesis with a cold "so there!" stare and Tienkie gave one right back and returned to sorting mail.

All the candidates had their own campaign managers by this stage: Oubaas had Alpheus, Dominee had Brumilda, Lady Lambert-Lansdowne had Dotty Gilmore (who was more of a campaign underling, she wanted her to be aware, but the same principle applied), and Pompies de Wet had Tienkie, whether or not he knew it. And already Tienkie was setting about creating a little mischief and unrest in the village of Hillman ...

Tienkie Groenewald was good at that. On the final evening of the Miss Pasture Cattle Feed Pageant in 1978, Tienkie had ensured that any competitors who may have stood between her and the crown were dealt with in quite spectacular fashion. During the intermission, after the final five contestants had been announced, Tienkie produced a small saw from her bag, and while all the other girls were fixing their hair and make-up, got to work on the heels of the other contestants' shoes. She also unpicked the straps of the evening gown of Trudie Lamprecht, the hot favourite to win the competition, until they were only just attached to the dress. That done, she passed around a bakkie of home-made chocolate biscuits to all the girls. After six weeks of stringent dieting everyone tucked in heartily and voted Tienkie "Miss Personality" for the pageant on the basis of her generosity and baking prowess. Unbeknownst to them, however, the cookies were laced with a powerful but tasteless emetic and in the final parade the judges were stunned to see four of the five finalists stumbling around on stage, green at the gills and holding on to their sides. In what was a death-knell for Trudie Lamprecht as far as the title went, the poor girl's dress came undone just as she reached the end of the runway and the last the audience saw of her was as she attempted to run off the stage, in shoes that no longer had heels attached to them, desperately clutching her apricot taffeta dress. The final humiliation came when she vomited in the potted palm to the side of the judges' table, much to their stunned disbelief. Tienkie stood smiling throughout and appeared suitably shocked and amazed when she was announced as Miss Pasture Cattle Feed (Vereeniging).

It being 1978 and Vereeniging, however, the other contestants were none too savvy when it came to reporting their suspicions, but a few months down the line one of the girls mentioned to somebody who told somebody else that she was sure that Tienkie Groenewald had "poisoned" them and in a matter of days a reporter from the *Vereeniging Herhout* and a representative of Pasture Cattle Feed were both banging on Tienkie's door, demanding to know the truth of events on the night of the pageant and threatening to strip her of her title. Without waiting to see just how shattering the fallout from that exposé would be, Tienkie Groenewald upped sticks, and climbing into her little yellow Beetle with the "Love Is ..." sticker on it, headed directly for the country, where she decided to lay low for a little while until it blew over.

This time round, however, Tienkie was going to be more cunning, and she would take every precaution to ensure that nothing she did to aid Pompies in his campaign to retain the mayoral seat could be traced to her. A little "mistake" here and there would be all that was needed to sow the seeds of malcontent, and if anyone asked her, well, to err was human after all.

Inside the co-op, all appeared to be normal save for two things; the first being that Alpheus had turned up to work wearing a Madiba-style shirt in garish colours and now insisted on speaking to Pompies in Zulu. As was to be expected, neither Pompies nor Alpheus mentioned the latter's gaudy attire nor the matter of linguistics but Pompies did wonder to himself whether the boy wasn't freezing in his cotton shirt when the thermometer outside the co-op was registering 5°C. Still, if that Dingaan chappie could run around in a grass skirt and a headband in weather like this, barefoot nogal, then Alpheus probably wasn't finding it cold at all.

In point of fact, Alpheus was freezing! He wished he'd listened to his grandmother and had worn the jacket and the gloves she had offered that morning, but now that he'd set the precedent he'd have to stick to it, at least until the election was over. He was asserting his cultural position and even if Nelson Mandela was a Xhosa he was still an African, and a great one at that, and the people of Hillman needed to recognize that fact.

The second noticeable change at the Hillman Co-op was that there seemed to be a marked drop-off in customer traffic from a normal weekday morning. Perhaps everyone was just tired after all the excitement of the previous couple of days, thought Pompies, but that disquieting feeling of agitation had by now taken up permanent residence in the pit of his stomach and showed no sign of abating.

Oubaas sat on a bench outside the co-op with his gloved hands wrapped around his cane, watching everything that was going on in the village. In fine weather, he would sit here with his friends in the morning and catch up on local gossip while Aggripina cleaned the linoleum and sorted out the laundry. Today, however, nobody else was there on account of the bitter weather and he cut a solitary figure as he sat on the bench, bundled up in the jacket, woolly hat, scarf and gloves that Aggripina had insisted he wear.

"Môre, Oubaas," beamed Doffie, blowing on his hands to keep them warm. Even in freezing weather, Doffie never left his station for the warmer interior of the co-op.

"Morning, Mr Dorf," replied Oubaas. The boy may not be the brightest candle in the pack, but he was always polite and Oubaas appreciated that.

"Jissie, maar you look like a sneeuman, Oubaas," said Doffie. "If, you know, snow wasn't white."

Oubaas chuckled. Doffie never meant any harm, even if the things he said didn't always come out quite right. The two men then watched as Dotty Gilmore came striding down the street in Wellington boots, riding breeches, a well-worn woollen jumper, and a woolly hat with an enormous pom-pom on it, handing out pieces of paper to everyone she met along the way.

"Morning, Mr Mthethwa, Dorf," she said as she reached them, promptly thrusting pieces of paper into the hands of both men.

"What's this, tannie?" said Doffie, holding the paper upside down.

"It's our very first newspaper, Dorf," said Dotty, beaming. "And it's free!" she said, before marching into the co-op purposefully.

Oubaas regarded the piece of paper in his hands. It had been printed on one side of an A4 page on an inkjet printer and wasn't quite dry yet. At the top, in bold Garamond font, was the masthead: *The Hillman Herald* and underneath it was the banner headline "Hillman's Proud Legacy" followed by a short story, greatly embellished from the few, scant details she had unearthed from the Internet on Sunday, about brave Walter Ambrose Hillman (as the eponymous Hillman was now being referred to) from Chatham in Kent, who had left a family (now comprising a devoted wife, Eloise, and four small children) to venture at Her Majesty's bidding to southern Africa in 1899 to save the country from the evil intentions of a handful of loutish renegades. By the time the article went to press, W. A. Hillman had not only distinguished himself in battle, he had been awarded several medals for bravery, including the Victoria Cross, which he won posthumously after perishing as he single-handedly saved the little mountain village from certain attack. The embellishments, said Eleanor Lambert-Lansdowne, were entirely necessary to give the story authenticity and the requisite gravitas, and besides they were probably all true; Dotty just hadn't located the details at that point, suggested Eleanor. The article was also liberally peppered with the words "political" and "historical" so that people knew that both of these criteria were being met in the case for the continuation of the name "Hillman".

Underneath the article, on the left, was a calendar of events, which included the various meetings of the HLANC, an announcement about flowers for the Hillman chapel and a teaser notice about the Hillman Winter Ball, as Eleanor's dinner party was now being referred to, which was, the notice said, "By invitation only". To the right of this was a small advertisement for the Hillman General Co-op, which promoted the Selati Sugar special, and another for the Hillman Ale & Arms, publicizing that establishment's forthcoming 70s Quiz Night. Both of these inclusions had been entirely deliberate; Eleanor and Dotty wanted to ensure that the newspaper would be circulated at both places as they both had the greatest concentration of human traffic in Hillman.

"So you'll put this in your shop, won't you, Mr de Wet?" Dotty had said, phrasing it more as a statement than a question.

Pompies scratched his head. What the blerrie bliksem was going on here? If he said no, then more people would hate him and not vote for him, but if he said yes then it sort of meant that he wasn't too firm in his position on the whole Dingaan Berg thing. Dotty tapped a finger at the advert for the co-op and said, "You'll see you have a *free* advertisement there, Mr de Wet. This newspaper is a hundred percent impartial and unbiased."

At this, Pompies capitulated. Publicity was publicity and there did seem to be a dearth of customers all of a sudden. "Ag ja, sure, Dotty. Why not, hey?" And with that Dotty Gilmore left triumphantly and went over the street to the Copper Kettle Coffee Shop and Tuisnywerheid.

There, her reception was not as acquiescent as it had been at the co-op. Brumilda van Vouw crumpled her copy of *The Hillman Herald* into a ball and threw it into the wastepaper basket saying that Dotty should read the sign on the door. At that, Dotty turned to Prudence Robinson who was unpacking her cheesecakes into the glass fridge behind the counter. There was a tense moment as all three women eyed each other, two English-speakers to one, but that one being a formidable woman whom most people never dared to cross. Prudence defused the situation by saying she'd keep copies on "her side" of the counter on days when she was on duty at the coffee-shop and Dotty left, but not before giving Brumilda van Vouw a perfect replica of the "so there!" stare that Brumilda had given Tienkie just an hour before.

At the post office, Tienkie was unequivocal in her refusal to carry or display *The Hillman Herald*. "This is a government building, Mevrou Gilmore," Tienkie said, knowing that the "mevrou" would annoy Dotty immensely. "You can't just go sticking up any old nonsens in an official post office. See the sign on the door: it says 'official postal business only'."

Dotty left, but snuck around the side of the post office and slipped folded copies of *The Hillman Herald* into every post box on the wall. As she did so, the postal mistress stood on the other side, removing them one by one as they entered each box. You'd have to get up *verrrry* early to catch Tienkie Groenewald napping, she thought.

At the Ale & Arms, Dotty got an effusive welcome, however. Neels van Vouw literally shrieked with delight when he saw *The Hillman Herald*. He instantly recognized the huge potential that such a journal offered. With the *Idols* auditions virtually around the corner, he could use the paper to publicize his audition and even to garner sponsorship, especially if Lady Lambert-Lansdowne was behind this publication. The possibilities were endless. It was too, too divine!

"Ag, of course, skattie," enthused Neels, "you can put a *hewge* pile here. The Ale & Arms is completely neutral in this whole oorloggie, you know," he said, and promptly got to work on creating a *Hillman Herald* display.

Esmé Gericke might have something to say about the presence of *The Hillman Herald* on the noticeboard and on the reception desk of her hotel, but Neels would point out to her what Pompies had astutely divined, which was that publicity is publicity, especially when it's free! Besides, with Tienkie playing 2IC to the mayor these days, Mrs Gericke's affections towards Pompies had not exactly evaporated, but they had certainly waned a tad.

Koekie van Vouw was now installed behind the reception desk of the AA, and managed to look as bored as was humanly possible without actually falling asleep. She was not nearly as excited as her brother about the whole *Hillman Herald* thing, especially as there was nothing in there about Heinz Winckler, Steve Hofmeyr or anybody even remotely exciting and—forget this dead Mister Hillman ou—the stupid rooinek cow had completely forgotten to mention that the reigning *Miss* Hillman was back in town!

At the Hillman Farm & Feed Store, Klippies was torn. He wanted to support his friend Pompies, but he was scared of Dominee because he was always so kwaai, and he liked Dotty Gilmore because she got all her feed and tack for her horses from him. Already Wessel van Vouw had been there that morning dressed like some boere-soldaat and had asked—no, *told*—him that they would be putting a sign over the word "Hillman" so that his feed store would now say "Jacobusville Farm & Feed". Klippies had agreed, but not because he had any choice in the matter, and because Wessel hadn't even been ordentlik about it, he agreed to let Dotty put her newspaper in his store window.

Back at her propaganda-free post office, Tienkie was distributing a few messages in her own inimitable fashion. Into Dominee's mail she dropped a letter addressed to "Liefling" from "Jou engel" of Pietermaritzbug. "Liefling", she happened to know, also went by the name of Koekie van Vouw. One of two things were guaranteed to happen: either Dominee would realize that somebody was writing to his virginal daughter thoughts so impure they left no doubt as to the virtue of the girl, *or* Brumilda van Vouw would think that Dominee had taken a fancy-lady on his many trips to the cattle shows in Martizburg. Hah!

Into Doffie's mail she dropped the letter that was to have been mailed to Koekie's paramour in Pietermartizburg, tantalizingly and ambiguously addressed to "My liefie". While Doffie's reading skills left a lot to be desired, he would still get the gist of the missive and was very likely to shout out to Koekie about having received the letter when he was over at the Ale & Arms. Doffie would do that in all innocence, Tienkie knew, and nobody would hold it against the boy, but the story would get back to—or be heard by—Dominee and before long the Van Vouws would be at each other hammer and tongs. If any of it got back to Tienkie, she would just say that the letters must have been improperly addressed. Oops!

Into Klippies' mail she dropped a receipt for the darts and dartboard which Dominee had ordered from the United States at a time when he told Klippies he couldn't settle his bill with the Farm & Feed Store because money was tight. She thought of putting a

Voortrekkers' newsletter into Alpheus' post, but decided that he was too much of a live wire right now and in any case she'd find other ways to destabilize the Mthethwa camp. Oubaas never got any mail anyway so she knew it would be pushing the envelope, so to speak, to try and put anything in his post. For her final item of business for the day, Tienkie slipped into Lady Lambert-Lansdowne's mail the periodical-in-the-brown-paper-wrapper that came once a month for Farmer Robinson, knowing full well that Florence would cut open the envelope without looking at the address and place it on a tray for Lady Lambert to look at with her morning tea.

By the very next day letter bombs would be going off all over Hillman, and with a final wipe down of her counter Tienkie Groenewald locked up and went home.

Things fall apart

It was now the 3rd of June, three full weeks since the fateful meeting in the Town Hall and three weeks to go until the big election on the 24th, and Hillman was a town in chaos.

Since Tienkie's letter bombs, many of the recipients of the incendiary items gave the others a wide berth or were openly hostile. The only person who was happy with the state of affairs following said mail drop was Doffie, who had, to Tienkie's immense surprise, kept quiet about the missive he had received, convinced that Koekie had a secret crush on him. Doffie was delirious with delight! Not so the other players. Klippies had summoned up the courage to tell Dominee that he had to settle his account immediately or no further purchases would be permitted and Dominee had opposed the motion saying that his account *would* be continued, citing clause 2 of Operation *Volk en Vaderland* vis-à-vis leg breaking. Klippies backed down, but he now hated the man more than ever. Koekie van Vouw was under house arrest when she wasn't at the Ale & Arms and had had her cell phone taken away from her; she, too, currently hated her father more than ever. Lady Lambert-Lansdowne, supposedly fully recovered (with the aid of Dotty's much-vaunted "Rescue Remedy") from the shock of opening *Desperate Housewives*, the monthly publication "for discerning gentlemen", now gave Farmer Robinson a wide berth in case he had sent it to her as an indication of what he had in mind for after-dinner amusements at the dinner party on the 23rd. She needed his vote but that was the extent of the input she required from the man!

Dwayne Donovan, at the urging of Lady Lambert-Lansdowne who

had argued that under no circumstances should he proceed as he had been for the "long-term sake of Hillman", had ceased his refuse collection, and piles of black bags now sat outside homes, farms and businesses, reeking of decay and awaiting a collection that never came. It should also be mentioned, however, that refuse collection *did* continue at the homes and farms of Hillman's English-speaking residents, paid for by the kind-hearted and infinitely benevolent Lady Eleanor. The message was clear: if you want to meddle with Hillman, then clean up your own bally mess!

More than fifty percent of Pompies' trade had dropped off instantly in the aftermath of the meeting on the 13th of May. No longer would Pompies be suspicious of any Friday the 13th; it was *Saturday* the 13th you had to watch out for! Most of the Afrikaans farmers and even some of the English ones, too, were now going to Underberg to buy supplies and stock up on petrol, and Doffie found himself standing out in the bitter cold for most of the day with not a customer in sight.

At least some of the farmers, however, had had the decency to come and speak to Pompies about their various predicaments.

"Ag, sorry, man," Jossie Vermeulen had said to Pompies. "It's just ... ag ... you know how Dominee gets, man. I mean he threw me with a dart and nearly took my eye out, you know? He gets moer of a kwaai, Pompies. It's just easier to keep the peace."

Pompies assured him that he understood. He had let Dominee win the 2003 Darts League Final for the very same reason.

Stoffie de Villiers had also come to see Pompies, somewhat sheepishly and looking constantly over his shoulder in case somebody had seen him enter the co-op.

"Jammer, man, Pompies," he'd said. "I feel kak, jong, but what can I do? The ouk is lank pals with everyone in Maritzburg and if I can't sell my sheep at auction next season, then I can't pay school fees for the kids, you know?"

Pompies thanked him for coming to see him and assured him that he understood. But still, it was such a shame as he had stocked up on extra candles and paraffin for the winter, which was getting colder by the day. The candles now stood like forlorn wax soldiers all in a row on the specials display shelf, waiting for customers who never came. Even the specials display shelf looked sad and dusty because Alpheus had quit the co-op two weeks ago to manage Oubaas' campaign fulltime. Pompies was very sorry to see him go; he was a great worker with lots of good ideas, but at the present rate he would have had to let him go anyway as there wasn't enough business to pay for additional staff.

Klippies, however, ever-loyal to his friend, continued to shop at the co-op and to fill his bakkie at the petrol station, but he had a nagging suspicion that it was no coincidence that all four of his tyres had been let down or that a rock had mysteriously found its way into the window of his shop front, shattering the glass. (Although, in fairness, that could have been one of those asteroid thingies like what Bruce Willis was trying to stop in that lekker flick, Armageddon. Asteroids were bad news, Klippies knew. They even banned them at the Olympics sometimes. They made women look like ouks, with chest hair and everything, he had heard, and evidently they were very bad news for shop windows, too. Klippies was pretty sure Brumilda van Vouw had been taking asteroids. On the rare occasions that she took part, she had never been beaten in the Ale & Arms Arm Wrestling Competition and it was mos a bit odd that she always wore cardigans, hey?)

The Afrikaans farmers had stopped short of wearing the khaki uniform that Dominee had suggested, but even though they weren't in uniform many of the farmers were observed giving the four-fingered salute to each other, each finger representing one of the Vs (Pompies would always give them a two-fingered salute of his own in return). The problem with this salute was that they split their four fingers into a V, which made anyone giving it look like a boere-Trekkie and not a bit like a hardened soldaat of the volk. Spock would be proud; Retief not so much …

Wessel had done a good job of erecting hand-painted signs everywhere that he could bearing the name "Jacobusville". The Hillman Farm & Feed Store became Jacobusville Farm & Feed; De Leeuk became "De Leeuk, Jacobusville", and every farm where the Van Vouws either found sympathy or where the farmers were too wary of Van Vouw to protest became signposted "Jacobusville". The roadsign at the bottom of the Valleikloof Pass now had an extra board hanging below it, which read "Jacobusville 8½" and the welcome sign just beyond the lookout point now had an extra board tacked above it, which read: "Welkom in Jacobusville. Gevestig deur Jacobus van Vouw, 1899".

It wasn't all good news for Dominee, however: Van Vouw's farmhands, with the exception of Wilson, Patience and Perseverance, had stopped coming to work and said to the de facto farm manager, Godliver, that he should tell Dominee that they refused to work for a man who supported outmoded and dictatorial ideals. (Well, in words almost to that effect; what they actually said was that the man was a crazy effing bastard, that this was 2006, not 1806, and that he could stick his Vierkleur and his four Vs where the sun don't shine!) Wilson and Perseverance only continued to work because they were getting money for jam, literally, and Patience *had* to continue working because she had three children to support and knew that it was only men who could afford principles and moral outrage.

Operation *Volk en Vaderland* continued undaunted, however; many of the farmers' tractors were now sporting banners and flags sewn by Brumilda van Vouw with the word "Jacobusville" embroidered on them and some die-hard Van Vouw-ists even had the four-V logo painted on their bakkies, prompting Lady Eleanor to think that the St John's Ambulance had overdone it a tad.

The campaigners for Hillman, however, not to be outdone, had done their best to make their mark in as tasteful and dignified a fashion as possible. A sign was printed in Harrismith at the expense of Lady Lambert-Lansdowne announcing, in an elegant font: "Welcome to Hillman, established by General Sir Walter Ambrose Hillman in 1899". Dotty Gilmore, honing her journalistic and marketing skills more and more these days, had come up with a positioning statement for the Hillman campaign, and below the masthead of her now-weekly newspaper appeared the tagline: "Hillman is Heaven".

Lady Lambert was very busy planning the Hillman Winter Ball and was content to leave Dotty doing the sterling job she was doing for the meantime. Lady Eleanor had a strategic advantage in that, because her house was so high up the mountain, everyone for miles around could see the Union Jack flying above the trees of Grasscroft. But Lady Lambert had domestic issues of her own to sort out beneath her flag. Florence had handed in her notice, telling her now-ex-employer that she couldn't continue to work for a neo-colonialist harridan who was a fascist at heart and devoid of any human decency (or words to that effect). Lady Eleanor had nearly fainted at this torrent of bile and abuse. "Devoid of human decency"? Dear God, the milk of human kindness fairly flowed through her blood! Hadn't she given Florence the afternoon off on Christmas Day? And hadn't she wished her a "Merry Christmas" very sincerely and said she could have the leftover turkey that very same day? Ye gods, there was ingratitude for you! But Florence was not to be persuaded and had marched off in high dudgeon nonetheless, leaving Lady Eleanor with the wearisome task of finding somebody else *and* having to make her own tea and meals in the meantime. It was so typical of the working classes to pick exactly the *most* inconvenient time to throw a tantrum just to make some measly point. Well, Eleanor Lambert-Lansdowne wasn't one to be dictated to! Florence had also said something about reporting Lady Eleanor to something called the CCMA, but if they were anything like the YMCA they would probably just give Florence a Gideon's Bible, a room for the night and then send her on her way. Still, all in all, it was proving very difficult to find someone with the right degree of pliability and servility to fill Florence's very capable shoes. And Phineas, although he hadn't resigned, had very unhelpfully said it was against his culture for a man to do any housework. Lady Eleanor, however, keenly attuned to just how far cultural limitations go, had smartly identified the ceiling of said cultural mores and offered him double pay to wield a vacuum cleaner around Grasscroft and do other menial tasks around the mansion that she simply didn't have the time, motivation, or physical strength to do. Phineas had decided his cultural pride could tolerate that for now. With money, mused Eleanor, most things are possible and indeed she should know; back in Scunthorpe she'd had no money, ergo no possibilities. Add money to that equation and, hey presto, just about every door had been opened and the world became alive with possibility. People had always told her that money couldn't buy you happiness. Fiddle-faddle, pish-tosh and complete and utter horsefeathers! It may not buy actual "happiness", whatever the hell that might be, but it bought a damn good facsimile of it, as well as a bally nice Christian Dior handbag with matching ostrich gloves, and it could also get the dishes washed when people called Florence let one down. Still, who was she going to find who could make vichyssoise like Florence did for the Winter Ball? Ho hum ...

Over in the Mthethwa camp, Alpheus was hard at work on his grandfather's campaign. He had painted one side of Philemon Nthuli's minibus with the word "Dingiswayo" in enormous letters diagonally across the length of the bus, and the words "Mthethwa for Mayor" in English on the other; he wanted the citizens of Hillman to understand what was going on and most of the whites couldn't speak a word of Zulu, even though they lived in Africa and in a Zulu province, at that. It really was shameful, he said. He even painted a fresco around the bus showing fearsome Zulu warriors in battle regalia and wielding assegais, and on the rear window had the words "Dingiswayo: our past, your future" painted on the glass. Philemon thought it a work of art and made extra journeys to Underberg and Himeville so that all the other taxi drivers could see his beautiful bus.

Alpheus also made signs of his own, one of which he fashioned out of one of Aggripina's bedsheets (to her absolute fury), which he stretched over three rungs of the Vodacom tower announcing "Dingiswayo" to everybody on the eastern side of the mountain, and Beatrice Ndlovu's children even made an enormous statement on the hill where their house was on the western side, spelling out "Dingiswayo" in big stones painted white, which could be seen for miles around. Los Angeles may have its Hollywood Hills, thought Alpheus, but here they had the Dingiswayo Mountain and a thing of beauty it was, too.

Alpheus now wore his uniform of Madiba-shirt, Ray-Bans, and gold watch on a daily basis and even though the winter wind cut straight to his bones he wore his bright, cotton shirts everywhere he went. Money was tight, though, and he still had to pay the Markham's debit order every month, he knew, or the Markham's credit police would come looking for him. It was sad that he couldn't carry on working for Pompies, really—he was a good man at heart, thought Alpheus, if a little slow—but desperate times called for desperate measures and he couldn't, under the circumstances, devote the time necessary to his grandfather's campaign while still working fulltime. In light of his new employment status, however, Alpheus decided that perhaps it was time to revisit the plan he had been trying to execute in Durban just prior to his swift departure from the city, namely the redistribution of wealth, so to speak.

Alpheus wasn't the only one with plans of affirmative shopping in mind, however. Everyone was feeling the pinch as a result of the new circumstances, and for the first time in the history of the Hillman Anglican Chapel money started disappearing from the collection plate, rather than going into it. When Cedric Parsons mentioned this, in as polite a fashion as he could during one of his long sermons at church one Sunday, Pompies felt a swift shot of retribution course through his veins. Serves you right, you doos (sorry God). That's what you get for talking ugly about me "lording it over" the people of Hillman, he thought. *Now* see if you can make it through the week with only twenty rand on your plate, pel!

Pompies own campaign was a much more low-key affair than the others. Tienkie had said she was "helluva sorry Pompies" but because it was a government building she couldn't rename the post office the Dingaan Berg Post Office until it was a fait accompli, but Pompies had put a sign of his own at the co-op saying Dingaan Berg General Co-op and Petrol Station. Klippies said he would have put up a sign saying Dingaan Berg Farm & Feed but that the weasely Wessel had got there first. And Esmé Gericke said that while she'd like to help Pompies by putting up a sign saying Dingaan Berg Ale & Arms, too many of her customers were Van Vouw supporters so she was going to leave it as it was until the whole thing was decided. There was also no mention of any more pampoenkoekies, he noticed ...

Even at Hillman Primary, renamed for the time being as the "Hillman Dingiswayo Jacobusville Dingaan Berg Primary School" so that no child felt in any way marginalized, Lynette Butler found herself having to deal with strange new divisions within her school. During art class, the children would split off into separate factions of their own accord and create posters—not of flowers, houses, dogs, fairies, Power Rangers and families, as they had before—but of Hillman as they saw it, or rather, as their families saw it. Ronan van Vouw was new to the class, having temporarily relocated to Hillman during the "operasie" as his father termed it, but his posters were so disturbing in content that Miss Butler wondered if she should seek professional advice as to what to do about it all. At playtime, her pupils would also "act out" on the playground their version of current events and what Lynette saw troubled her. Whereas before the children would play "cops and robbers" or "cowboys and Indians", now they played "impi and boere soldaat" or "colonialists and robbers", and Josephina Nguni's grandson had even sprained his wrist in one particularly lively battle enactment. Fortunately, Dr Miller and Mrs Coleman had been on high-alert since this whole thing started and were able to put Bongani's arm in a sling, so not too much came of the incident.

These divisions weren't only at play in the classrooms of the HDJDB Primary School. Within the ranks of the previously content little HLANC group, different factions had arisen, and there were now breakaway groups that met on different days of the week according to their political affiliations. Even at the Tuisnywerheid and coffee shop, formerly a happy enterprise of like-minded women who enjoyed serving their calorific treats to appreciative customers for a little extra pocket-money, battle lines were now drawn in the sugar. Mondays, Wednesdays and Fridays were designated "English" days, (or "rooinek dae" as Brumilda had written it up on the roster) and Tuesdays, Thursdays and Saturdays were Afrikaans days (or "guttural hybrid language days" as Dotty Gilmore had countered on the same sheet). Thank goodness Aggripina Mthethwa, Josephina Nguni and Florence Dlamini were not yet supplying the Tuisnywerheid with their cakes as they had often talked of doing, because that would have meant only two days each for all three groups and how could you make any money out of *that*? Only Cedric Parsons could get away with those types of working hours!

It was a disconsolate Pompies who went outside his empty store on that glacial Saturday morning in June to join Oubaas Mthethwa on the bench in the freezing weather. He took two cups of coffee with him, one for himself and one for his supposed adversary.

"Ja, ou man. How is the day?" said Pompies, taking up a seat next to Oubaas.

"Good, thank you, Mr de Wet. And how are you?" said Oubaas, taking a sip of the coffee.

"Could be better, Oubaas, could be better. Everything's vrot in Hillman, Oubaas. Everyone's lelik to everyone else and nothing is like it was anymore. Somebody stole Dominee's John Deere tractor last night and all of Farmer Robinson's silverware was taken from his sideboard the night before. And that stuff was hairlooms, you know? Did you hear about that? We never had this kind of problems before, hey Oubaas? Now Hillman is horrible, man," said Pompies, shaking his head.

"This is true," said Oubaas, warming his hands on the cup and looking out onto a deserted street, which should have been filled with busy people exchanging weekend pleasantries and commenting on the weather. "So, as you are the mayor, Mr de Wet, what are you going to do about it?"

Pompies looked into his cup of coffee in the hope that the answer was going to appear in the grounds at the bottom of it. It was a good question; a fair question; a question he couldn't blerrie well answer. What *was* he going to do about it?

Strangers in our mist

If Pompies was hoping for an epiphany, none came, and Hillman lurched from the chaotic to the criminal. The only person untouched by all the mayhem and anarchy was Neels, who had almost perfected Celine Dion's *My Heart Will Go On*, except for the *very* high notes, and had been hard at work on a silver lamé suit for his audition (which would also double as his outfit for when he MC'd the election, a role he had now secured. "Ag sure, Neeltjie," Pompies had said, "Why not, hey?"). He was also very busy—unbeknownst to his father—in another new role as a party-planner for Lady Lambert-Lansdowne, who had asked him to co-ordinate her little rendezvous in exchange for a considerable sum and her "eternal gratitude". He wasn't English, she and Dotty lamented, and therefore might lack some of the finesse that the event called for, but the boy did have the flair and pizzazz that "comes naturally to the type", said Lady Eleanor, and in the absence of Florence he would suffice nicely.

Doffie was also immune to the bedlam around him, and had started picking flowers, which he took to a very surprised but appreciative Koekie on an almost daily basis. He may not have the city-slicker appeal that Wynand (who was a junior manager of the Steers in Pietermarizburg) had, but he had a certain country-bumpkin charm, she thought. (Although her actual words were: "Ag sjeim, he's oulik, Neels, stop picking on him, man! Jy's vieslik!") And it did brighten her day to be brought flowers, even if they were from the flowerbeds of the Ale & Arms. Even his notes were pure poetry: "Roses are red, violents are blue. Melktert is sweet, and Koekies is also". That chappie Blake (or was it "Bloke"? She couldn't quite remember; matric was *soooo* long ago) could have taken a leaf out of Doffie's book, thought Koekie dreamily.

As romance blossomed over the reception counter of the Ale & Arms, so everything else withered in the rest of Hillman. There were skelms about, of that there was no doubt; people no longer felt safe to sleep with their doors unlocked as they had previously, and each group blamed the other for every incident of theft and vandalism. Klippies' tyres had been let down and his shop front smashed; Prudence Robinson's wedding silverware had been taken from the dresser in her dining room; money had gone missing from the post office, the co-op and the Copper Kettle; laundry had been taken off washing lines around Hillman; vegetables uprooted from beds in every garden in the village; some "monstrous individual" had shaved Lady Eleanor's poodle, Lavinia; one of Josephina Nguni's goats had been stolen (although she was ready with a bottle for when she found the skebenga); and Dominee van Vouw's prize tractor had been pinched.

The only part that Alpheus had played in any of this litany of lawlessness was the theft of Dominee's John Deere tractor, but then, if you're going to leave the keys in the tractor ignition, he thought, it was all but an actual invitation to drive it away and could hardly be construed as "stealing". The theft itself had been highly unsuccessful; for one thing, the tractor—despite its racy cup-holder and leather seat—had a top speed of about 50kph, which didn't make for a very fast getaway at all, and because Dominee was no longer filling up at the Hillman petrol station he'd let the tank get very low and Alpheus had run out of petrol before he reached the other side of the mountain. He left it where it had spluttered to a halt and walked home dejectedly in the freezing night air, thinking that the life of a car criminal was very definitely not for him. At five o'clock in the morning, on discovering that his beloved John Deere 6603 tractor had been removed from his property, Dominee had phoned Farmer Robinson and enquired of the man if perhaps he had a tractor-kleptomania problem. (He seemed to be forever "borrowing" tractors and then returning them and Dominee hadn't forgotten that Robinson had "borrowed" old man Kloppers' tractor back in '86). His phone call and the accusations contained therein served only to further erode whatever lingering goodwill had existed between the English- and Afrikaans-speaking camps.

Later on the same morning, however, Pompies had found the tractor exactly where Alpheus had left it, with the keys still in the ignition, and had filled it up with fuel before returning it to De Leeuk. Dominee was forced, somewhat grudgingly, to thank Pompies for returning his tractor to him, with a full tank nogal. He offered Pompies money for the petrol, but Pompies said he was "just doing his duty" and Van Vouw had to swallow his pride, the very act of which gave him maagpyn, and thank him again.

The following week got off to an inauspicious start with five Zulu women gathering outside the Town Hall on Monday morning to toyi-toyi about the spiralling crime in Hillman. Included in their number were Florence, Beatrice and even Josephina Nguni, who had told Pompies that she would be late for work because she and her friends were staging a mass rally.

Lady Eleanor had seen this display on her way to post her victuals and beverages orders for her party (one simply couldn't leave things like that to chance; what would happen if Phineas arrived in Durban and its various emporia had insufficient stock of Cornish game hens or Stolichnaya?), and she thought that perhaps it was some kind of traditional dance organized as a cheap tourism gimmick by that bounder of a mayor who would stop at nothing to push through his tawdry plan to curry favour with the natives in Hillman and those boors in government. She immediately phoned Dotty, who phoned all the other English ladies of the HLANC, and within twenty minutes a chorus of middle-aged women in sensible shoes, tweed skirts, cardigans and earmuffs were singing *God Save the Queen* and other old English ditties twenty feet from the toyi-toying party.

In the middle of this extraordinary cacophony, a vehicle with a GP registration plate glided up through the mist and parked in the parking-lot of the Ale & Arms. All singing and dancing ceased immediately as the women, joined by Pompies, Doffie, Oubaas, Tienkie Groenewald and the Afrikaans ladies on duty at the Copper Kettle, watched two men in sunglasses, sharp haircuts, city-wear and "fency-shoes" (as Brumilda called any men's footwear that wasn't vellies), get out of the car and walk into the Ale & Arms armed with what appeared to be a briefcase in the hand of one (who also carried a big tube of rolled-up paper), and a shiny metal case in the hand of the other.

SMSes were sent hastily all over the village and subsequently all over the valley. Hillman almost never had strangers in the village and those that came were invariably lost. These gentlemen didn't appear to be lost. Several parties speculated that they were from the Department of Roads and Transportation, while others surmised that they must be from the Department of Name Changing or whoever it was that Pompies had been so geheimsinnig about at the Town Hall meeting. Pompies, however, told the growing crowd that he had *no* idea who they were and they couldn't be from the government because 1) they were white and 2) their car registration was GP, which did *not* stand for "Government People", he told everyone, not "G", which did. Dotty, now with her journalist hat firmly on her head (it was the woolly cap with the big pom-pom) stood poised with a steno-pad and ballpoint pen in hand, wondering if perhaps she should go and interview them for the next edition of *The Hillman Herald*, and then decided against it in case they were having a nice cup of tea and didn't want to be disturbed.

Inside the Ale & Arms, Koekie was on high alert. This was exactly the type of intelligence-gathering her father expected of her and she wanted to do something right so that he would leave her alone about "daa'ie onnosele dons" as he referred to Dorf. She wished Neels was here because all of a sudden she wasn't sure what she was supposed to do anymore.

"Goeie môre, good morning," said Koekie, brightly. It was difficult to tell what stratum of society these men belonged to other than "City Folk". Best to sound them out first.

"Wotcher!" one of the gentlemen said back. Foreign, definitely foreign, thought Koekie. He sounded European, like American or something. Was he a "watcher"? And if so, what was that?

"Can I help you?" Koekie purred. When in doubt always resort to coquettishness.

"Well, can you start by telling us where we are?" said Number Two, smiling a little too nicely for a man with broken, yellowing seashells for teeth. He was up to something, he and his big metal case.

Koekie stared at him blankly. The sign over the counter said "Ale & Arms" in big brass letters. Perhaps Europeans from America couldn't read.

"This is the Ale & Arms, meneer," said Koekie incredulously, pointing at the sign and trying hard not to sound like she thought he was dof.

"No, no, I mean which town are we in?"

"O. Hillman, meneer." So they *were* lost after all.

"I see," he said, although clearly he didn't. "It's just that there are at least three different flags flying here and the signs all say different things. One says Din-gan-Berg, a few say Jacob-us-ville, the mountainside says Dinghy-sway-o, and the only mapbook we could find this place on says that this should be Hillman." The only name that came out right was "Hillman". Rooinek, perhaps?

"Ja ..." said Koekie, giggling nervously. What should she say? What should she say? Her sleuthing skills were not finely honed at all but if these men *were* watchers from some secret organization sent to spy on them then she probably shouldn't mention Operation *Volk en Vaderland*. Or should she? Where the bliksem was Neels?

"I mean you're in Hillman *now*," she said, "but if you come back in three weeks you might not be. It all depends." Koekie was trying her best to be helpful.

"On what?" said Number One.

"On who wins the war, meneer." This ou really wasn't the sharpest knife in the drawer.

The two men looked at each other, then back at Koekie.

"Tell you what," said Number Two. "Koki, is it?" Koekie blushed. If he could read her name tag, then obviously he could read after all, even if he said her name funny. "Tell you what, Koki, can we get some breakfast here and a nice cup of coffee to start?"

"Ja," said Koekie. Relief washed over her. A breakfast order she could handle. Eggs, bacon, sausage, toast. Ah, the toast ... her turn to ask the questions!

"White or brown, meneer?" she asked Number One.

"White, please." Koekie looked at him long and hard. Perhaps this was a secret signal.

"Brown, please," said Number Two. Hmm. This may be a test.

"And koffie, meneer?"

"Black, please," said Number One.

"And I'll have white," said Number Two. She was getting mixed messages here. Too confusing to decode right now. Only Neels could help.

"No, actually, make that tea, please," said Number Two. Tea? Her father was right; the Rooinekke *were* coming! "Do you have Earl Grey?" he asked.

"No, but we got a Lady Eleanor," she said. Spies, very definitely spies.

The two men looked at each other. Number Two thought he'd try again.

"Do you have Liptons, perhaps, Koki?"

Koekie was horrified. "Nee, meneer! I mean I thought I had it once but Dokter Miller gave me something and it cleared it up." This ou knew far too much already.

Number Two realized he wasn't getting anywhere and went back to coffee. Black.

"Oh, Koki? This Lady Eleanor: is she German?" said Number One.

"No, meneer, Pa says she's from Mars. Groot Grootoupagrootjie mos killed the German!"

Koekie went off to place the breakfast order with the kitchen and frantically phoned Neels. His phone was off, however, and Koekie assumed he was prancing around his bedroom pretending to be Celine Dion, when in actual fact he was measuring Lady Lambert's dining room for the "acres and acres" of blue, red and white chintz he was going to positively drape the room in. It was going to be *heaven*!

While Cook made the breakfasts, Koekie tried to listen in on their conversation. It was very difficult, however, as they had closeted themselves in front of the inglenook fireplace and every second word was drowned out by the crack and pop of logs on the fire.

As she had walked away from the table, she'd heard Number One ask, "So what is the plan?" and what followed went something like this ...

Number Two replied: something ... something ... "like we did before with the ..." ... whiz ... bang ... something ... snap ... something ... "well it's a great idea" ... something ... another pop ... "build it from the ground up" ... something ... fizz-bang ... "right here" ... pop ... "Have you looked at the" ... something ... "from all angles?" ... something ... something ... explosion-in-the-grate "the other side of the mountain" ... snap ... pop ... big explosion ... "the ... site" ... pop ... snap ... "both sides" ... fizz ..."start digging" ... "We could start" ... bang ... pop ... something ... "up by the Vodacom tower" ... crackle ... pop ... "the whole of the valley" ... snap ... bang "everyone's opinion" ... pop ... snap ... "then everyone will want" ... fizz ...crack ... "to come here" ... bang ... crackle ... "resort" ... "build the foundations of" ... pop ... crack "very complex" ... something ... something ... "take the photographs first?" ... pop ... bang ... "Sun City".

She definitely heard that! Sun City she definitely recognized! She had always wanted to go there and had wondered for a long time if it was bigger than other cities she had been to like Pietermartizburg or Vryheid.

When she came back with the coffees, the two men were huddled around their big sheets of paper. They looked like maps of the area and in the top left-hand corner, partially obscured by Number Two's cellphone were the words ... something ... Plan.

He quickly rolled up his papers to make room for the coffee and shut his laptop on which appeared to be a lot of numbers and names in a big long list.

"Koki," said Number One, "do you know much about the history of this town?"

Again with the questions. This guy was very nuuskierig.

"Ja, meneer," said Koekie; best to tell it to him as per the facts, then nobody could shout at her later. "Jacobus Johannes Ezekiel van Vouw started it in 1899 with his three sheeps. But we only knew it was 1899 in 1998."

"Really?" said Number Two. This was getting weirder. "Then perhaps you can tell me why it's called Hillman?"

It was a trick question. "No, sorry, meneer." If she mentioned that other Hillman guy, her father would donder her. "But I'm Miss Hillman, if that helps."

"Are you?" Number Two looked at her askance. Her name badge said Koekie van Vouw.

"Ja, but only until May next year," she said, as if that clarified everything.

"Oh? Are you getting married?" said Number One.

"Haai, meneer! Sies! He hasn't even asked me yet!"

"So, Koki," Number One continued (it was clear he wasn't going to get very far at this rate), "does that mean you are a descendent of the founder of this town?"

"Of course, meneer, he was my great, great, great-grandfather."

"But ..." Oh, never mind, thought Number One. "So where can we find the role players in this whole story, Koki?"

"Um, at the Tuisnywerheid, meneer," said Koekie. "That's where they mos do all the baking."

"OK, then ..." He looked at his friend, who shrugged. "And when is this election taking place?"

"End of this month, meneer. But first, Lady Eleanor is having a ball. And a lot of English people is going to get vrot, Neels says, and they're all going to stand under Unicorn Jack and sing songs about a queen, but Neels says it isn't him. And Alpheus says the only reason why all the whites is wearing costumes now is because we all look alike and it's the only way to tell us apart." She knew she was saying too much, but they were clearly hanging on her every word and she was loving the attention.

"So, really, we should come back here towards the end of the month, then?" said Number Two.

"Depends when you want to start digging, meneer."

The two men conferred quietly and the words she heard were "Sun City" (again), "The Wild Coast Sun" and "Kruger".

"Koki, is the mayor available?" said Number One, as he handed his plate to Koekie.

"Hard to say, meneer. We all wonders that. His wife died *lonnng* time ago, but he kuiers with Tienkie Groenewald a lot and even Mevrou Gericke's staying away now."

The two utterly confused gentlemen paid and left, promising that they would return when they were ready to go ahead and could they take some photographs of the townsfolk in the meantime? Koekie said she didn't think they'd mind because there wouldn't be any people out anyway on account of they all hated each other now.

And indeed when they emerged from Ale & Arms not a soul was on the street. This was not due to any enmity, however, but because it had started to snow and a bitter wind was blowing up the Valleikloof Pass, freezing everything in its wake. Not even the hardy toyi-toyi-ladies nor their intrepid HLANC counterparts could stand it any longer and everyone had pocketed their curiosity and their principles and gone home.

Koekie, not wanting to forget a word of what had just transpired (which was sadly already far too late), wrote a shorthand version of what she could recall of the various conversations. She was thrilled that something she had learnt at that "schupit" secretarial college was finally of some use and when Neels finally flounced into the Ale & Arms, glowing after a *di-vine* morning swagging cloth all over Lady Eleanor's grand salon, she relayed to him the following:

"Two men. Foreign. European. American. Wanted rolls. Got toast. One wants everything White and Black. Two wants everything Brown and White. Fishing, relative Lady Eleanor. Had *big* plans. Going to start digging, starting Vodacom tower. All over the valley. Resort. Foundations. Very complex. Done this before. Sun City (two times). Wild Coast Sun. Building something. Site. Asked election, mayor. *Big* box. Lots of numbers; dates. Possibly friendly; mentioned Kruger. Coming back end June. No photographs."

By the time the Greater Drakensberg Translation Squad had interpreted the message, however, and edited out that which didn't make any sense whatsoever, it was relayed as follows all over the valley: "Two men visited Hillman today: one American, one European. One of them was a '*Big* doos', (probably American; Sol Kerzner?). Big plans for Sun City–style resort at Hillman site with fishing, like at Wild Coast Sun. Massive complex. Have done this before, twice at Sun City. Doing the numbers and working on dates. Will start digging foundations at site, end June. Keen on the multi-racial angle, but also 'Kruger'-friendly. Refused to have photographs taken. They're toast!"

As the foreign correspondent for *The Times of London* and his photographer drove very, very slowly down the Valleikloof Pass, they reflected on what had undoubtedly been a superb breakfast, but an extraordinarily confusing and unproductive morning. As this was their last assignment before they returned to the UK, they each wanted to go somewhere warmer than Hillman to soak up some sun before getting back to Blighty. The correspondent would go diving at the Wild Coast Sun, the photographer to photograph wildlife at Kruger National Park, and they would both meet up at Sun City for a spot of gambling before heading back to Hillman to complete the story. It was a very complex story, they agreed, the foundations of which were rooted in antiquated ideals and they did not want to have to resort to the old "black versus white" angle, although clearly some of the old ideas were still hanging about from the former regime and some factions seemed to be violent, especially towards Germans. They needed to build the story from the ground up and get opinions from everyone on both sides of the mountain however, which they would do before the election, but they didn't want to go digging around too soon and risk spoiling the story. This was a village that seemed to have an enormous identity crisis and be stuck in some sort of time-warp and, if the waitress was anything to go by, the people here had a very low level of understanding about events elsewhere. Furthermore, the facts as the villagers saw them didn't really tally with the information on the Boer War battle maps or the data that they had. It was a great story, though, they both agreed, but they wanted to keep quiet about it or every other bloody reporter would want to get their hands on it and come to Hillman. And if a Nazi, or a Nazi sympathizer, was indeed living in the village posing as a Peer of the Realm, well then, that *would* be the scoop of the century!

The sale of Hillman

If Pompies thought that everything had gone bananas after his campaign announcement at the Town Hall in May, it was nothing compared to what happened once word spread that Sol Kerzner and his band of merry men were going to turn Hillman into the next Las Vegas. *The Hillman Herald* of that week ran a vox-pop (Dotty was an old hack by now, familiar with all the journo-jargon) on *two* sides of an A4 page, and made sure that everyone had their say. But as with the name-change issue, opinion within the village was greatly divided.

Van Vouw said that over his cold, dead boerelyf would they get him off his farm—never!—while Brumilda van Vouw said she was thinking of going into mass production of melktert and supplying the Sun resort on a daily basis. Farmer Robinson reckoned they could definitely get him off his farm, but they would have to pay him a truckload (or something that sounded like "truckload") of money; he wasn't getting caught out like he had been with those slippery Vodacom buggers. His wife commented that she didn't at all like the idea of gambling coming to the mountain because gambling was naughty, but nonetheless she was going to start planting lots of potatoes at Broadacres where their horses usually grazed, because she'd heard that casinos like Sun City use thousands of chips a day.

Neels van Vouw thought that this could definitely be a step-up for him professionally; he could go from manager/maître d' at the Hillman Ale & Arms, to resort manager of the Hillman Sun. Or the Dingiswayo Sun. Or whatever blerrie Sun it was going to be (although he was pretty sure it wouldn't be the Jacobusville Sun …

don't print that!). Whatever it was, it represented upward mobility for Neels, especially with the "event-management" experience in his current portfolio (*nor that either, dear!*). Alpheus also saw opportunity leap before his eyes and wondered if this was all to do with 2010? If they had "big plans" for the valley, did those plans include a football stadium for the World Cup? It wasn't too late, not by a long shot. Never one to miss a potential opportunity, Alpheus also added the distinctive Sun International logo to Philemon's minibus, just in case those guys came back any time soon.

Lady Lambert-Lansdowne said she wasn't having any tacky "roulette-o-rama" built in her bally garden and spoiling the jolly view, and Dotty Gilmore herself wanted to know where she was supposed to exercise her horses if they built a huge resort in the valley? Josephina Nguni was already mentally spending the money she would make on the deal (because her house was right in the middle of the valley) and she had designs on a very nice skirt and matching blouse that she'd seen at the PEP in Harrismith. Esmé Gericke said that Meneer Kerzner would have to pay her a moer-of-a-lot of money to buy out her goodwill for the Arms & Ale and that she'd sue if he didn't. ("Yes, print that. I want him to know who he's dealing with here.") Her hotel was there first, Solly-boy, and she wasn't going to take any nonsens from a German who spoke like a play-play American, especially after he was so ugly to poor Annelien. Of *course* he was German with a name like Kerzner!

Klippies said he didn't mind, really, but would he have to move? He'd lived in Hillman all his life and he didn't like the sound of having to move, and Aggripina Mthethwa said she was worried that they were starting at the Vodacom tower because where was she going to hang her washing? The mayor himself was quoted as saying, "Ag, sure, why not hey?" but in his heart he was troubled. As mayor of Hillman it was difficult enough to keep the town under control in present circumstances, but what would happen if there was a big, fancy resort on the mountain full of drunken people who lost all their money gambling? Crime was out of control as it was. He had a bad, bad feeling about all of this.

Tienkie van Vouw insisted that she would have to get a bigger post office and more staff, and that all the toeriste and other skorries would have to queue *outside*; she wasn't having them clogging up her nice, clean post office. Doffie said he didn't mind: everyone needed petrol, he said, even "fensie" casino people, but it made no difference to him so long as Koekie was there. And Koekie said, "Oh, Dorf ...!"

Only one person mentioned the thing all the others had forgotten. "For myself, I will wait and see what will happen," said Oubaas, "but shouldn't we know who we are first, and what we are called, before we sell ourselves to the Sun people?"

But it wasn't only Hillmanites who reacted to the sensational news. For the first time in years, people (well, people other than Cedric Parsons, that is) came from Underberg, Himeville and Bulwer to see what all the hullabaloo was about in Hillman, and to "see it one last time before everything changes".

"Ja, swaer," Pompies observed. "We weren't good enough for inclusion into the regional Darts League tables, but ever since there's talk of Sun City, now *every*body wants to come here! *Eeeev'ryone* wants in on the action now, hey Tienkie?"

Tienkie said, "Ja."

And it was true. The Copper Kettle was full of people all day long and the ladies of the HLANC had to bake twice as hard just to keep up. Brumilda van Vouw *almost* buried the hatchet and *nearly* agreed to a truce with the "rooinek dames" in order to keep supply in line with demand, but Dominee said something about where he'd bury a hatchet if she did that so she just kept on baking double the amount.

Despite the freezing weather, the Zulu Women's Informal Peaceful Protest Organization (or ZIPPO) as Florence, Beatrice, Josephina,

Beauty and Portia now called themselves, took advantage of the influx of people to the village to step up their peaceful protest and now toyi-toyied to "End Krime", as their lone placard said, outside the Town Hall every day from 12pm to 2pm (after which time Josephina had to get back to work and the other ladies had to sort out children and ironing etc). But, much as Lady Eleanor had thought, any outsiders thought they were part of a tourism drive (what with all the dancing and singing and general jollity) and ended up putting money in Florence's hat every day. She didn't mind at all; since she'd left Lady Eleanor's employment money had been a bit tight, so she was grateful for the extra cash, but she shared it with the other ladies and everyone was happy. It had now shifted in focus slightly from a peaceful protest to a profitable one.

The Hillman Ale & Arms was also full of tourists (residents from all over the Drakensberg) who wanted to see what all the fuss was about in Hillman, and who promptly wanted to escape the bitter cold the minute they got there, and Neels found he was just run off his feet with customers, which annoyed him tremendously as he had a party to plan. To make matters worse, the Ale & Arms was seriously understaffed as most of the workforce (of four) had followed the lead of Florence Dlamini and Van Vouw's farmhands and were striking in protestation of "neo-colonialist ideals". Even Sylvia Mthethwa had stopped going to work at the insistence of her brother. Mrs Gericke wasn't aware that this was an official strike, however, and thought that they were just being lazy and not coming to work. None of the goings-on fazed Koekie too much, though; she just ignored the customers most of the time and carried on reading her *Huisgenoot* magazine and drawing little hearts on the hotel stationery with the letters "D" and "K" in the middle.

Dominee and his friends felt very crowded by all these interlopers in their local and when Drummond Cruickshank from Bulwer stated loudly that the Ale & Arms didn't look like much of a Sun hotel to him and asked of no one and everyone if he could start gambling yet, Dominee challenged him to a darts play-off, "right here, right now". Instant hush in the AA, and the theme tune to *The Good, the Bad and the Ugly* almost whistled down the length of the bar counter. The hapless Drummond not only accepted the challenge but beat Dominee soundly, prompting a war of words between villagers from the two towns which was finally settled with fists and vellies in the parking lot afterwards. Drummond fared less well in that round, however, but fortunately Neels packed snow onto his head and Dr Miller was roused from his bed to bandage him up, assuring him that no permanent damage had been done, except to the nose.

The co-op also now had more customers, but none of them wanted candles or paraffin and Pompies found he had to keep stocking up on batteries and camera film because everyone from outside wanted to take pictures of all the signs in Hillman. The mayor now joined Oubaas every morning outside his shop for coffee on the bench and together they watched the amazing scenes of life in Hillman as it had become. Pompies himself wondered if these were the "end times" that the Bible spoke about, and Oubaas agreed that he'd never witnessed so much craziness in his entire life.

Oubaas shook his head, saying, "Well, Mr de Wet, I think between us we have unleashed a beast."

"Ja-nee, Oubaas," said Pompies contemplatively. It always confused Oubaas a little when people said that; it was very difficult to know if they were agreeing or disagreeing with you.

Things were still going missing every day: a kettle here; an iron there; umbrellas; teapots; Tienkie Groenewald's "Love is ..." coffee mug; handcuffs and a riding crop from Farmer Robinson's bedroom cupboard. Even Eskom's doggy bowl was taken from outside Pompies' kitchen door. The strangest items were going missing all over Hillman and the general consensus was that whoever the Hillman Pilferer was, he either had very strange tastes or had started with an empty house.

And as if it wasn't bad enough what with all the crime, the picketing protesters outside the Town Hall, the discord between the villagers, and all the wide-eyed onlookers from neighbouring villages coming to gawk at the upheaval in Hillman, the town then became besieged by journalists who'd got wind of the story, leaked to them by Petronella Stevens who was convinced more than ever now that what was happening in Hillman had ominous overtones for Himeville. Petronella Stevens had been very annoyed when the person manning the newsdesk at *The Mercury* asked where Hillman was and then added insult to injury by asking where Himeville was. The reporter on the newsdesk at *The Daily News* had just laughed and said that they had enough stories about name-changing due to everything that was happening in Durban, but thanks for letting them know.

A staff writer for *The Estcourt Echo* and another from *The Pietermartizburg Advisor*, however, descended on the village en masse and booked out the two rooms at the Ale & Arms to "cover the event", although there were huffy suggestions from Dotty Gilmore that this was just a nice little "jolly" for them, paid for by their employers, and that they had no serious journalistic intent. Her nose had been very put out of joint to find both individuals interviewing people on the street. That had been her idea!

The flood of journalists from both papers made Tienkie Groenewald very nervous indeed and she had Koekie ask them both if they'd ever lived in, worked in, or even been to Vereeniging. They both said they hadn't, but Tienkie decided to give them a wide berth anyway. As it was, she now had more work than ever at the post office and couldn't even devote the attention to Pompies' campaign that she would have liked.

Tienkie wasn't the only one with concerns as regards the influx of press hounds. Lady Eleanor had heard about the presence of hacks in the village from Dotty Gilmore, but took succour from Dotty's assurances that both reporters looked like they hadn't even been born in 1969.

"Why on earth do you want to know *that*, Ellie?" Dotty had asked.

"Well, it's obvious, surely. If they weren't even around when man landed on the moon, how can they possibly cover this election with any sense of what a news story really is?" Dotty had thought this a sensible enough answer. Still, one could never be too careful, and Lady Eleanor did wonder if perhaps they also had a computer like Dotty's that had access to all sorts of information at the touch of a button. She, too, decided to give them a wide berth and elected to stay out of the village centre as much as was humanly possible. Besides, there was far too much riff-raff traipsing around the streets of Hillman these days, and she had a party to plan.

In the middle of all this, the five Grade Seven pupils at Hillman (HDJDB) Primary, under the auspices of Lynette Butler, decided to move the school's bi-annual fundraiser from July, when the second cake sale was usually held, to June, in order to take advantage of all the extra people swarming the village. With at least twenty extra people coming to Hillman every day, and about twice that at the weekends, they were bound to have a bumper event. Maybe they could get that carpet for the Dewaldt de Wet Library that had been set up in the corner of the classroom after all. However, this time it was decided that instead of a cake sale they would hold a flea-market, because many of the mothers wouldn't provide cakes if they were going to be sharing a table with cakes made by women on the opposite end of the political spectrum. When Ronan van Vouw had gone home to De Leeuk with the exciting news that the school was having a flea-market the following Saturday in the Town Hall, Dominee had laughed at the lad and ruffled his hair. "Nee, Ro, it's not a 'flea-market', my boy. Nobody wants to buy fleas! This is sheep-farming country, seun, so we have 'fleece markets'."

You see, said Dominee to his son, *this* was what South Africa was coming to. The level of education had dropped to such an extent with all the dumbing-down and standardization that even the teachers couldn't get "fleece market" right. He gave Wessel a stern lecture, saying he must consider home schooling.

Wessel said, "Ja, pa", but he wasn't so sure that Lientjie would be up to the job. Lientjie was an angel and was *every* bit as classy as Patricia Lewis, but he had heard her refer to Koekie as an "intellecshal" because she read *Huisgenoot* every week. "So many words, Wessie! Every week!"

Posters went up all over Hillman, jostling for space between signs for Hillman this, Jacobusville that, and even next to the Dingiswayo Spaza shop in Beatrice Ndlovu's back yard. Painted in bright colours in poster paint, the childish handwriting advertised the "Flee Market" at the Town Hall on Saturday the 17th of June to "Raze funs for the HDJDB Primery".

The Hillman Primary bi-annual fundraisers were historically always well supported by the townsfolk, nearly all of whom had attended Hillman Primary in their youth. And even with money so tight, Pompies knew that people would be lining up outside the Town Hall in the bitter weather on Saturday to support the children of their village. At five o'clock on the evening of Friday the 16th, Pompies went to lock up the Town Hall and make sure that everything was ready for the next day. The Grade Sevens, who were charged with running the event as part of their "Social Responsibility" studies, had laid out all their goods neatly on the tables but what Pompies saw made his heart drop: arranged on three trestle tables along the walls were teapots, cups, a few kettles and a couple of irons, Prudence Robinson's silverware and her husband's riding crop and handcuffs, several items of second-hand clothing and linen, Tienkie's "Love is ..." mug and her post office petty cash tin (with the money still in it, ready to be used as change the following day). Even Josephina's goat was curled up on Dotty Gilmore's floral picnic blanket, tethered quite happily to a pot plant in the corner of the room next to a box containing grass and cabbage leaves and Eskom's water bowl, in which was water sufficient for the evening. A note tied to the goat's collar said "Raffil prize. Tikets R2 each".

It was a heartsore Pompies who called the parents of Tilly Forrester, Bongani Nguni, Pieter Vermeulen, Thulani Ndlovu and Dietrich Schoeman and asked them to bring their children to the Town Hall immediately.

Telling any parents who wanted to wait for their children that they must do so outside the Town Hall, Pompies took the children inside and asked them what was going on.

"Vlooimark, Oom," said Pieter Vermeulen, shrugging.

"Uh-uh, Pieter," said Pompies. "Flea-markets is when you sell old stuff that nobody wants any more and that they *give* you to sell. All of this stuff belongs to your parents or to other people. This is stealing, jong."

Tears welled up in Tilly Forrester's eyes and spilled down her cheeks.

"Nobody wants to make cakes anymore because they're all fighting and we need to raise money for school," sobbed Tilly.

"And nobody has any money because nobody's working anymore, because everyone's fighting," said Bongani. "We only took old stuff, like you said, that people had used already. Mrs Robinson's knives and forks are *very* old. We didn't take anything new. Except for the goat. The goat is almost new. But she's a very nice raffle prize," he added with a big smile, hoping that that would somehow ameliorate the situation.

How on earth had it come to this? Everyone fighting. Nobody working. Children stealing. Children crying. And all for the sake of pampoenkoekies, thought Pompies.

"Are we going to jail?" wailed Thulani.

"Nee, jong, nobody's going to jail. Not because of Oom Pompies se onnosele ideas."

That evening, with a heavy heart, Pompies put all the contraband into his bakkie and returned each and every item to its rightful owner, saying that the goods in question had been found in an old barn near Himeville. (Ja, they wanted to roer kak in Hillman? He'd roer a bit in their direction!) Everyone was delighted and said that Pompies was a "good man" (which only made him feel worse) and no questions were asked, not even by Josephina who might well have wondered how her goat had survived in a freezing barn for over a week. Neither Lynette Butler nor the parents of the children were told of the situation and in the morning Hillman woke up to the heaviest snowfall on record since 1919.

A note tacked to the door of the Town Hall said simply "Hillman (HDJDB) Primary Fundraiser Postponed on Account of the Weather".

White out

The snowfall, which began in earnest on the night of the 16th of June, as Youth Day drew to a close, showed no sign of abating. Once it started, it snowed. And snowed. And snowed. And snowed. Every inch of Hillman was blanketed in the stuff, transforming the town into a scene from a picture postcard (if Hillman sold postcards, which it didn't) or a Christmas card (if South Africa had Christmas in winter, which it doesn't). The forests of pine trees around the mountain appeared to be frosted with a thick layer of icing and an eerie silence hung in the air as though Hillman itself was holding its breath. Which it was.

On Sunday the 18th of June, the hardier residents of Hillman went to church as they always did, but this time each was aware that it may be the last time they all gathered together at what they had always known as the Hillman Anglican Church, and everyone put their hostility on hold for an hour and greeted each other, not necessarily with warmth, but with the kind of respectful courtesy that people extend to one another around the dead or the dying. From the outside, the little chapel resembled the fabled gingerbread house from the children's fairytale, with its frosted roof, liquorice leading in candy-pane windows, and long icicles frozen in suspended animation like sugared lace around the eaves. Koekie had mentioned this observation to Doffie as everyone filed into church (although what she actually said was "Looks jis like ice-cream, hey Dorfie?" to which he said "Ja, Koekie") and halfway through the chorus of *The Lord is my Shepherd* Pompies received an SMS from his son frantically imploring him to come and detach Doffie from the icicle to which his tongue had become attached when testing whether or not they actually tasted like popsicles. It turned out that they do not.

Cedric Parsons said a special blessing for the town and its residents for its Big Day the following Saturday, wishing everyone divine guidance, peace, tolerance and understanding (which the congregation answered with grunts and a grudging "Amen"). He also added that he might not be able to host the service the next week if the weather worsened, and sitting in his pew next to Tienkie and a very embarrassed Dorf, Pompies thought it might be quite nice if the requisite amount of snowfall *did* fall in time for next Sunday so that for once, just once, he could stay in bed late (sorry God). After coffee and cake in the foyer of the church, the cramped confines of which forced everyone to huddle together whether they liked it or not, the members of the Hillman Anglican parish put on their hats and scarves, and an ever-so-slightly-lighter overcoat of prejudice than that which they had donned earlier that morning, and ventured back out into the bitter cold.

By Sunday afternoon, the snowfall only seemed to get heavier, and those who hailed from the nether regions of the valley went back from whence they had come while they still could. Almost overnight, the curious onlookers stopped coming to Hillman for fear that they wouldn't be able to leave, and by Sunday night the only "foreigners" left in Hillman were the two reporters from *The Pietermaritzburg Advisor* and *The Estcourt Echo*, respectively, who were holed up in the Ale & Arms, three sheets to the wind, the former relaying stories to an enrapt audience of Hillmanites about the genuine chaos that had resulted when all the street names changed in Martizburg. While the reporter was gifted as a raconteur, and his stories were certainly told with the express intent of amusing everyone in the pub, nobody laughed. The events of the previous weeks were no laughing matter and the thought of people wandering around in a state of utter confusion as they were obviously currently doing in Pietermartizburg, just didn't seem so funny anymore.

By dawn on Monday morning, the fields of De Leeuk were patchwork carpets of white, and shivering sheep clustered together like cottonballs, their chorus of melancholy bleating the only thing to attest to any sign of life in the frozen landscape. Dominee's sandbagged trenches were covered in snow, and as far as the eye could see the vista was white, white, white. Pure, bright, dazzling, sparkling white. Dominee took this as a sign from God, that this was what He wanted. To which Koekie replied, "What pa, for everyone to be blerrie cold? Jissie!"

On Monday, Lynette Butler shut the Hillman Primary School "until further notice" as it was far too cold in the classroom, so all the children gathered on the hillside near Beatrice Ndlovu's house with cardboard boxes from the co-op and held tobogganing competitions down the slopes, their makeshift sleds gliding effortlessly over the thick layer of snow, beneath which the painted stones had spelled out "Dingiswayo" on the mountainside just days before. Peals of childish laughter rang down the valley and for an entire morning everyone in Hillman under the age of thirteen forgot that they were supposed to be squabbling.

The ladies of ZIPPO stayed indoors and suspended all toyi-toying for the time being. Having had all their pilfered items returned on Friday, there no longer seemed to be any point in braving the weather to protest anything, especially as all the foreigners had gone away and Florence needed her hat back to wear on her head. Even Alpheus, at his grandmother's absolute insistence, finally capitulated to the might of nature and wore a heavy coat and scarf over his Madiba shirt, and the two-and-a-half men comprising the VVVV army also donned woollen jumpers and zip-up fleeces over their "uniforms". As their armbands would not span the circumference of all that outerwear, the only visible crest was that on Dominee's hatband, which became covered with snow the minute he stepped outside, which in the main he did not.

Three days before the election, the Valleikloof Pass was deemed impassable and virtually no vehicles entered or left the village. With the snow continuing to fall and temperatures continuing to plummet, the Valleikloof had become a frozen zigzag of ice that only the suicidal, the insane or the Swiss Olympic Luge Team would even dare to venture down. The minibus of Philemon Nthuli (who fell into the second category) was the last vehicle to venture up the treacherous Pass on Wednesday the 21st of June, while his passengers on that particular journey held hands and prayed fervently that they did not fall into the first. What they did nearly fall into was the gorge near the top of the lookout point and more than twice the vehicle slid back down the ice to the terrified screams of Philemon's passengers and the maniacal laughter of Philemon himself, his deep baritone ho-ho-ho solo in contrast to the castrati chorus of his fellow journeymen.

Aside from the thirty-three terrified-yet-grateful passengers that alighted outside the Town Hall, Philemon also brought with him (at Dotty Gilmore's specific request) the last newspaper, outside of its own weekly publication, that the residents of Hillman would see for over a week. The banner headline of the weekly journal, *The Northern Natal Express*, read "White Out!" accompanied by a picture of children making snowmen in Bulwer, the caption of which read "Freezing in Bulwer, but the kids are having fun". The copy of the feature article was in essence one long weather report listing the maximum and minimum temperatures all over northern KwaZulu-Natal (which essentially ranged from highs of freezing-bloody-cold to lows of break-out-the-thermals-Mildred-or-we're-all-going-to-die); some travel, heating and safety advisories for the days ahead (including a sensible, if somewhat portentous, rumoured recommendation from national electricity supplier, Eskom, that everyone should get a generator), plus the chilling but enlightened caution that hypothermia "can be dangerous". There was also a forecast from the Met Office, which insightfully predicted "snow", and a line-drawing showing the elevation of the Drakensberg mountains with pointers indicating where most snowfall was expected. The place on the map where Hillman should be showed that the highest snowfall was predicted there, but helpfully excluded the name of Hillman. And in the bottom right-hand corner of the page, in what was Hillman's first-ever recognition in an "outside" newspaper, were two lines stating that "outside sources" had informed *The Express* that the Underberg town of "Hillmin [sic] near Himeville" was earmarked for development by Sun International and that more would follow as the story developed.

What the newspaper did *not* have, as had been reported by Petronella Stevens, was a headline stating "Whites Out!", nor a report detailing the "chaos and upheaval" in Hillman and the imminent expulsion of all Caucasians, accompanied by an artist's rendition of how the new Sun casino and resort was going to look. It also did not have a picture of the children of Hillman standing forlornly in the snow, nor a caption reading: "They're dreaming of a white Christmas".

The back page of the same newspaper, however, also featured an article headlined "White Out?" which ran a story speculating that Jake White was rumoured to be getting the boot before the World Cup in 2007, despite the Boks having beaten the Poms in Bloemfontein the previous week. It was perhaps an indication of just how tired the people of Hillman were growing of the whole election-name-change-Sun-City saga that it was *this* article that got pinned to the noticeboard outside the Town Hall and not the other.

At Grasscroft, Lady Eleanor was oblivious to everything except the continued preparations for her "little soirée". She was silently grateful that she had not listened to Saint Winston just this once and had saved all the gas canisters to heat her cavernous house. The last time she remembered feeling this cold was in 1944 in ~~Scunthorpe~~ Mayfair when ~~Mother couldn't pay the gas bill~~ the Germans bombed their London townhouse, when she was ~~seventeen years old~~ just born.

She had a creeping fear that if Phineas couldn't get *down* the mountain in the Bentley, how on earth were the party people going to get *up* it in cars of infinitely inferior quality? Fortunately, Doug and Rosie Forrester's eldest son, Roger, had already arrived in Hillman on the Wednesday, as had Dotty Gilmore's son and daughter-in-law from Howick, so at least the barest trickle of reinforcements had started arriving. Thank God! She had not so much a school of salmon as an entire university of the stuff in the freezer, twenty-four pheasants, all braced for their raison d'être, an equal number of Cornish game cocks, and a damn sight more Bollinger on ice in preparation for the Hillman Winter Ball, and while one could always make a plan with the Bolly, what in the blazes was she going to do with a barnyard-full of dead poultry if the other whining cowards didn't make it up the jolly Pass? They must come, they simply must! Otherwise, what was the bally point of all that salmon swimming upstream in the first place! Besides, her dining and ante-rooms were in the process of being transformed by that lovely boy Eels into a venue fit for the very ambassador of England on St George's Day! They would come, wouldn't they? Lady Eleanor wasn't so sure all of a sudden and knocked back an extra screwdriver to calm her rather frayed nerves.

Oubaas didn't venture out to have his morning coffee with Pompies for the moment. Aggripina said she didn't want him falling in the snow because she still needed him to fix the windy-dry and she wasn't old enough to be a widow yet, so Oubaas stayed at home, in front of his fire, and watched his great-grandchildren tobogganing with their school friends down the slopes of Beatrice Ndlovu's hill. Why is it, he wondered, that adults try to teach children, when in truth more lessons were to be learned the other way round?

Even Eskom stayed at home, loyal to his owner at last (if purely by virtue of the weather), venturing out only to accompany Pompies to the co-op where he lay in front of the electric heater at the mayor's feet, stirring now and then for the occasional biltong treat tossed to him by his grateful master. As power lines creaked and groaned under their burden of snow and ice, the villagers of Hillman braced themselves for the blackouts which they knew would surely come. One by one people tramped through the snow towards the General Co-op to stock up on the candles and paraffin that they would doubtless need, and by the Thursday before the election every family in the village had sent at least one representative to the co-op to get supplies in case winter, in all its wisdom and wonder, finally cut Hillman off completely from the outside world.

Even Dominee came to the co-op in the end, although he sent Ronan inside while he stood on guard at his bakkie, watching for insurgents (or, as Ronan relayed it: "watching for detergents"). Pompies pressed into Ronan's little hand two Wilson's toffees as the boy took the bag of candles and the bottle of paraffin and Ronan said, "Dankie, oom." Then, hovering by the door, he turned to Pompies and said, "Oom? Oom het mos nie vlerke nie, nê?"

"Wings? No, I didn't got any wings, Ronan, only arms. Why?"

"Oupa says you're a left-wing, tree-hugging, radi ... radish-something."

"Oh, OK. Well, I'm sure your oupa knows best, Ronan. But just between you and me, man to man, I don't *really* have any wings."

"It's OK, oom. Sometimes I hug trees, too." And with that, he was gone.

Still the snow fell. And fell. And fell. Burying houses, cars, tractors and fields. It covered everything, including the painted signs that for just over five weeks had loudly, if not proudly, advertised the bitter divisions within Hillman, but as everyone stayed rather more sensibly indoors, few were around to witness the very natural neutrality which the snow had visited upon their little village. It was as though Nature herself was silently painting over the bigotry and folly of the townsfolk, providing Hillman with a fresh canvas from which to start.

Crossed wires

On the eve of her party, and with just forty-eight hours to go before the election, the telephone rang in the sunroom at Grasscroft. The lady of the house was stationed comfortably in front of a roaring log fire and was on her third (or was it fourth?) Manhattan of the afternoon. In the kitchen, Phineas was whipping up a fresh batch (for medicinal purposes for Meddem), while Dotty Gilmore basted poultry and prepared wild rice stuffing for two dozen Cornish game cocks, all for a party of people Dotty was sure could not possibly arrive. How she had gone from campaign-manager-and-newspaper-editor to chef-de-partie she did not know, but such was the power of Eleanor's persuasion that here she was, with her hand up the rear of a rather startled looking pheasant.

"Grasscroft, good afternoon."

"Hello? May I speak with Lady Eleanor Lambert-Lansdowne, please?"

"This is she. And who might you be?"

"This is Tim Hawthorne of *The Times of London*."

"What did you say your name was?" *Why* don't people enunciate any more, hmm?

"Hawthorne, ma'am. Tim."

Well, things *were* looking up; usually only Queen Elizabeth got "ma'am"!

"Hawthorne? You're not related to Lord Roderick Hawthorne, are you?"

"No, ma'am, I don't believe I am."

"Well, why ever not? You should be! I knew him, of course."

"Ah. I see. Who was he?"

"'Who was he?' 'Who *was* he?' What kind of an imbecile are you? *Everyone* knew Lord Hawthorne! Drank like a fish. Absolute bounder. Where did you say you were from again?"

"*The Times*, Lady Eleanor."

"Well, where the bally hell is that?"

"London, ma'am. But I'm in South Africa."

Lady Eleanor was dumbfounded. She didn't have time to waffle on all day with some twit who didn't even know where he was!

"Well, make up your mind, man," she snapped. Absolutely infuriating!

"I'm the South African foreign correspondent for *The Times of London*, ma'am," said Hawthorne, slowly and clearly. "The newspaper."

"*Ohhhh!*" *Finally!* The gentlemen of the Fourth Estate! Heavens above, it was like drawing blood out of a stone. "Well, why didn't you bally well say so in the first place, Tom?"

"Tim, ma'am."

Bloody fool didn't even know his own name! Lady Eleanor needed to move this along sharpish. That boy Eels or Neill or whatever they called him was coming to hang the swags in the dining room in twenty minutes and she wanted to be sure it wasn't *too* O.T.T. You know how carried away their sort can get. Besides, she needed a nice Bloody Mary and/or similar down her throat before they got down to business.

"So I take it you got my letter, then? And you know all about what's happening here? The gumboot dancing and all the Irish people?" Come, come; let's move this along; one wasn't going to waste time covering old ground.

On the other end of the phone Tim was starting to wonder if this wasn't all a wind-up. "Well, our editor did, ma'am. That is why I'm calling you."

"Good, good. Well, get a move on, then. There's no time to waste with just forty-eight hours to go. Are you sending troops?"

"Troops, ma'am?" The old dingbat was off her flaming trolley!

"Yes, troops, young man. You *do* know what troops are, don't you?" What kind of feeble-minded, slow-witted dullards were they letting into *The Times* these days? It really was exasperating.

"I don't believe so, Lady Eleanor. Look, we're having tremendous difficulty getting up the Valleikloof Pass."

Ah, so *that's* why reinforcements hadn't arrived! First people were phoning with all sorts of mewly sob-stories about getting stranded at the bottom of the hill, and now not even Her Majesty's Armed Forces could make it up the Pass. This really was intolerable!

"We are running a story on this Hillman election," he continued, "and I wondered if I could ask you a few preliminary questions over the phone in case we don't get up the Pass in time?"

"To pass the time? Well if you absolutely must, but the cocks are about to get stuffed and I'm going to have a fairy in for hanging in around twenty minutes, so you'll have to do this chop-chop, I'm afraid."

"A fairy, ma'am?"

"Yes, well, you know what they're like. We're going to do the hanging in about twenty minutes. *Lovely* boy." Dear God in heaven! If this is the level of journalism in England today you could jolly well keep it! "And I absolutely must be there to watch, especially now that Florence is no longer with us. Traitor! So let's move swiftly along, shall we?"

Tim Hawthorne wondered if perchance *everyone* in this town was nuts. Perhaps they were all raving, barking bonkers, from the waitress in the pub to the crazy lady in her house on the hill, and God help you if you happened to wander in off the street or cross them in any way.

"OK, well my first question, ma'am, is how confident are you of winning on Saturday?"

"The July isn't until next month, Tom-Tom. Everyone knows that. And I'm betting on Badger Babcock's horse, *Banshee*. Excellent filly. Jolly good chance, I should say."

"No, I meant the election. In Hillman. On Saturday?"

"Oh, that again?" Talk about labouring the point! "Well of course we'll win. We're right!"

"I see. I believe, Lady Eleanor, that you're having a ball?"

"Well, not exactly a ball, yet, but give it one or two more Manhattans and one may well be in the ballpark area."

"I mean at your house tomorrow night?"

"Oh, *yes*! *Lovely* little gathering. Very exclusive. Only white inside, you know. The other colours will be outside. Very chic." That had been Neels' idea. A "winter palace" in the dining room: white table setting, white dinner service, white swags of cloth. Ice sculpture for the Norwegian salmon. "Very, very Winter Palace in Doctor Zhivago," he'd gushed. And then a riot of blues and reds for patriotic colour on the periphery.

"So you're saying that only whites will be allowed inside?" Hells-bells, he needed to get this straight for the record.

"Well, not so much 'allowed' as that's where they'll be concentrated. Otherwise it's too much of a mixture. Anyway, it was Neill's idea. You'll have to speak to him."

"Would that be Neels van Vouw, son of the self-styled leader of the VVVV?"

"Yes. Father's a dreadful oaf; v-v-bourgeois. No style at all, if you ask me!"

"And ma'am, are you, or have you ever been, associated with the Nazi party or any right-wing organization?"

"You cheeky rotter! Of course I won't be associated with any nasty parties! My parties are always *lovely*! Very tasteful. Ask Dinky Babcock, she'll tell you! Plenty of fizz; that's the secret."

"No, ma'am, the Nazi party."

"What about them? Dreadful fellows!"

"I asked, ma'am, if you have ever been associated with them?"

"Good God, no! Hate the bally Jerry. Except for Klaus von Reiniger, of course. Bloody good laugh, what!" Where was Phineas? Time for a top-up.

"Klaus von Reiniger, ma'am?"

"Yes, do you know him?" He didn't know Lord Hawthorne, the fool, so what hope could she possibly have of him knowing Klaus.

"I know *of* him, ma'am. He disappeared in South America in the 1970s. Believed to have been a Nazi, ma'am."

"Who? Klaus?" she said with disbelief. This Tim-Tom was a blithering idiot. "Absolute poppycock! He came from Henley."

"Henley, ma'am?"

"Yes, *Henley*, boy! Henley-on-Klip. You know: the regatta?" Saints preserve us, she was going to have to write the blessed article for him.

"Did you know him, ma'am?"

Was TimTam not paying attention or was he being deliberately obtuse? "Of *course* I bally knew him. Drank like a fish. Absolute gas at a party. He designed my seal, you know."

"Oh? The one on your letter, ma'am?"

Hah! She *knew* that would impress the socks of the chaps at *The Times*. "Yes. Quite breathtaking isn't it?"

"Indeed, ma'am, it's a swastika."

"It's no such thing! It's proper sealing wax! I have it imported from Northampton. I won't have you calling my seal a sticker."

"No, ma'am, it's a swastika. The symbol of Nazi Germany."

"It bally well is *not*! It's my initials, you daft little twerp! L.E.L.L. Look, I don't have all day to shilly-shally with you on the telephone, dear boy. If there is something you specifically want to ask, then ask it. I need to put shrouds over the pouffes before we get hanging."

Lady Eleanor simply had to get Phineas to cover the ottomans after he'd finished making Manhattans, although God knows when that would be! She wasn't going to get grubby footprints all over them when Eels was standing on them to hang the drapes.

"And you hail from where in England, ma'am?"

Hmm. This *was* taking a nasty turn. "Look, I don't know what you're implying, you impudent little upstart, but I've never even been to Scunthorpe!"

The old bird was absolutely doolally! Time to get one last question in before all her faculties failed her. In the background he could hear a muffled exchange and then Eleanor Lambert-Lansdowne came back on the line.

"Look, Jim-Jam, I really must go. The peasants are about to get stuffed."

"The peasants, ma'am?"

"Are you deaf as well as daft? I said pheasants."

"Last question for the time being, then, ma'am. What should I call you?"

"Well, how very forward you are! You can call me what everyone calls me. Lady Lambert-Lansdowne. Or Lady Eleanor, if you insist, seeing as we *have* been talking for what feels like a bally eternity."

"No, I meant in the article: what shall I call you in the article, ma'am? Only, my research has thrown up that in fact you are not, in fact, a lady at all, and that you used to be known as Ellen Mavis ... hello? Hello?"

The party faithful

Before you could say "Jack Robinson" (who, incidentally, had been Farmer Robinson's elder brother until he fell off the Valleikloof), the election weekend was upon them. All around Hillman, last-minute preparations were underway for E-Day, and behind closed doors, in the warmth of cosy houses all over the village and in the valley below, people were putting the finishing touches to speeches, pressing their battle attire, airing jackets and opinions, polishing shoes, and sharpening tongues, knives and other assorted weapons in readiness for their Big Day. It had all the apparent atmosphere of Christmas Eve about it, but none of the festivity; almost as though the chief players had a sneaking suspicion that Santa Claus would bypass Hillman, despite an abundance of cookies. And cookies there would be …

Brumilda van Vouw had decided that if the potent combination of xenophobia; perceived threats; a paralyzing fear of change; and simple pride in 'n trotse geskiedenis was on its own not enough to convince people to vote for her husband, then she would win them over the only way she knew how: with lard, sugar and eggs. She had had a cookie-cutter specially made in Harrismith, and while Dominee rubbed an oil-cloth over every gun in the cabinet, Mrs van Vouw stamped out an army of V-shaped biscuits into endless batches of almond, raisin, peanut, ginger and coconut dough, with a furious vengeance that hinted at her unvoiced concern that the end of the world was indeed upon them.

Farther up the mountainside, however, in her snow-covered, thatched bungalow, Tienkie Groenewald harboured no such concerns. While her attempts at postal subterfuge had not yielded the hoped-for results, Tienkie knew of more proven methods to secure victory at the polls, and had decided that now was the appropriate time to bring out of mothballs the only sure-fire, tried-and-tested approach the postal mistress knew to winning anything. The same tactic had won the day for other celebrities: Caligula, Stalin, Pohl Pot and Saddam Hussein, to name a few, and look how far they got! Yes, elimination of the competition would work for Tienkie Groenewald, too.

At 6.30pm on Friday the 23rd of June, she left her weapons of mass destruction cooling on long ribbons of wax paper laid out across the length of her lounge floor, got in her yellow Volkswagen Beetle and made her way through the snow to Pompies' house, where she would help him go over his speech one last time. They had to be *absolutely* certain this time; tomorrow there would be no margin for error. The Dingaan thing had been an unfortunate oversight, but this time there could be no errors lurking undetected, waiting to ambush them like in the last speech. This time they—she and Pompies—would be prepared. And although he did not know it, Tienkie had just baked all the reinforcements they would need to bolster his argument: two hundred and fifty very special chocolate-chip cookies.

The other Koekie was on duty at the reception desk of the all but deserted Ale & Arms, hypnotized into a virtual trance by the screensaver on her cellphone as she waited for the SMS that would tell her that Doffie was closing up the petrol station and coming over the road for a nightcap. In the pub itself, the two journalists who were responsible for the "No Vacancies" sign which now hung over the door for the first time in living memory, sat by the fire in the empty bar, regaling a captivated Esmé Gericke with yarns of all the exciting assignments they'd covered thus far as staff writers for *The Estcourt Echo* and *The Pietermartizburg Advisor*, respectively: the High Schools' Choir competition; an impromptu performance by Dozi at the Spar in Estcourt; an injury during a regional rugby match that had resulted in the prop forward having to wear a neck-brace for an *entire week*! It was the cutting edge of journalism, no doubt, but *this* story—the Hillman Sun-City-name-change débâcle—was a scoop-and-a-half. For both of them this was their first story of Regional Importance, and they were the only ones with access! These were interesting times indeed. They needed sharp pencils and sharper wits about them tomorrow, and they had started honing the latter on a bottle of Jack Daniels about two hours previously.

At the very top of the hill, Alpheus was doing a little sharpening of his own. As Aggripina finished ironing her husband's Sunday trousers and Alpheus' favourite Madiba shirt, her grandson stood in front of the mirror in his bedroom brandishing a ceremonial assegai and practising the poses he would use for the photographs in the newspapers, which ranged from CIA-bodyguard steely-cool to 50-Cent steely-cool (it was all in the position of the hands). If nothing came of being the star of the Dingiswayo Sun Football Stadium, he could always try and be a rapper, he mused. It seemed to him you didn't even need to be able to sing; what you needed was to be able to grope your nether-regions frequently (presumably to check they were still there), look angry much of the time, and say "yo" a lot. He could do that. Yo.

As he vogued his way through a variety of profile and straight-to-camera poses, he lamented that the reporter from *The Daily Sun* had also become stuck in the gridlock of vehicles stranded at the foot of the Valleikloof. Alpheus had contacted the paper when he read a front-page story in *The Daily Sun* about a tokoloshe (including actual photographs of a real, live one!) and realized that the media is a powerful tool for spreading the truth. It was sad that the reporter was unable to make it up the Pass, but he was placated by the journalist's assurances that *The Daily Sun* was in no way affiliated to Southern Sun or its partner companies, so it wasn't as though Alpheus was going to lose out on both scores.

In her mansion on the leeward side of the mountain, however, Lady Eleanor Lambert-Lansdowne said her own votive thanks to the Almighty, with two Bloody Marys and a Glory Be that the bloodhound from *The Times of London* had not made it up the Pass with his snaparazzi photographer in tow. She toyed with the idea of sending Phineas with the 12-gauge to make sure that the devil's minions didn't make it beyond the lookout point, but with just two hours to go before the Hillman Winter Ball she needed him on hand to pour the sherries and generally play butler for the evening. It was sad that Phineas' talents couldn't extend to performing both tasks, but she took comfort from the notion that any tabloid-wannabes fool enough to wander about in the snow around Hillman that evening would either fall off the edge of the mountain or die of cold. This was the only happy thought rattling around her head, however, and that part of her cerebellum that had not already been anaesthetized with alcohol was consumed with disappointment that more people hadn't made an effort to get up the Pass one way or another; with crampons and bally ice picks, if necessary. Hardier, more patriotic souls would have! Even local Hillman folk stayed away in droves, whining like ninnies about being stuck in snow and not being able to see "further than the windscreen". Oh, boo-hoo! And even Dr Miller and the terminally boring Widow Coleman, usually both dead certs, sent apologies, but due to the weather blah, blah, blah, they would both need to be on standby. Balderdash!

It really was the last straw when Dinky Babcock of all people phoned to say that she and Badger couldn't make it up the Pass and that they were going to check into the Mountain Park in Bulwer, take a couple of sherries and see if it got any better in the morning.

"What do you *mean* you 'can't get up the Pass'?" Lady E had ranted. "You're in a sodding Roller. If that car can't make it up this little hillock, I shall eat my hat!"

"Then eat it you shall, Ellie, for it's not getting up there and no amount of yelling at me is going to change that," said Dinky, quite taken aback at Eleanor's tone.

"Shame on you, Dillys Chamberlain Babcock! Where's your sense of duty? You can *walk*, for Pete's sake, can't you?"

But no amount of gentle persuasion in dulcet tones could convince any of the feeble cowards to come to the aid of her party. Whatever happened to the basic tenets of Churchillism and all that "we shall fight in the hills etc. etc. we shall never surrender" business? "Never give in", his edict had been, "never, never, never, never, in nothing great or small, large or petty" and yet there they all were, beating their retreats faster than a fox on Hunt Day, and all because of a little snow. Talk about petty! Bone bally idle, is what it was! Her magnificent, dramatic statement of a party had been reduced from an initial list of forty-eight politically simpatico dinner guests, to a paltry list of eleven, none of whom were any fun at all. Pearls before swine, and salmon before simpletons! It was enough to make one weep!

As Lady Eleanor finished her toilette, Neels put the finishing touches to the dining room, and although he was on the verge of nervous collapse the boy had outdone himself. Having cleared away the redundant place-settings so that the disappointing turnout wouldn't appear to be such a defeat, Neels had filled the space in the atrium, which would have been filled with people swapping anecdotes about important things like polo, with a statue that he and Phineas had dragged in from the garden and draped with swathes of blue and red chintz. The room was now dominated by what appeared to be an approximation of the Statue of Liberty, minus the spiky crown-thingy. The barren length of the obscenely long dining table was now covered with candelabras borrowed from every room in the house and the overall effect was that of a séance or a synagogue at Hanukkah. The ice-sculpture hadn't quite worked, so Neels had gone out into the snow, trooper that he was, and brought in buckets of the stuff which he packed together to fashion a shape on which to arrange the smoked Norwegian salmon. The somewhat Freudian result of his snow-sculpture efforts, however, was a rendition of an enormous phallus, with a strategically placed garnish of parsley.

Just as he put the last sprig of green *just so* the doorbell chimed and the first guests of the evening arrived. Phineas teetered to the door, much of the sherry that was intended for the vichyssoise having taken a detour down his throat. (Phineas had also kindly proffered the bottle to Neels earlier in the day, seeing that they poor chap was on the brink of emotional disintegration, but not even distress on the scale to which he was presently subject could induce Neels to steady his nerves with anything called "Cockburns", he said.)

Farmer and Mrs Robinson loitered in the foyer of Grasscroft, the former looking like he had to be coerced into leaving his house to come to this event, which was exactly the situation. Mrs Robinson, who had been brought up properly and never went to a party empty-handed, held out a Tupperware of home-made shortbread to Phineas, who knew his Meddem well and promptly went and hid it in the pantry. Their arrival was followed shortly by that of Dotty Gilmore and her son, Michael, his wife, Robin, and her "best friend", Sharon. The last to arrive were Doug and Rosie Forrester, with their daughter Tilly (of flea-market fame) and eldest son Roger, who was in his second year of a Performing Arts diploma.

Roger attended what used to be called the Natal Technikon but which had also changed its name to the somewhat misleading "KwaZulu-Natal University of Technology" because either: 1) the word "Technikon" offended the political sensibilities of someone with a very sensitive barometer of offence, or 2) the faculty didn't have enough to do with their time or enough stuff to spend their allotted budget on, or 3) some joker in administration just wanted to be able to say he worked at KNUT. Or mayhap these days it just made a lot of people who couldn't get into law school feel less bad about their situation to hoodwink them into thinking they attended a "university" even though everybody knew they didn't *really*.

The guests hovered nervously in front of the fire in the formal lounge, talking—as English-speakers are wont to do—about the simply *appalling* weather. Dotty Gilmore was secretly thrilled that the snow continued to fall unabated, however, because without it as a talking point they would have precious little to say to each other. It also gave everyone a perfectly plausible excuse for leaving if the party got as morose as she suspected it might.

Although Neels may not have been from Mayfair, he knew that this motley gathering was sub-par and that Lady Eleanor, when she emerged from her preparations upstairs, would be mortified that all ~~his~~ her hard work had amounted to this, but there *was* a silver lining to the dark cumulonimbus that hung over the festivities and it came in the form of the festive party-favour that was Roger Forrester, draped in a cape covering v-v-thespian attire of palazzo pants and a pirate shirt with puffy sleeves and a ruffle down the front. The last time Neels had seen Roger he'd been a pubescent, pimply-faced little squirt who said he didn't know what he would do if he didn't get into Forestry at Saasveld (he didn't); but here he was, looking positively *ravissant* and clearly at one with his life a world away from deciduous pine forests. Maybe all was not lost …

Fashionably late, as was protocol (hers at any rate), the hostess herself appeared at the top of the sweeping staircase that led from the entrance hall to the upstairs rooms. Looking remarkably like Queen Elizabeth (the First), Lady Eleanor had opted for an emerald-green, full-length evening skirt with a long train and a silver blouse with a high-necked ruffle, giving her head the appearance that it was being served on a platter of platinum lettuce (which, Farmer Robinson commented, sotto voce, might give everyone something else to talk about). What was uttered considerably more audibly, however, was Michael Gilmore's enquiry as to whether or not this was a fancy-dress ball, which comment received a swift kick to his shins from one of his mother's high heels.

At the top of the staircase, Lady Eleanor eyed with derision the rag-tag group assembled in her house. One was very definitely not amused. Farmer Robinson, while he wasn't wearing the denim overalls he usually wore six days a week, was in corduroy—*corduroy!*—and Prudence was in some nasty little two-piece from Milady's with what appeared to be some vegetable or other pinned to her breast. The Forresters had made an effort as best they could and Tilly looked appropriately girlish in her tartan frock and matching hair-ribbon, although Roger did appear to have come dressed as d'Artagnan for the evening. Very queer costume. Dotty Gilmore had at least put on evening shoes, as opposed to the galoshes or riding boots she wore most of the time, but her son was attired in chinos, a sweater, and some awful, fleece-lined canvas jacket, and his fey little wife was in a ghastly Edgars off-the-peg Chanel-imposter of an outfit. Most hideous of all was Robin Gilmore's frightful shambles of a friend, Sharon, who came to the party in jeans, bangles that appeared to have been made out of grass, and a "Make Poverty History" T-shirt, the sight of which nearly made Lady Eleanor collapse. (And who on earth invites somebody called "Sharon" to a formal dinner-party anyhow? If that was the "best" Robin Forrester could do in terms of friends, it was a very lamentable state of affairs indeed.)

The *only* person properly attired in a dinner jacket was Eels and he wasn't even English. The whole bally country was going to hell!

Lady Eleanor smiled stiffly and Phineas, reading the familiar warning signs, ran off to fetch his employer something with ice and as little soda as was decent, while the hostess greeted her guests and made small talk before Neels announced that dinner would shortly be served.

Once everyone had taken their places, Lady Lambert stood and said a few rousing words about the significance of the evening and the solemn duty that was to befall everyone the following day. The dinner guests seemed to look uneasy, however, and not even the veritable river of Bollinger that was available seemed to be stirring their passions or getting these people in the mood. At the end of her little oration, Lady Eleanor suggested that everyone rise to sing *God Save the Queen*, although the Union Jack under which they were supposed to sing it was now draped across the previously naked breasts of the statue from the garden.

"Except you, Eels, dear. You don't have to sing it because you're not English," she said.

"He bloody well *should* sing it," said Farmer Robinson. "He's going to need a bit of saving when his father finds out where he's been tonight!" Neels coloured instantly, but at heart he knew the man in the *hideous* mustard corduroy pants was right.

Prudence Robinson put her hand up and said timidly, "I don't want to sing it. I'm not English, either. I'm South African and she isn't my queen." Other people at the table grumbled their concurrence, and the succubus-in-a-T-shirt, Sharon, said, "Besides, I absolutely won't support any oppressive monarchies and their system of autocratic rule."

Why oh *why* wasn't Phineas stabbing her with the ice-tongs, hmm?

In the end, it was decided that everyone should sing *For She's a Jolly Good Fellow* instead, which wouldn't offend anyone's sensibilities and which everyone hoped would invest the party with a more convivial atmosphere. Their hopes were dashed.

Midway through his vichyssoise, Michael Gilmore commented that the "veggie soup" was good (God help us; the man probably thought "burgundy" was a colour!) and Tilly Forrester asked if there was any pizza. Then, as the entrée was served, things took a lively turn for the worse when Saint-Sharon-of-Perpetual-Idiocy announced that she was vegetarian and couldn't eat the "chicken". *Chicken?* Sweet Jehosophat; it was imported Cornish cock, costing, per metric kilo, the entire GDP of whatever tatty little West African backwater she was trying to save!

The only party guests who seemed to be getting into the swing of things at all were Roger-the-thespian and Eels (who was the hired help, saints preserve us!). But there they were: one pale and arty, Neels hale and tarty, and both of them up for a bloody good party; the fairies were bally good fun! Everyone else, however, steered clear of the real topic du jour, the election, for fear that somebody would say out loud what everyone secretly suspected, which was that it was looking ever more likely that tomorrow they would all be living in Dingiswayo. As the conversation droned on around her about mind-numbing subjects like the Ladies Auxiliary and a sheep-shearing competition in Himeville in the spring, Lady Eleanor's attention wandered. It was perhaps a little presumptuous to break out the Bolly, but in the circumstances there really was no other sensible course of action. With a powerful cocktail of gin and champagne coursing through Lady Lambert-Lansdowne's veins, however, it really was the final straw when the United Nations envoy that was Sharon Whoever-the-hell-she-was announced loudly that the wine served with the "chicken"—a *very* expensive Blanc de Noir from a private bin, no less—was an "unusually politically progressive" choice for this particular gathering. And just as Lady Eleanor reached out and grabbed a lethally sharp carving knife—originally intended for the pheasants, but lately destined for the breastplate of Our Lady of Grass Bangles—all the lights went out.

Blackout

At 9.33pm precisely, just as Lady Lambert was about to plunge a carving knife into her dinner guest's breastplate, all of Hillman was plunged into darkness. Well, all of Hillman, that is, bar the house at the very top. In 1937, when Hillman was electrified, the powers that be had not thought to extend the power lines just 300 feet further so that Oubaas' father, Joseph, could have electricity in his house, too. While Joseph Mthethwa doubtless thought that it would have been courteous to at least have been asked, the absence of electrification didn't really bother him all that much. He'd never had electricity, he said, so he didn't miss it. He felt the same way about the possession of a car, a watch, reading glasses and an ice-box. But a coal stove for Mrs Mthethwa would be quite nice, he had said, as would a new Sunday hat and a say in how the country of his birth was run. In his lifetime, sadly, Joseph would only see two of these three dreams come to fruition.

Oubaas now lived in the selfsame dwelling, without electricity, and managed very nicely in spite of its absence, just as his father before him had done. He resisted all pleas by Aggripina and the rest of his family to modernize the house, and it was only when the Mthethwas acquired a lovely black and white Telefunken television in 1990 that Oubaas Mthethwa capitulated in part and got a petrol-powered generator, which now sprang into life every night from 5.30 until 10pm. Oubaas liked it this way. With powered appliances available at only certain times of the day the children played outside in the fresh air until it was dark and then the family ate together, sat together, prayed together and spent time together, not glued to nonsense, watching programmes where people got all dressed up just to throw each other in swimming pools or smash things in their big houses. As patriarch of the family, Oubaas ensured that his wife and daughters had enough electricity to cook the family dinner at night, and that there was enough light for the grandchildren to finish their homework by. There was also sufficient power to charge cell phones, run the electric heater for a while, and for someone to read from the Bible before they all settled down to watch *Generations* and *The News* together (although frankly there was often more violence on *The News* than there was in the programmes that Josephina Nguni liked watching so much). Then at ten o'clock sharp Oubaas would go outside and switch off his generator and everyone would go to bed.

At 9.33pm Oubaas was sitting on a wooden chair in front of the old trunk that was permanently stationed at the foot of his bed, unaware that at that very moment the village and valley below his house had been thrust into darkness. The trunk was open and Oubaas had assembled around him its contents, which were family heirlooms too priceless to be put on display where little hands might damage them. The trunk had been the property of Joseph Mthethwa and indeed many of its cornucopia of treasures were things that Joseph had collected in the course of his seventy-eight-year lifespan; worthless bric-a-brac to others, but objects of enormous sentimental value to Mthethwa senior: old photographs, now sepia with age; a few badges of some description; an old helmet; and ancient newspapers, yellowed and fragile. To his father's store of riches, Mthethwa had added over the years mementoes of his own, including a porcelain plate with a picture of Jesus and the apostles on it, from his sister in Durban; a ceramic photo frame with roses around the border, from his late brother in the Transvaal, with a photograph of younger versions of the two of them frozen in time at his brother's wedding; his children's birth certificates and school reports; an old encyclopaedia, and a bedspread hand-crocheted for Aggripina by her mother at the time of their marriage.

Ordinarily the old brass fastening on the trunk was locked to ensure that great-grandchildren couldn't plunder the family treasures on rainy days when ennui set in. But on the eve of the election the trunk was open and its contents laid bare, as Oubaas searched for the answer to the question that had been troubling him for six long weeks. Whenever Oubaas was at odds with the world, which admittedly wasn't very often, he would retreat to his bedroom and riffle through the happy memories and pillage the cache of nostalgia stored in the trunk for rainy days of his own, and generally this would sort out whatever troubled him. Tonight, he had open on his knees the old leather-bound Bible, which ordinarily nestled in the trunk on top of the old newspapers and underneath the plate with its image of Jesus at the Last Supper, a Good News Bible having replaced this ancient tome as the family Bible more than thirty years ago.

At that precise moment in her little mansion on the hill, Lady Eleanor Lambert-Lansdowne announced to Dotty Gilmore that this was positively the *last* supper she was *ever* hosting in Hillman, the village—and its residents and guests—being simply too déclassé to appreciate fine dining when it was handed to them, not so much on a plate as on bone bally china! And that Dr Miller—Judas that he was—could go to hell for leaving her "on her own" to suffer the brain-numbing small talk of the Robinsons and people "of their ilk". Lady Eleanor cast a withering glance at Dotty's son as she said this, who had removed a candle from one of the myriad candelabras at the other end of the dinner table the minute the power went down and stuck it in one of the poussons on a platter near him so he could continue shovelling pommes gruyère (or "cheesy spuds" as he insisted on referring to them) into his maw.

The interruption of the electricity supply also meant that the dessert of Cointreau almandine soufflé gently baking in the oven collapsed with a sigh, never to be resuscitated back to life, and with its last breath the party also succumbed. Sharon of the Eternal Grandstanding (who, it turned out, despite her bohemian jewellery and "Make Poverty History" T-shirt, came from a very wealthy Durban family, lived in a duplex purchased by daddy—who was in textiles—and drove a nifty little Mercedes A-Class when she wasn't out saving the world by expression of opinion alone), used the moment to launch into a monologue about how the previous administration was responsible for everything, including—no, *especially*!—tonight's power failure. Everyone else used Sharon's diatribe as the launching-point for their departure from the party, including in their litany of feeble excuses the fact that they simply must get back to their houses or people "would use the cover of darkness to loot their homes in the current political climate". Lady Eleanor thought that none of them had a bally thing worth stealing anyway but wished any burglar fool enough to try and make it up or down the mountain in this particular climate—with swag in hand, no less!—the very best of British.

She toasted the departure of her dreadful dinner guests by breaking open the champers in earnest, their exodus being true cause for celebration, appreciation and good old-fashioned inebriation. Phineas had already beaten his mistress to it and had fallen asleep in front of the fire in the kitchen, his somnolence having been greatly hastened by the remainder of the cooking sherry, and in the end the party of eleven was whittled down to just three, Neels and Roger having stayed behind to "help clean up".

And then, as if by magic, the party really *did* get going! Roger, it turned out, could tickle the ivories with some aplomb, and both he and Neels, unsurprisingly, knew all the show tunes of which Lady Eleanor was so terribly fond. Within the hour, the threesome had cut a swathe through five bottles of Bollinger, with another crate on standby, and were ripping through *Luck be a Lady Tonight* with gay abandon by the time they finally heard Farmer Robinson's truck splutter back to life, more than twenty minutes after their original departure. They then set sail on *Showboat*, had a merry go around *Carousel*, and, as the candles slowly melted all around them, moved on to their own interpretation of "the divine Barbra's finest role, *Hello Bolly!*", which found Lady Eleanor herself draped across the Steinway and Neels with the Union Jack wrapped around his head in a Carmen Miranda headdress, which he finished off with bunches of grapes that had been intended for the cheeseboard. Lady Eleanor's dismal failure of a political rally was redeemed by two chaps in a cape and a turban, and would end, as she had always hoped it would, with a bang!

This too, was how Dominee van Vouw's evening was to end. At 9.33pm, as his wife put hundreds-and-thousands on her last batch of vanilla shortcake, Dominee had just finished loading his Ruger Blackhawk .357 magnum pistol (his philosophy being that four-armed is forewarned), when the power went out. In the instant darkness, he fell over the ammunition case, which he had left in the middle of the lounge floor, and the weapon in his hand discharged, unleashing a bullet, which went straight through Dominee's veldskoen and into his foot, causing him to let loose a salvo of profanity unbecoming in a would-be man of divinity. That evening, Dr Miller and his clinic assistant, Mrs Coleman, got the medical emergency that both had anticipated and almost had another when the good doctor attempted to retrieve the errant bullet from Dominee's foot. It was only a swift whack to the head with the butt of one of Dominee's own rifles from a quick-thinking Mrs Coleman that prevented Dr Miller from becoming the first fatality of the entire Hillman skirmish. There were no witnesses and it was dark, she told Dr Miller, so nobody could say what had actually happened ...

Fast action was not only the preserve of first-aider and closet ninja, Mrs Ethel Coleman, that evening. At 9.33pm the power went down in the Ale & Arms (and Doffie could verify this as the time the electricity went off because that's what the backlit LED screen on his Pokemon digital watch read). This prompted Doffie to finally say to Koekie the thought that had been uppermost in his mind for a goodly while now: "Hey Koekie, how come they is always talking about 'global warming' when it just gets colder and colder, hey?" Not ten seconds later, Koekie van Vouw, overawed by Doffie's insight and brilliance, sprung into action and used the power-outage to hurry their courtship up a notch, much to the surprise of Dorf de Wet who wondered for a fleeting second if perhaps Koekie was looking for the light-switch in the strangest of places. She was; knew where it was; found it, and turned it on ...

At the exact point at which Doffie had looked at the time in Pokemon Land, his father had just finished reciting the third paragraph of his rousing election speech to Tienkie who mouthed each word as he said it. The speech was essentially a reworking of the 13th of May speech, but instead of "standing on a threshold of change" they had now "crossed the threshold of change" (best not to give people a choice in these matters, he had learned). They had also decided to dispense with any mention of "evolution" because maybe that was what had caused all the kak in the first place, but by paragraph two there was a jolly good justification for the inclusion of Dingaan in the new name of the town, because this time round he had actually gone back and read the boring encyclopaedia and knew a bit more about the man in the headband and grass skirt. Pompies had just got to the good bit in paragraph three where he quoted General Jan Smuts, "Let this monument of our genesis be a symbol not only of the past but of our reconciliation" (how could Dominee argue with a real general, hê?), when the lights went out.

Both he and Tienkie instantly saw this as a perfect opportunity, but from very different perspectives. Tienkie was hoping for something along the lines of the sort of fire-stoking action in which Koekie van Vouw and Doffie de Wet were currently engaged in order to keep each other warm, whereas Pompies saw this as the perfect moment to do the right thing by the little village of which, at least until 2pm the following day, he was still the mayor.

The first thing he had to do, he said, was phone Eskom (the company, he clarified, not the dog) and inform them of the power outage. However, the same fate that had befallen the power lines had been visited on the telephone cables as well, and not a single phone in Hillman was working. Indeed, in the morning, the residents of Hillman would find power and telephone poles toppled over and cables strewn across fields and roads, like so many soldiers perished in a battlefield. Pompies still had a cell signal, but knew it wouldn't be long before even the cell tower succumbed to the elements; when he'd last been able to see the cell tower it looked like an enormous Christmas tree covered in snow. He phoned the faults line for Telkom, the irony of which was not lost on Pompies. "If your phone isn't working, how can you phone blerrie Telkom to report the fault, hey Tienkie?" Telkom were virtually begging people to get cell phones instead! But after two minutes of the doo-doo-de-doo music and a lady's voice assuring him that his call was very important to Telkom and that an operator would be with him soon (well soon-ish; well, if somebody could wake up the one individual whose duty it was to be awake that evening), Pompies decided to give up on the national telephone monopoly and phone the national electricity monopoly instead. You could die of cold, Pompies reasoned, but you were less likely to die from being unable to use the telephone. Unless of course you were dying of cold and needed to tell someone; that would be a kicker, hey Tienkie?

Calling the Eskom fault reporting line, Pompies went through the familiar succession of number punches along the lines of "Press '1' if you want to report a fault, '2' if you think it's our fault, '3' if you think it's the fault of the previous regime, '4' if power cables in your area have been stolen and '5' if you would like to sell our cables back to us" and eventually got hold of a real live human who said that there was nobody around to deal with the situation and could he call back in the morning.

"No, I *can't* call back in the morning. It's minus two here and there's snow everywhere, man, and people could die! I can't 'wait until morning'. Somebody needs to come out here *now*!"

"Where did you say you're calling from again, sir?"

"Hillman," Pompies said, then added, "It's near Himeville" just in case.

"Can you spell that please?"

"H I L L man-this-is-irri-tating!"

"I have Hibberdene, Highflats, Himeville and Hlabisa on my list, sir. No Hillman. Are you sure that's where you are?"

"Of course I'm blerrie sure that's where I am. So are you coming or not?"

"Not until the morning, sir. If you can call customer services from 9am ..."

Pompies banged the phone down in frustration and went to grab his coat, his torch, and his keys. He knew that most people in Hillman had generators, but he also knew that most people, with the exception of Tienkie, Klippies and Oubaas, probably had no fuel for their generators because for six weeks they had boycotted his petrol station. Still, this was no time to harbour grudges; people could die in this weather and Pompies would have no part in that.

Telling Tienkie gravely, "I'll be back," he swept out of his house, climbed into his bakkie, and ventured out into the thick pall of night. Tienkie fairly swooned at the sight of her hero off to save the day, with his trusty rescue/sniffer-dog at his side (although in truth the only thing Eskom had ever been known to sniff was other dogs' behinds). Arriving at his co-op, Pompies took all the one-litre Coke bottles that were waiting to be returned and filled every one of them with either petrol or diesel. He then loaded the crates of fuel-filled Coke bottles in the back of his bakkie and phoned his nemesis,

Dominee, with the last remnants of battery power on his Motorola. Mrs van Vouw answered Dominee's phone and said that her husband was unconscious, which Pompies took to mean that he had drunk himself to sleep again. (And before the election, too; nee, sies!) He hastily told Brumilda van Vouw that this was a "State of Emergency" and that he was "coming to everyone's house immediately with both types of fuel in Coke bottles for their generators" and that she must SMS as many people as she could and tell them. Of course, by the time Brumilda had relayed this message most people in the village had been apprised that Hillman was now "a state of Germany" and that Pompies was "bringing coked-up fools to everyone's houses for their detonators". When Pompies did turn up, he received a very warm welcome from some very chilly people who had been expecting a drug-addled Kaiser Wilhelm and a Panzer or two to come rolling down their driveways. Within four hours, Pompies had ensured that every family in every home in the village had fuel for their generators if they needed it, and if indeed he hadn't actually saved the day, he had certainly rescued more than two hundred citizens from a night of perishing cold and discomfort.

By 9.45pm, around the same time that Pompies was arriving at his co-op to fill his Coke bottles, Alpheus had gone outside to look at the village of Hillman one last time before it became Dingiswayo. Standing in his grandfather's yard at the very top of the hill, he could see that the entire village below him was in darkness and that all the rectangles of light, which usually shone from the houses down the valley, had been extinguished. As far as the eye could see the vista was black, black, black. Pure, impenetrable, dark, jet black. Alpheus understood this to be a sign from God; that this was what He wanted: pure, total, Black power. It was the confirmation Alpheus had been waiting for, and having received it, he went to bed.

At 9.55pm, as Pompies was filling his Coke bottles with fuel from his petrol pumps, Oubaas was putting the last of his treasures back into his father's trunk in readiness for bed. Having gotten the answers he sought from God and from his own mortal father, Oubaas put away the old helmet and the leather-bound Bible, and put the photographs and the badges back into the old Mazzawattee Tea caddy in which they were stored for safekeeping. He wrapped up the photograph of his brother in the newspaper in which it had originally been wrapped all those years ago and patted his favourite brother goodnight, his fingers tapping lightly on the words "*Vereeniging Herhout*, 24 Junie 1978". He then ran his hand across the plate from his beloved sister before wrapping it once more in the newspaper in which it, too, had been wrapped to ensure its safe passage all the way to Hillman. Finally, he put the family treasures back into the trunk one by one and the last thing to go in it was Aggripina's crocheted bedspread, which Oubaas laid gently over his sister's plate, wrapped as it was in the same newspaper in which it arrived from Durban nearly thirty-eight years before. The last thing Oubaas read as he laid the bedspread over the Mthethwa family heirlooms before shutting the lid was the headline of *The Daily News* of the 18th of July, 1969: "Ginger Snaps!"

To the polls

And then the day of reckoning was nigh. On Saturday, the 24th of June, just four hours after Pompies delivered the last of his fuel, dawn broke over Hillman and the townsfolk awoke to more than six inches of snow and the detritus of fallen telephone poles and cables strewn all the way down the mountainside. News of Pompies' heroism had spread across the valley long before the people of the Drakensberg mountains sat down to their ProNutro, and the Hero of Hillman himself was woken by Petronella Stevens, who wanted to know if it was true that he had single-handedly saved Hillman from German invasion. He said no.

The blizzard had finally ceased and all was calm, and by eight o'clock the sun was doing its best to thaw the crisp, frozen landscape of the Hillman Mountain. Across the village, grateful residents were doing a little thawing of their own in front of their generator-powered heaters, sipping piping-hot coffee made possible by their own personal Santa Claus of the mountains.

Oubaas had woken at his usual time, having slept right through all the fuss and commotion while Pompies was crusading through the blizzard to deliver diesel and petrol to those stranded without power. He now listened quietly as his great-grandchildren chattered excitedly about how the portly white man had gone to everyone's house "like the Christmas Father", handing out free Coca-Cola to everyone who needed it. After hearing the extended version of the same story from Aggripina, Oubaas was now more certain than ever about what needed to be done ...

Not everyone woke in Hillman with a clear head and a sense of purpose, however. At Grasscroft, Phineas woke up in the freezing kitchen, the fire having died at around 3am, with a head that felt far too large for the skull in which it was encased. His white uniform with its high-buttoned mandarin collar was stained with the few splashes of sherry that hadn't made it to his mouth, and on the kitchen table stood two full Coke bottles that he didn't remember putting there the night before. (Meddem never served Coca-Cola; she said it was "the beverage of Americans and the working classes, neither of whom would be dining at Grasscroft".) Stumbling through to the atrium, Phineas found Lady Eleanor fast asleep on top of the grand piano, underneath which was a pile of fabric, to whit one floor-length maroon velvet cape and one enormous, crumpled Union Jack, from which poked four bare feet. It was not the first time Phineas had come across such a tableau the day after a Lambert-Lansdowne party, and he knew it was best to leave the white folk as they were, tidy away the eleven empty bottles of Bollinger strewn across the room, and go to bed himself.

At De Leeuk, Dominee woke up *on* the kitchen table where Dr Miller and Mrs Coleman had performed minor surgery on his person the night before, surrounded by mountains of biscuits and in enormous pain. His head was bandaged, for reasons he couldn't remember, and his foot was in a plaster cast. In the chair next to the table, was his wife, fast asleep in her dressing gown and curlers, and hugging a loaded shotgun.

In the Hillman Ale & Arms, the two reporters woke much as Phineas had done, next to a cold fireplace, Messrs Daniels and Walker having addled their brains beyond the point of walking any further. Sunlight that was far too bright to be tolerable came streaming through the lead-pane windows, casting a golden spotlight on the sleeping form of the Ale & Arms receptionist, who appeared to have gone above and beyond the call of duty the night before with AA patron, Dorf de Wet, fast asleep next to her.

Mrs Gericke had at least had the good sense to stumble up to her warm bed at around eleven, but when she awoke the next day—with a very unfamiliar head that demanded the immediate attentions of Panado and several litres of undiluted water—vague memory bells chimed in her painful cranium and she could have sworn that she had seen Koekie van Vouw administering CPR to somebody as she'd staggered up the stairs.

At one o'clock in the afternoon, the actual bells of the Hillman chapel pealed out across the valley to announce to all interested parties that there was just one hour to go until the all-important election. One by one the villagers trudged through the snow to the little Town Hall for what everyone agreed was likely to be a momentous occasion for the village one way or the other, and in light of the events of the previous evening many felt that the outcome of the election was now by no means a done deal.

Josephina Nguni was the first one in line outside the Town Hall, determined as she was to get a front-row seat this time in case people started pelting each other with snow or anything else remotely exciting, but it was generally a far more sedate and orderly crowd that gathered behind her than that which had assembled at the Town Hall six weeks previously.

The doors of the Town Hall were closed and a handwritten sign on the noticeboard read: "Hillman Mayoral Election 2pm, HOSTED BY HILLMAN (or whatever) POP IDLE, NEELS VAN VOUW", leaving voters standing in line in no doubt as to which was the more important feature of the day's events.

At quarter to two, the doors of the Town Hall were opened by Neels himself, dressed in a dazzling silver lamé jacket with sequinned trim, and with a generous application of Koekie's kohl pencil outlining very bloodshot eyes. As people filed into the hall they greeted Neels politely, who responded with "Ooh, don't shout, dear" to even the meekest salutation.

It had been decided that, as an entirely neutral party, Neels would preside over the entire event so that no candidate appeared to be getting preferential treatment. His relationship to one of the chief contenders was irrelevant, he claimed, because everyone knew that he would never align himself politically with anyone who thought that a safari suit is a legitimate and acceptable form of apparel.

At the back of the hall, Tienkie Groenewald and Brumilda arranged their respective baked goods on a trestle table with icy civility, their coolness towards each other showing no signs of diminishing even as the ambient temperature increased. Tea and coffee would only be served after the speeches and prior to the votes being cast, so Tienkie estimated that she had plenty of time to mix her confections in with those of her adversary so that nobody would be able so say for sure whose cookies had done the damage.

As people took their seats as close as they could to those with whom their political allegiance lay, Pompies was interviewed at the back of the hall by the two reporters from *The Estcourt Echo* and *The Pietermaritzburg Advisor*. Sharp the hacks were not today, but interviewing a community man about something he had done for their community was much more within their remit as journalists than covering a contentious election, and for the first time that day they both felt relatively familiar in their own skins. Pompies responded to their questions as all heroes do in every report ever written about any act of heroism anywhere: "I just did what anyone else in my position would have done." The two reporters were agog; this was editorial gold and they both secretly doubted that there were any circumstances that could have induced either of them to venture out into a blizzard to deliver fuel to people, especially if the people to whom one was delivering the fuel didn't seem to like you very much. In the time-honoured tradition of hacks the world over, they then milled about at the back of the hall, filling the gaping hole that had been burned into their stomachs the night before with chocolate biscuits purloined from a platter at the edge of the table.

At five minutes to two, Lady Eleanor Lambert-Lansdowne arrived at the Town Hall, looking pale and a tad fragile. She entered the hall with as much authority and grandeur as a person wearing large Jackie-O sunglasses on a winter day could muster, supported as best he could by Phineas, who didn't look too sturdy on his feet, either. Walking very slowly and deliberately to the seat that had been reserved for her in the front row, she cast a cursory glance at the English contingent present for the election. Those present seemed to include all the usual suspects but none of the non-Hillmanites: Roger Forrester was still where Neels had left him, positively unconscious under the Steinway, and Dotty Gilmore's wimpy daughter-in-law and abomination of a friend, Sharon, had decided not to come because Sharon insisted that "without an independent observer present to monitor the proceedings the election is bound to be rigged in favour of the capitalists". Dotty's boorish son just wanted to stay in and watch a rerun of *Magnum*. Never again, vowed Lady Eleanor solemnly to herself, would she go to the enormous trouble of hosting a lovely dinner party for people who had no sense of reciprocity, duty and patriotism. Never!

Oubaas Mthethwa sat surrounded by his family and an orderly phalanx of loyal supporters, every one of whom was quietly confident in the knowledge that today was Dingiswayo's day of glory. Alpheus had eschewed the Madiba-shirt-fashion-statement in favour of the gangsta-rapper-fashion-statement because that way he could at least wrap up warmly without losing face.

As both he and Lady Lambert-Lansdowne tried to make their way to their seats, Alpheus brushed past her, almost knocking her over.

"What ho!" said Lady Eleanor tersely.

It really was awfully uncouth to be mowed down by somebody dressed as the Yeti, especially when the world felt so dreadfully off-kilter as it was.

Alpheus eyed the old woman quizzically for a second.

"No hos here, yo," he said. "Hos is in Ethekwini, y'all. Yo." He realized that he really needed to watch a bit more MTV in order to get the lingo right before pitching himself as a rapper to the people from Southern Sun, and Lady Lambert, who had no time for foreign languages today, pushed him aside, taking her seat with a cluck of indignation.

Dominee was the last candidate to arrive. He, Wessel and Ronan had planned to arrive in uniform as an impressive and united Van Vouw front, but with his foot in plaster and his head bandaged he could no longer get his hat on. He was forced to make a much less impressive entrance on crutches that he'd had to borrow from Klippies, who still had them left over from the time between losing his foot and gaining his prosthetic back in 1986. Dominee could also no longer salute his party faithful, because every time he tried to stand on one leg to give a salute he either fell over or poked somebody's eye with a crutch.

With everyone finally seated, Neels took to the stage, which had been hastily draped with whatever fabric was left over from his silver lamé ensemble. He had planned on doing something much more "zhuzh" for the occasion but what with all the snow and the mad panic to get things done for Lady Eleanor yesterday, and with a head that today felt like it belonged on someone else's body, Os du Randt, perhaps, he thought he'd done remarkably well under the circumstances.

"Good afternoon, ladies and gentlemen," Neels said hoarsely. He'd rehearsed a much more theatrical opening to the day's proceedings, which included greetings in three official languages and an ice-breaker that involved a rabbi, a priest and Van der Merwe. However, as he could barely talk today, never mind string whole sentences together in anything other than his mother-tongue, he opted for a more low-key opening on the day.

He welcomed everyone as best he could with a barely functioning tongue that tasted as though several small animals had lain down on it to die, and ran through the agenda for the election. This included the singing of the national anthem followed by speeches from the four candidates in which each would have to outline why they thought Hillman should either keep its name or change its name. Each candidate would also have to state what they would do if they became mayor for the next four years and what their position was on "the whole Sun City/casino/development gedoente, warra, warra, warra". After the speeches, everyone would break for tea, coffee en koekies while the votes were being cast.

Once a decision had been reached, he said, everyone could then go home and get accustomed to calling Hillman ~~Dingiswayo~~ whatever the majority of voters decided. *Orrait? Fêbulous.*

Neels had originally planned on doing his first public performance of *My Heart Will Go On* as a dummy-run for the *Idols* auditions, but knew instinctively that although his heart may well go on, his voice almost certainly would not, so the vocal debut of Neels van Vouw, superstar of the Underberg, would simply have to wait. Sjeim ...

It had been decided weeks ago that, as ladies always go first, Lady Eleanor would be the first candidate to speak, followed by candidates in order of age: Dominee, Pompies and Oubaas. In the case of the first and last candidates nobody could actually verify their ages (and indeed in the case of the first nobody would dare), but Oubaas was assuredly the eldest of the male candidates and everyone seemed happy enough with the running order. It didn't matter where you started on the track, everyone thought, so long as you finished first!

Once all two hundred and thirty-eight citizens were apprised of the sequence of events, they all stood to sing their national anthem. However, when Lynette Butler picked out "e" on the old upright piano as a starting note, what followed were simultaneous renditions of *Nkosi Sikelele, Uit Die Blou Van Onse Hemel* and *God Save the*

Queen from various sections of the hall. Hell hath no irritation like a hungover maître d'iva, however, and Neels, whose delicate head simply couldn't cope with the cacophony of noise over and above the relentless pounding in his own eardrums, screamed at everyone to "Shut up and blerrie sit down. Skaam en sies, julle!" and instructed the candidates to "just flippin' get on with it! Jissie!"

At that precise moment—and before a single candidate had spoken—Tienkie Groenewald's doctored cookies began to work their magic on the alimentary canals of both journalists, who bolted in the direction of the toilets, missing the rest of the day's events entirely. The election coverage in each of their papers would read "as reported by D. Gilmore, *The Hillman Herald*".

One man, one goat

A hush descended on the group assembled in the Hillman Town Hall. The last time it had been this packed with humanity was after Kobie Gericke's funeral, only then the atmosphere had been much more festive. With as much gameshow-host-flair as Neels van Vouw could muster, he ushered Lady Lambert-Lansdowne up to the lectern to deliver the first speech of the day, but with running eyeliner circling eyes the colour of an abattoir floor, and hair that had been gelled to within an inch of its life, the flagging silver-clad Neels looked more like a chorus extra from an off-off Broadway production of *The Rocky Horror Picture Show* than the arbiter of Hillman's most serious election.

Lady Eleanor Lambert-Lansdowne climbed the five stairs to the lectern with a sobriety that belied what her innards were telling her. "Evil, evil fairies!" she cursed silently, glaring at Neels. A couple of Nancy-boys, a bottle of Bolly and a sound knowledge of Rodgers & Hammerstein and there was one's political career gone pouf! Thank goodness her speech was almost wall-to-wall Winston. The prols and the trolls wouldn't know vintage Churchill if it bit them on the bally behind, and as she knew every last word by heart at least she didn't have to think too much; thinking hurt, as did breathing, sitting, standing, coughing, walking, smiling, and even her hair. *Especially* her hair! Best just to get this over with and get home to bed. It was now obvious that one faced defeat, if purely on the mathematics of the thing, but one must still go down fighting.

"Ladies and gentlemen," she began, seriously doubting that either was present in the rabble in front of her, "never in the field of human conflict was so much owed by so many to just one man: W. A. Hillman. Without Wilfred Albert Hillman, none of us would be here today."

"I thought his name was Walter Ambrose Hillman?" said Klippies.

How utterly *typical* of the lower classes to nitpick over every last piffling detail.

"Without *Walter Ambrose* Hillman," Lady Eleanor continued through gritted teeth, "none of us would be here today. Leaving his wife Evelyn ..."

"Eloise!" shouted Farmer Robinson. "The paper said Eloise."

Dear heaven, whose side was this buffoon on? You give a man a lovely dinner and some fabulous vintage wine squeezed between the very toes of peasants in Provence and this is how he repays you! Treachery! Yes, "treachery" was the mot bally juste.

"*Eloise*," she corrected. "He came to these shores to ..."

"We doesn't have any shores. We're *mos* miles from the sea!" Stoffie de Villiers chimed in.

Oh for the love of God! *Where* was Phineas and *why* wasn't he stabbing these people with the ice pick that she *specifically* instructed him to bring to deal with hecklers?

All at once, the floor in Lady Eleanor's world listed sharply to the left and she felt an unsettling sensation she had last felt en route to Africa on the *Union Castle*. In her flustered state, she grabbed onto the lectern, dropping all twelve pieces of paper on which were written the myriad wondrous, noble qualities of W. A. Hillman and the many services he'd performed for mankind (and for Hillman, in particular), as well as every justification as to why his good name should be retained for time immemorial.

It was hopeless; nobody would come to her aid. Her loyal factotum, Phineas, was asleep in row five on the left of the hall, the ice pick in his pocket; Florence was sitting looking very smug in the row in front of him, and Neels, her would-be fairy-godson was himself concentrating very hard on staying upright in the corner (which he was accomplishing with only moderate success). And as stooping to pick up her notes was out of the question (one doesn't stoop for anything other than the queen), the future of all that had been Hillman lay in a scattering of little lavender rectangles around the lectern. A sea of open-mouthed goldfish stared back at her.

Lady Eleanor gathered her composure and segued on to what she would do if she became mayoress, which included the only salient points she could remember with a head that threatened to explode, these being flying the Union Jack and the banishment of "all foreign languages, except for French" (and even that only "where appropriate"). On the issue of the casino she stood firm: under no circumstances was it going to be built in her garden or in any place that would spoil her view!

Was it possible, she wondered, for one's head to literally crack open, and if so what could be done about it?

As she pondered this, she moved swiftly on to her conclusion, which had been adapted from one of her favourite prime minister's very own speeches, thinking that at least a rousing finish would salvage something of one's reputation and good standing:

"Let us therefore brace ourselves to our duties, and so bear ourselves that, if Hillman and its Commonwealth last for a thousand years, men and women will still say, 'This was their finest hour'. For what is the use of living, if it be not to strive for noble causes and to make this muddled world a better place for those who will live in it after we are gorn?"

And with that, so was she. Lady Eleanor's stirring election speech, which should have lasted almost fifteen bracing minutes, had lasted less than three. The floor rose up to meet her face, as she had rather feared it would, and as she grabbed too late for the lectern to steady her the startled crowd watched aghast as Lady Eleanor Lambert-

Lansdowne collapsed in a heap, her heavily lacquered coiffure the only thing that broke her fall as her head hit the top step. Dr Miller, Mrs Coleman and Pompies were swift to react and lifted her at both ends, moving her inert form rather unceremoniously to the trestle at the back of the hall, amidst the urns and the piles of biscuits. And for the second time in as many months, Lady Eleanor was laid out on a trestle table in the Town Hall, while Neels did his best to lower her skirts so that the people of Hillman didn't see quite as much as the patrons of the CoCo Gentlemen's Lounge had back in 1946. It was an inglorious moment in the annals of Lambert-Lansdowne history, and that was really saying something.

Nobody knew the protocol in such a situation. Does one clap or not? Probably not. So instead they did what people the world over do whenever something a bit embarrassing happens: they stared straight ahead, pretended as though nothing whatsoever had happened, and carried on completely as normal. No applause necessary.

Neels rushed back to the stage, lamé trousers schlick-schlacking as he did so. Had he been feeling better than he did, *now* would be the perfect time to break into his cover version of Freddie Mercury's *The Show Must Go On* (he did a *faaa*bulous "Queen" impersonation and even had the white Lycra leggings for it back at De Leeuk), but in the absence of fine vocal form (and said leggings) he opted for the less theatrical: "*Orrait* pa, you're next."

As introductions go it was not all Dominee had been hoping for, and to make matters worse what he had not factored into his great oration was the perilous combination of stairs, crutches and only one functional leg. He had prepared for this day by watching his video of the Nuremberg Rally and knew that history's great speeches did not begin with their orator hopping up stairs on one leg. Nor would it do to seek assistance with getting up there, either. You can bet your bobotie that General Smuts didn't address the Assembly of Nations on crutches and with a doek on his head, nor did anyone help him get to the lectern. Ja swaer ...

As Wessel and Ronan moved into their at-ease positions at the front of the stage, they both gave Dominee the four-fingered Spock-salute, which he answered with a sigh and a weary wave of his right crutch. Dominee began the great trek up the stairs and those on the left of the hall held their breath, wondering what calamity would come of this misadventure by the middle-heavy white man lumbering up the stairs on sticks. Josephina Nguni was enjoying this immensely: one candidate down, another an almost dead-cert. It was even better than Jerry Springer. Elections were such fun! Too bad they only happened every four years. Or five, depending on the election.

At the lectern, Dominee glanced around the Town Hall and felt his father's disapproving eyes boring into him from the photos on the walls. If Jacobus van Vouw III had known that his son would address a crowd of rooinekke and farmhands on one leg and with a moffie-band around his head, he'd have impaled himself on the spade in his hand rather than pose with it for the photograph taken in 1954 when the first sod had been turned at the Hillman Agricultural and Domestic Science College. Brumilda, however, did her best to look every bit the proud wife, but even she had to admit that the man at the front of the hall did not inspire the awe and confidence that they had all so hoped he would.

"Dames en here," began Dominee.

"Nee, sorry, pa. English only today," interjected Neels with an I-don't-make-the-rules-pa-I-only-enforce-them sort of shrug. Dominee gave his younger son a look in return that implied that if he didn't have both hands otherwise engaged he would throttle the very life out of him.

"Ladies and gentlemen," he started again, addressing the right side of the hall. "I don't have a fancy speech prepared for today like some other people will." He glared at Pompies.

In truth, Dominee had had a *very* fancy speech prepared. He'd been working on it for weeks and had even rehearsed with Brumilda, in front of the mirror, every finger-jab, point, gesture and pause to enhance the dramatic impact of his stirring words. P. W. Botha, "the last man with any blerrie backbone in this country", had been the greatest living exponent of the well-timed finger-point and Dominee had paid close attention.

However, in the early hours of this morning, it had become abundantly clear that Dominee would no longer be able to hold his prompt-cards while balancing on one leg and holding crutches. Furthermore, the back of his head hurt uncannily like somebody had hit him with a rifle butt, although he could no longer remember why or how. He clearly couldn't rely on his recollective skills and he was physically unable to hold any prompt cards so another approach had to be found. It really was such a pity; the other speech had all sorts of inspiring stuff in it including the irrefutable claim that only a Boer might "rightfully carry the white light of Christendom", ek-sê-tera, ek-sê-tera, plus a list of Jacobus Ezekiel van Vouw's many singular attributes and an even longer list of all the reasons why the town of Hillman should justly be renamed after him. Ag sjeim ...

"Ja-nee, I mos don't do fensie speeches. I'm just a simple sheep farmer. We *all* simple sheep farmers here in this town."

Neels bristled, as did Lady Eleanor who had now recovered from her attack of the vapours and was sitting at the back of the hall with a wilted Neels, the pair of them doing their best to look as together as two hungover queen-clones possibly could after ingesting over four litres of fantastically expensive champagne apiece. Hungover they may be; sheep farmers they most certainly were not!

"Even you, Oubaas, even you was a simple sheep farmer when you were young." The tacit implication being that Oubaas was now old. Very old. *Too* old. But Oubaas just nodded.

"If my groot oupa-grootjie Jacobus never came here with his three sheeps, we wouldn't be here today. None of us!"

He glared at Lady Eleanor. Nobody knew who the hell this Hillman oukie was, but Dominee would get the crowd where it mattered: their sheep. Their farms. Their history. Their very livelihood!

"So you should all think about that so long, hey? No Jacobus van Vouw: no sheep, no farming, no town. And you lot would be down the mines," he looked at the left of the hall, "and *you*," he said to those on the right, "you would all be working in the post office."

It was all an incensed Tienkie could do not to pelt him with her cookies, but she knew she would need them in about thirty minutes time.

For some reason he couldn't quite fathom, Dominee had a sneaking suspicion that he wasn't quite capturing the hearts and minds of the crowd in front of him. But why? He was an imposing form. What he said made perfect sense. He had an air of authority and gravitas. Must be the crutches and the blerrie doek. What he needed, he realized, was to throw in a nugget; something to sweeten the deal.

"*When* I become mayor, we should all get back to doing what we do best."

As far as Alpheus could tell, that was limited to drinking a lot and throwing very short spears at a stationary board very close to them. Nothing like Shaka or Dingaan's spear-chucking prowess. Now *those* two could throw *lonnnng* spears from far away and *still* hit a man running for cover!

"What this town needs is better sheep-farming skills. It's too bad those onnosele mense shut down our Agricultural College but we must make a beurs so that the young sheep farmers of tomorrow can learn what we all had to learn the hard way. Our past is our future, mense!"

He'd tried to cap off the bursary thing with something that sounded impressive, but nobody really knew what it meant, least of all Doffie and Klippies who both wanted to ask but knew better than to provoke the big man with the sore head and a hole in his foot. Maybe it was one of those "peroxides" Pompies had spoken about when he made his other speech? Koekie smiled at Doffie with an I-also-don't-know-what-that-means look, which made Doffie feel better, and gave another but-if-you're-up-for-a-repeat-of-last-night-then-I'm-game sort of look, which made him feel even better yet.

Dominee was getting into his stride now. He had impressed the vellies off the voters with talk of the bursary and the whole verbally clever past-and-future motif and he was about to go into his viewpoint on the Sun City development, which he actually remembered verbatim from his rehearsals, including exactly when to punctuate with vigorous pointing. "Not. Until. They *sign* on the *dotted* line." That sort of thing.

In his zeal, however, Dominee forgot that the only thing holding him erect were two pieces of aging aluminium and just as he was about to launch into the bit about how you can't trust Germans bearing gifts ("and ja, 'Kerzner'; how much more German can you get, hey?") the rubber foot at the end of his right crutch slipped on the parquet flooring that Neels had ordered polished to a shine and down went Dominee in a humiliating crash of twisted metal and shattered plaster-of-Parys. His head was the last thing to crash onto the bottom step and not even the sterling mummification provided by Mrs Coleman's bandage could stop the darkness that instantly replaced Dominee's erstwhile brilliant "white light". Rushing to his aid, Wessel and Ronan refused all external assistance and solemnly carried their fallen general to the trestle table at the back of the hall, amidst the urns and the piles of biscuits. There, for the second time in as many days, Dominee was laid out on a table to recover from his injuries, attended to by the ever-vigilant Dr Miller and Mrs Coleman, the latter now very relieved because the damage to Dominee's head was happily so much worse than that which she had caused with the rifle butt.

Josephina thought it just couldn't get any better than this! White people seemed completely unable to stay upright; it was fascinating! Perhaps all that leaning to the right made them unable to remain vertical. They fell off horses; they fell onto pitchforks and into swimming pools; they fell off stages; they fell out of bed and out of favour. They even fell down when they had not one, but *two* sticks to keep them up! Haibo!

Neels sighed. This election was a yawn. A bit like a Heinz Winkler konsert, really. With two candidates down it was becoming the two-horse race that it was destined to be from the very beginning. He needn't have bothered to dress for the occasion. In fact, he should have just stayed kaalgat under the piano. That was much more fun. Hillman was so utterly provincial. These people didn't appreciate style and glamour: they just wanted to see people falling down. It was so ... what did Lady Eleanor call it again ...? So very "Boer-jois"!

Fed up with the whole thing by now he didn't even bother to get up to invite Pompies to the stage and instead just waved a hand dismissively at the general stage area, which the mayor (well, he was still the mayor!) took as his cue to say his piece.

Pompies climbed wearily to the lectern at which he had stood six weeks previously when everything had gone horribly wrong. He, too, had prepared what he thought was a brilliant speech and had also rehearsed with Tienkie until it was word-perfect and sounded like a much more convincing argument than the one he'd put forward the last time. But now he was tired. He was tired from driving around all night in the snow. He was tired from having just four hours of sleep. He was tired after six weeks of everybody hating him; well, nearly everybody. He was tired ... actually perhaps he was tired of being mayor. Ja, maybe that was it! He was tired of listening to what everybody wanted all the time. What about what Pompies wanted, hey? What about that for a change? But in that instant he couldn't think what that was.

"Ladies and gentlemen," he began. Neels rolled his eyes. Could nobody think of anything more original that that as an opener? Dull, dull, *bor-ing*!

"We in Hillman have crossed the threshold of change." Pompies breathed a sigh of relief; so far so good. Even Klippies had managed to keep quiet. But then, just as quickly as assurance had come to him, Pompies drew a blank. A vast, cavernous, empty nothingness replaced the space in his brain where just last night over a page and a half of clever words had bedded down. He scanned his mental notes frantically but the words wouldn't come. How was this possible? Last night he knew it off by heart. He didn't need any notes! And now? Nothing! He looked at Tienkie who was mouthing frantically at the back of the hall but he couldn't understand what she was trying to say. People fidgeted in their seats. This was going horribly wrong. Again.

Tienkie grabbed a piece of paper and wrote "monument of our genesis" holding it up for Pompies to see, but it made no sense. Hey? What monument? And what the hell did Phil Collins have to do with anything? Come on Pompies. Best to say something. Anything.

"Um, I was going to tell you about Dingaan. He was a great man."

Why? Why was he a great man? Pompies couldn't for the life of him remember why at all ... Oh yes!

"He killed a lot of people." Oh no! That wasn't it!

"I mean he killed a lot of people, but he was still a great man. Even if he wore a skirt."

Pompies heart was racing. The Zulus were looking a little unreceptive to the idea of their great leader in ladies' apparel.

"Ja, he was very brave. Lots of people thought he was great. Well, not everybody, of course, because his own people killed him in a forest in the end, hey?"

Shut up, shut up, shut up! Why was he rambling like this? He wished he could just stop! But he was tired. So very, very tired. Like Lady Eleanor he just wanted to get this over with and get home to

Eskom and his bed. And sleep! Heerlikheid, he would sleep for forty-eight hours if given the chance. Nee! Kom aan, Pompies. Stay awake, stay awake, stay awake! Talk about something else. Anything. Then a flash went off:

"I believe in democracy."

Yes, yes! *That* was in the original speech. But what came next? Think, *think*! O ja …

"I *believe* in one man, one…" One what? *What*? How did that saying go again?

"I believe in one man, one goat." *Hey*? What did he just say?

In her seat Josephina sat bolt upright. For the first time in her long, long association with her employer, he had finally said something that made sense. Votes were very nice and she was very glad she finally had one of her own, but a goat: a goat was dinner!

Pompies was sweating. This was not at all how it was supposed to be. How could he get it so wrong twice in a row? Blerrie bliksem! (Sorry, God.) What should he say next? Wasn't there something about the sun? Sun? What sun? Oh yes!

"And another thing. I don't like Sun City coming here. We had enough problems this past six weeks; what's going to happen when all the skorries come here with their drinking and their nonsens, hey? And us with no hospital and no police station. And no policeman. And …"

At that Pompies simply ran out of steam. He knew he had blown it, but he just couldn't remember the words, and he was simply too tired. He looked out at the villagers in front of him and to his surprise the eyes that looked back at him contained none of the hostility that had been there in previous weeks.

"Ag, I don't really know what else to say, except … thank you, everyone. It's been nice being your mayor for all these years. Perhaps it's time for me to do something else anyway. Why not, hey?"

And with that he sighed and walked away from the lectern. Had it been a Hollywood movie, Tienkie (played perhaps by that lady with the Afrikaans surname, somebody Streep) would have run from the back of the hall into his arms (in slow motion with some uplifting music swelling to an emotional crescendo in the background) and the audience would have started cheering for the man who had led them for so many years. But this was Hillman, not Hollywood, and Pompies was terribly fatigued. So when he turned to leave the stage his foot caught on the silver lamé draped around the pedestal of the lectern and, like Lady Eleanor and Dominee before him, he tripped and tumbled down the stairs, the brick wall breaking his fall, and very nearly his head. However, to add to his indignity he was still conscious and fully mobile so the audience just gasped, rooted in their seats. Nobody came to carry him to the back of the hall and he lost out on his chance to have a nice sleep on the trestle table like Lady Lambert and Dominee had done. It really wasn't fair. If only he could sleep, he'd realize that this had all been a bad dream and he could at least wake up and get it right tomorrow. He was just so moeg, so very, very moeg ...

Secrets and lies

As Pompies took his seat, Oubaas got up slowly and walked three paces, stopping at the front of the stage for what was to be his first-ever public address. He had decided that the lectern was too much like church and the stairs seemed to have posed too many problems for the first three candidates, and Aggripina had warned him again today that mayor or not she still needed him to fix the windy-dry.

The atmosphere was electric and the hall was so still you could have heard a grenade-pin drop. Expectation hung in the air like piñatas; everyone on all sides was waiting to hear what the old man was going to say, and for the first time ever Oubaas felt an unwelcome sensation, rather like the feeling you get when you eat mbusi that hasn't been cooked properly or bananas that aren't quite ripe yet. For a second he thought about Nelson (not the one from the little scuffle at Trafalgar; the other one) and wondered if he had felt nervous the first time he spoke in public after his release from Pollsmoor Prison. *There* was a challenge, thought Oubaas: one minute you're in solitary confinement, talking to yourself just in case it *isn't* like riding a bicycle and you might actually forget how to do it, and the next the whole world's listening to you! Well, if another old man could manage *that*, reasoned Oubaas, then Ephraim Mthethwa could say a few words to the people of Hillman.

"Good afternoon, ladies and gentlemen," he began. There was a collective sigh of relief from the right side of the hall, as though they had perhaps been expecting him to make his speech in Zulu and then nobody would understand if he said anything about "Land Reformation" or "impis" or anything that might require Brumilda van Vouw to bring out her Robertsons black pepper.

"In six weeks nobody has thought to ask me: 'Why Dingiswayo?' In fact many of you here today, including my own grandchildren and great-grandchildren, probably do not even know who Dingiswayo was."

Pompies wondered if this was like Quiz Night and almost put his hand up, thinking that if he got the answer right it might stand him in better stead come voting time. He'd gotten his own speech horribly wrong but he *had* read something about Dingiswayo when he was doing his research (it came right after "Dingaan" and before "dinghy" and "dingo" in his encyclopaedia), but now, aside from the headband, the pointy stick and the grass skirt, he could no longer remember any details so he put his hand back down again.

"Dingiswayo was an Nguni chieftain," continued Oubaas, "a great leader of the Mthethwa army—possibly its greatest leader—and a noble warrior himself."

Sitting in the third row, Josephina Nguni looked very pleased with herself. She would remember this the next time Pompies asked her to clean the skottel. She was descended from royalty, she would remind him, and royalty doesn't do skottels! While, in her seat on the other side of the hall, Lynette Butler imagined Oubaas learning about the legend of Dingiswayo from his father, who had heard about the great warrior from his father before him. This was the "real Africa", she mused: secrets imparted around the campfire; raconteurs passing down the tales of the ages in unwritten records that transcended time. She made a mental note to put together a lesson plan on Dingiswayo next term and all the children would make shields out of paper plates and glitter.

In point of fact, Oubaas had learned about Dingiswayo the same way Pompies had: from the old encyclopaedia in his father's trunk. It was that one dog-eared, mouldy, well-thumbed book that started his lifelong romance with all others and as a child he had stumbled upon the history of his heritage while looking up what he thought was "dinamite", which sounded like something all ten-year-old boys should have access to.

"The Mthethwas of old were fighters," said Oubaas, "but we, in Hillman, are not. The truth of it, ladies and gentlemen, is that the Mthethwas who came here, driven westwards from the Umfolozi Valley into the Drakensberg mountains, had no stomach for fighting; they could not see sense in war. Our forefathers were an anathema to the rest of our family."

Doffie wondered why Oubaas had four fathers and Klippies wondered what an "athema" was. As did Pompies, Dominee, Farmer Robinson and several other people who all tried to look like they understood exactly what Oubaas had just said. It sounded like "asthma", thought Klippies, but whatever it was that Oubaas' four fathers suffered from, the rest of his family obviously didn't like it very much.

"Did you know that 'amaZulu' means 'the people of heaven'?" said Oubaas.

Dominee most certainly did not! But just the thought was making him sweat inside his cast. First the Jewish people take first pick with their "chosen people" gambit and now the Zulus were pitching themselves as "people of heaven"! How was it possible that the Afrikaner had missed out on a great marketing opportunity back at the time of the Trek? Too busy building ossewas to spend time on moffie taglines and public relations, he supposed. Still, it had been an oversight; they could have become known as "God's Farmers" or something like that had they thought it through properly.

"People of heaven should not fight, and the Mthethwas who came to settle in Hillman were not fighters. *Nobody* who has ever come to settle in Hillman has been a fighter. In fact, the past six weeks have demonstrated how bad we all are at fighting with each other."

Alpheus didn't like the sound of this! It had started so well with all the "noble warrior" stuff and the whole "Mthethwa army" build-up; now he didn't know what direction his grandfather was going in, but it didn't bode well for Alpheus' career as a gangsta-rapper if news went around that he was descended from a bunch of conscientious objectors.

But what Oubaas had said was true; he just didn't tell the *whole* story to the crowd assembled in the Town Hall ...

In 1900, several years after a faction of the original Mthethwas had headed west for what was to become known as Hillman, Rufus Lambert-Lansdowne—uncle of Rupert, gentleman layabout and reluctant participant in the Boer War—had seen enough on the battlefields to know that warfare didn't suit him, especially when it was so insufferably hot and you couldn't get a decent brandy anywhere. In fact, he'd had an absolute bally bellyful of the whole beastly warmongering business and after a particularly vicious battle with the bearded blokes in the floppy hats in which he'd had an eyebrow singed "right orf" he had taken a little impromptu sojourn from Her Majesty's service.

Taking refuge in a remote little village that nobody had ever heard of, he came upon some "awfully accommodating and bloody good chaps, what" and the Mthethwas of the mountain gave Rufus sanctuary from the battlefields (and bottomless bowls of some "tremendously amusing sorghum beer") until word finally came that it was all over. And they'd won! Hurrah! At last Rufus could go home, which he did, arriving back in Northumberland to a puzzled family who'd already held a stiff-upper-lip memorial service for their war-hero son who'd supposedly perished on foreign soil fighting the "Boors". For six months after his return, Rufus feigned dementia (this was long before somebody coined the whole "post-traumatic stress" lark) and everyone just assumed that poor old Rufus had gone a bit doolally on the battlefield. Twenty-five weeks and a lot of medicinal brandy later, however, Rufus exhibited a dramatic recovery and everyone was so thrilled at the turnaround in his mental faculties that nobody ever asked any questions. All was tickety-boo and Rufus lived to the ripe old age of eighty-nine in style and comfort.

What was known only to Rufus and his unlikely hosts in the mountains of Natal (aside from his absconding from the business of war), was that Rufus had left behind his helmet in which was tucked a letter from his good friend William Arthur Hillman to Lieutenant Hillman's fiancée, Emily, which Rufus had promised to send to the poor girl in the event of William's demise. Along with this letter was the Victoria Cross awarded to Lieutenant Hillman posthumously after said demise at the ironically named "Geluk". Not so lucky for poor old William. However, in the absence of any postal service in his host village, Rufus had been unable to send the items to the young lady for whom they were intended, and they remained in his helmet for safekeeping while Rufus enjoyed the abundant hospitality of his hosts. Around the campfire, Rufus told Oubaas' great-grandfather, Indoda, and a group of enthralled villagers stories about William's courage under fire and his incredible bravery on the battlefield. In a woollen jacket at that! The Mthethwas of the mountain weren't too keen on war themselves, but they liked a good yarn as much as the next man and this Hill Man seemed like somebody of whom Dingiswayo himself would have approved. Everyone was very impressed.

In 1901, when word came that all the ballyhoo was behind them now, Rufus said a fond "salakahle" to his hosts, having distinguished himself from his fellow countrymen abroad only in his ability—and willingness—to speak the native lingo, and set sail for Blighty. Indoda Mthethwa hung onto the helmet, the letter and the VC, unsure what should be done with them. It was only long after Indoda passed away that Hillman got its own post office, but by its establishment in 1947 his grandson Joseph assumed that either Miss Emily Compton-James would be late of this world or at the very least she would have married someone else and would no longer have any use for the letter or the piece of shiny metal on the ribbon. If the queen had actually bothered to come to Hillman when she visited the Drakensberg that same year he would have given them to her, because maybe she knew this e-Mily person and could pass on Mr Hillman's greetings. But she didn't, and for the next fifty-nine years the letter and the VC would stay secreted in the helmet in Joseph Mthethwa's trunk.

A few months after Rufus' departure in 1901, some white men came up the Pass toting poles and a mallet and asked what the name of the village was. They had apparently won the war and were making maps of all the places that Her Majesty now owned. The Mthethwa villagers, however, had only been living on the hill for fifty years or so and had been so busy setting up house they hadn't thought to name the village other than referring to it as "entabeni", the "place on the hill".

"No, no," said the man with the mallet. "You can't use that; Durban already has one of those."

"Your village must have a name!" said the white man with the pole. "Wasn't there a great warrior who lived here or something like that?"

Colonization was predicated on great warriors, preferably dead ones (and ideally ones who'd died at the hands of their colonizers). In the absence of a politically non-contentious, dead warrior of some description, however, places could permissibly be named after people of great social standing who obviously missed "home" so much they kept trying to turn each place into which they stuck their poles and flags into a replica of what they'd left behind. Either that or they'd simply name a town after the very place they'd just left. If they missed it all so much, many wondered, why not just stay there?

The Mthethwas, however, didn't want their name used as they were very comfortable with their pacifist, pastoral existence in an anonymous village and didn't want any trouble, and the grumpy white man who had just started farming sheep in the valley below didn't want his name used because somebody in Harrismith was looking for a Van Vouw on some "trumped-up charges" relating to sheep-theft.

The Mthethwas shrugged and looked at each other and Indoda disappeared into his boma returning with the letter and the Victoria Cross.

"Perfect!" said the man. "I name this town Hillman!" And in went the pole.

And so it was that Hillman came to be; not because William Arthur had actually ever been there, but simply because the residents of the town didn't want to draw attention to themselves. Of all the current residents, only Oubaas knew this story, but before he passed on he would tell his eldest son, Elias, so that the history of Hillman would at least be remembered for posterity.

Oubaas now looked out at the assembled crowd and drew in a breath. Some of his family would not like what was coming next, but he had thought about this all carefully and his mind was made up.

"I believe three things: the first is that history is simply how we choose to remember it."

Lady Eleanor nodded in agreement. The history of a thing was always so much more presentable when trimmed with a little colour and a dash of gilding around the edges. It was still a facsimile of the past, of course, but with all the unseemly bits edited out.

"The second is that we are *all* foreigners here in Hillman; some of you just came from further away." Tienkie Groenewald nodded. Vereeniging was far.

"And the third is that in the new South Africa we must all be open to change."

This elicited a collective squirming from the people on the right. This was the moment everyone had been waiting for (or dreading, depending on which side of the hall you sat): the point at which Oubaas would announce that the time had come for Hillman to fall in with the rest of the country, shake off old identities and adopt the mantle of change.

"We must realize the mistakes of our past and we must right them …" said Oubaas.

Pompies thought about last night and how he had tried to make amends for causing all the kak in the first place. Tienkie wondered if Oubaas already knew about the koekies. Dominee reflected that he really should have erected a gun-turret at De Leeuk, and Neels decided that silver lamé was indeed a mistake; too wishy-washy. Mauve really was the way to go.

"… but as Jean-Baptiste Karr wrote," Oubaas continued, "'plus ça change, plus c'est la même chose'."

Lady Eleanor could scarcely believe her ears! She must be more pickled than she thought. The writer at bally *Times of London* didn't even know Lord sodding Hawthorne and here was this Ma-tet-wa chappy quoting Karr. *In French!* Whatever next!

Dominee fiddled with his head bandage; he didn't know who this "Kar" oukie was or what the hell nonsens he had said, but 1) he was a Baptist and 2) he spoke German, and together that just spelled out a world of trouble ahead. Or maybe he was Russian (Russian, German: same-same really) and therefore a commie and he'd been right about Oubaas all along.

Alpheus didn't know who Karr was either, but at least Grandfather Mthethwa seemed to be back on track with the whole "change" message. Time to cut to the chase …

"We must sometimes, ladies and gentleman, regardless of its consequences, accept change in whatever form it presents itself to us."

Bodies on the right stiffened and breath was inhaled sharply; Brumilda van Vouw was reaching into her bag for the peppermill. Here it comes …

"Today I am a candidate for change because I, too, have changed.

My mind."

The eyes of two hundred and thirty-seven eligible voters stared back at Oubaas in complete bewilderment.

"What did he say?"

"What does he mean?"

"What's he changing?"

"What's going on?"

"Is he still talking English?"

Never mind changing it, thought Alpheus, the old goat's gone and *lost* his mind!

"I have thought about this a lot recently. Dingiswayo was a great man, it's true, but our Mthethwas didn't fight alongside him." They didn't fight alongside William Arthur Hillman, either, but that was beside the point.

"So I propose that we keep the name of Hillman. It's a fine name and everyone knows it."

(Everyone except, of course, the good people of Eskom, Telkom, *The Northern Natal Express*, *The Mercury*, Brabys, the Democratic Alliance, cartographers across South Africa, and the people at the Provincial Administration.)

There was stunned silence across the hall.

"I say 'No' to developers. Like Mr de Wet I also say 'No' to Sun City and to a casino on our mountain. I say 'No' to lots of people coming here and messing up our nice town. For what do we need development? We all got on fine before all this talk of change, and some things are best left alone. We like our funny town with our bad road; it's what we all know as home. Hillman has always provided refuge for those of us who needed it; Hillman hides our secrets and protects those who need protection from the outside world."

As he said this, he looked in turn at Dominee, Lady Eleanor, Tienkie Groenewald, the children who'd been involved in The Case of the Disappearing Items, and Alpheus; all of whom stared at their shoes (or where their shoes would be, in the case of Dominee).

He knows! thought Tienkie Groenewald. The sly ou skelm knows!

And thanks to his mother's firm belief in wrapping paper you can read, Oubaas did. But thanks to his father's equally firm belief in keeping some things under your hat (or your helmet), he did that too.

"However, I like some of the suggestions I heard today and I think we should be brave enough to embrace some small changes. I think there *should* be a Hillman scholarship for young sheep farmers, and I think that Mr van Vouw is sufficiently involved with S.H.I.T. to make that happen. I think there *should* be a community police station in Hillman and I think that Mr de Wet has more than demonstrated his ability to run it. You never know; crime may actually come to this mountain one day and when it does we should be ready." He regarded the group of thieving children who all looked appropriately terrified at the prospect.

"In fact, in light of what Mr de Wet did for this town last night, I think that he should get some recognition for what he did for all of us, for the people of Hillman. Not just for his efforts last night, but also for his brilliant investigative work in the field of stolen goods recovery."

And reaching into his pocket he held up the VC originally intended for Lieutenant W. A. Hillman. On the cross itself were two words: "For Valour". Well, thought Oubaas, when temperatures reach minus two and the roads become glass you can safely call driving around in a blizzard at night on them an act of valour. And anyway, both Victoria and William were long dead so he was sure neither would mind.

Dominee, however, did mind. If he could have raised his hand he'd like to have reminded Pompies that he had won a medal long before him in the Best of Breed Category at the Pietermaritzburg Agricultural Show (or rather his sheep had; it was unlikely Dominee would win any accolades for Best of Breed). And his was at least a bronze medal, not grey. Not only that, but this medal of Oubaas' looked suspiciously like Van Vouw's own insignia, with four Vs placed perpendicular to each other. Everybody copied Dominee van Vouw, he thought; no originality whatsoever. Blerrie typical! Perhaps there was a copyright issue at stake there. He should look into that. Perhaps he could sue ...

As Pompies went up to the front of the stage to receive his medal for valour and self-sacrifice, the Town Hall erupted into cheers from every side and the ladies of ZIPPO broke into spontaneous song and dance. The Zulus hugged the English, the English hugged the Zulus, and the Afrikaners hugged each other, because *here* was a visionary, a man truly of the people. Sanity had prevailed; the village had won. Indeed, without a single vote being cast, *everybody* had won!

The only people not celebrating were Dominee (who was unsure what exactly had just happened and was still a bit miffed about the medal thing), Neels and Phineas (who were both asleep) and Tienkie Groenewald, who ran around while people danced and sang, frantically collecting chocolate cookies in a black bin bag. Lady Eleanor Lambert-Lansdowne, who had managed to regain some of her composure in the midst of all the hullabaloo, suffered a further setback, however, when she went to get a cup of tea to fortify her nerves during all the hysteria and hugging. Brumilda van Vouw, who was now playing the part of the gracious hostess with as much poise as she could pretend under the circumstances held out a cup of tea to Lady Eleanor and said, in all sincerity, "Would you like a koekie also, Lady Lambert? I got some lovely ginger snaps ..." And down went Lady Eleanor for the second time that day.

As Oubaas watched the celebrations, he patted his pocket in which rested an ancient photograph, crumpled and yellowed with age, which had lain for years between the pages of his father's leather-bound Bible. It showed Oubaas' great-great-grandfather, Indoda, posing with a smiling white man at the very top of Hillman mountain. It had been given to Oubaas by Rupert Lambert-Lansdowne some thirty years before and on the back was the inscription:

"Me and Indoda pheZulu Kwentaba
('the man on the hill') Mthethwa.
Bloody good chap, what.
Rufus LL 1901"

Epilogue

Extracts from *The Hillman Herald*
(The editor would like readers to know that "*The Hillman Herald*: for Heavenly People" is now also available online, electricity-permitting):

Wednesday, 24 January 2007:
The ladies of the HLANC are to hold a Hillman Arts and Crafts Fair at the Hillman Town Hall on Saturday, the 3rd of February. Ladies Auxiliary President, Mrs Florence Dlamini, a full-time Household Services Manager at Grasscroft, who took over as president of the HLA from Mrs Dorothy Gilmore when the former president resigned her position to pursue a career in journalism, has promised that a wide variety of cakes, biscuits, and handcrafts will be available on the day. All proceeds to go to the Klip Klop Prosthetic Fund after the loss of Mr Klippies Klopper's other foot in a freak accident involving fireworks outside the Hillman Farm & Feed Store (as reported in our New Year issue).

Wednesday, 14 February 2007:
Late Breaking News: Local police CHIEF (Community of Hillman Informal law Enforcement Force) Superintendent, Dewaldt de Wet, has announced his engagement to Hillman Postal Mistress, Ms Tienkie Groenewald. The happy couple are to marry at the Hillman Anglican Chapel on Saturday the 31st of March. In what was reported to be a fairy-tale Valentine's Day proposal, Mr de Wet got down on bended knee and popped the question in front of a crowd of at least

three people waiting in line at the Hillman post office earlier today, to which Ms Groenewald is said to have answered "Ag ja, why not hey?" Ms Groenewald is planning to wear a gown made for her by local Drakensberg couturier and wedding/party/conference planner, Neels van Vouw. A venue for the reception is being sought after Mrs Esmé Gericke announced that regrettably the Hillman Ale & Arms is already booked for that day.

Wednesday, 14 March 2007:
Mr and Mrs Dorf de Wet are delighted to announce the birth of their son, Jack Daniel de Wet, on the 11th of March 2007 in what former "Miss Hillman" Mrs Koekie de Wet (nee Van Vouw) said was a premature birth, at the Mimi Coertse Neo-Natal Clinic in Estcourt. Regular readers will remember the front-page Celebrity Wedding Special carried in *The Hillman Herald* following the couple's September 2006 wedding after a "whirlwind romance". Proud grandfather, Dewaldt de Wet, confirmed that no forceps were used during delivery, while the infant's maternal grandfather and local S.H.I.T. representative, Mr Kobus van Vouw, would like to remind readers that he was prouder than everyone and that he became a grandfather long before Mr de Wet.

Wednesday, 18 April 2007:
Mr Stoffie de Villiers has won the Hillman Darts League annual tournament in a nail-biting final held on Saturday the 14th of April at the Ale & Arms. Former title-holder, Mr Kobus van Vouw, has announced that the result is yet to be finalized pending an investigation regarding the admissibility of Mr de Villiers' darts, said to be Japanese imports that offer an aerodynamic advantage over those of the rest of the Darts League members. *The Hillman Herald* will carry more on the investigation as this dramatic story unfolds.

Wednesday, 16 May 2007:

Hillman Arts League President, Lady Eleanor Lambert-Lansdowne, is delighted to announce auditions for the Hillman Dramatic Society's forthcoming musical production of Oscar Wilde's *The Importance of Being Earnest*. The production will run for two nights at the Hillman Town Hall on the 15th and 16th of June. Art Direction and Costumes by Neels van Vouw (of "Maison Neels, Couturier to the Stars", next door to the Copper Kettle and Tuisnywerheid). Musical direction and arrangement by Mr van Vouw's close personal friend, Roger Forrester. There will be a sit-down, candle-light finger-supper as electricity cannot be guaranteed. Catering to be provided by Mrs Esmé Gericke of the Hillman Ale & Arms. A "bally good time for all" is promised. Neels van Vouw said that "*Idols*-format" auditions would be held at the Town Hall on Friday the 18th of May at 2pm. Everyone welcome.

Wednesday, 6 June 2007:

Hillman Primary Principal, Lynette Butler, has announced that the children of Hillman Primary are to stage an "authentic re-enactment" of the Battle of Isandlwana for Heritage Day on the 24th of September and invites the donation of feathers, paper plates, traditional weapons and glitter for the event. Ms Butler has said that the re-enactment will be true to the historical account of the famous battle, except that at the end all parties will shake hands and agree to be friends so that "the mistakes of the past are not entrenched in young minds". Dr Miller and Mrs Coleman of the weekly Hillman Medical Centre and Birth Control Clinic have assured all parents they will be on standby to assist should any injuries occur, as will local sangoma Professor Prince Chiya of the Hillman Traditional Healers' Working Group.

Wednesday, 4 July 2007:

Eskom recently warned residents across the country to prepare for power outages as part of its "load shedding" policy. Local refuse collector Dwayne Donovan has generously offered to collect several loads of Eskom's unwanted electricity in his bakkie if they just tell him where they are shedding it, but Eskom had not responded to Mr Donovan's offer by the time *The Hillman Herald* went to press.

Hillman General Co-Op Manager, Marketing Director and PRO, Mr Alpheus Mthethwa, would like all residents to know that the store has sufficient stock of candles and paraffin, both of which are on special for the duration of the blackout, although the Hillman General Co-Op "has the right to preserve quantities", he added. (Also on special, while stocks last, is a selection of Ray-Ban sunglasses and a range of quality time-pieces for "discerning shoppers only" said Mr Mthethwa.)

Wednesday, 1 August 2007:

Miss Buhle Nguni was crowned "Miss Hillman" in a glittering pageant held at the Hillman Town Hall on the 28th of July. Miss Nguni, daughter of domestic executive and ZIPPO Chairlady, Josephina Nguni, won over the panel of judges with her call for "world peace" and is looking forward to making good use of her first prize, a scholarship to the T&A Modelling Academy in Pietermaritzburg. In an emotional speech following her investiture, Buhle said that she wanted to thank Miss Hillman Pageant choreographer and coach, former beauty-queen Mrs Tienkie de Wet, for "all her help and excellent advice".

The other contestants are said to be recovering nicely after a freak bout of food poisoning felled all but the eventual winner on pageant night.

Wednesday, 12 September 2007:

A memorial service will be held at Hillman Anglican Chapel on Friday the 14th of September for Mr Philemon Nthuli, former proprietor of the Hillman Taxi and Limousine Service, who passed away last week in a tragic accident on the Valleikloof Pass. Mr Nthuli had been on his way to get a new gear-box from Harrismith when the brakes on his Isuzu minibus failed in the rain. Former passengers described Mr Nthuli variously as a "larger than life" character, "fearless" and a "raving lunatic". He rests next to his father, Elias, the founder of HT&LS at the foot of the Valleikloof Pass. Donations in lieu of flowers may be made to Mr Nthuli's widow, Courage.

Wednesday, 17 October 2007:

After sixteen months of legal wrangling and with the assistance of Legal Aid in Harrismith, a hearing has concluded that the medal awarded to Mr Dewaldt de Wet at the Hillman Mayoral Election on the 24th June 2006 did not infringe the Trademarks Act. The insignia of the now-disbanded VVVV was deemed by legal experts to have been crafted significantly after that of the Victoria Cross and was never registered with the relevant department in Pretoria anyway. Mr Bigboy Chaka of Legal Aid, Harrismith, has cautioned Mr van Vouw through a statement issued to *The Hillman Herald* that he needs to "stop bugging (his) staff and that the matter is now closed".

When approached for comment, Mr van Vouw countered with, "We'll see about that!"

Wednesday, 7 November 2007:

Hillman Police CHIEF Superintendent, Dewaldt de Wet, is to be issued with a catapult and a BB gun following a recent spate of thefts in the Hillman area. Mr de Wet says he blames the sharp increase in crime (up nearly 0.25% on previous months) on increased "skorrie" tourism as summer approaches, but has expressed his delight at finally being issued with an official firearm. Three residents have reported fruits and vegetables "disappearing" from their gardens and smallholdings, and for the second time in eighteen months Josephina Nguni's pet goat "Pompies" has been stolen. A reward is being offered depending on the condition of the goat upon return. Hillman has seen a dramatic increase in tourism since the start of the warmer weather with no fewer than four non-residents having been served at the Copper Kettle since the start of October, only two of whom were reported to have been lost on their way to Bulwer.

Wednesday, 19 December 2007:
The mayor of Hillman, His Worship the Right Honourable Ephraim "Oubaas" Mthethwa, would like to wish all the citizens of Hillman a "blessed and joyous Christmas and a Happy New Year" and cautions everyone that Christmas is a time for giving, not drinking. He also said that there is no truth to the rumour that he plans to abolish Christmas in favour of Kwanza nor has he at any time issued a statement, as reported recently in certain circles in Himeville, that Jesus was Zulu.

The editor and staff writer of *The Hillman Herald*, Mrs Dorothy Gilmore, would like to wish all readers a Merry Christmas/ Hanukkah/Kwanza/day-off-work and a Happy New Year. The paper will close for the Festive Season and will reopen on the 9th of January 2008 with a bumper two-page "What Happened in Hillman over the Holidays" edition.

Acknowledgments

My profuse thanks go to Chris and Kerrin Cocks and Jane Lewis at 30° South Publishers for their vision, good humour and hard work on this book, and to Bruce Dennill and all at *The Citizen* and The Write Co. for championing the idea of the book prize. I am also indebted to my editor, Julia Gault, for her excellent advice and meticulous attention to detail, and to Aideen for her support of all my endeavours, madcap though they almost always are.

My love and gratitude to Christopher for his tireless re-reading of the manuscript and for all the late-night chocolate runs in mid-writing frenzy; you make it all worthwhile.

Lastly, my thanks go to our government for providing me with such a richness of subject matter, and to everyone who voted in *The Citizen* Book Prize; may *Home Affairs* give you as much delight as your vote of confidence in it has given me.

About the author

Bree O'Mara was born in Durban on a Thursday in July, just in time for lunch. She started out life in the theatre and performed for all four performing arts councils before the diet of lettuce and watercress became too much to bear.

In 1992 she went to live in the Middle East where she worked as a steward for Bahrain's national carrier. After appearing in the television advert for the airline, the producer of the commercial got drunk on a flight to London and offered Bree a job as an art director in his film production company. She took this offer (written on a napkin in case he forgot the next day) and went on to become a producer of 35mm television commercials and documentaries, writing copy and scripts all over the Gulf and Middle East region.

Since then she has lived and worked in broadcast and print media in Canada, the United States and England. In 2004, she left the UK for Tanzania, where she lived for a year with the Maasai, working for a small charity. There she lived with no electricity and no running water and this made her homesick for South Africa. She now lives with her husband in the North West Province.

Bree speaks a variety of languages, plays the harp, doesn't like artichokes, follows Formula 1, and works in conservation. Her favourite authors are Joanne Harris, P. J. O'Rourke, Tobias Wolff and Stephen Fry.